# Pilgrims of the Fall

The First World

CHRISTOPHER C LEVY

Published by Christopher C Levy 2025

Black Hart Entertainment.
www.blackhartentertainment.com



Cover by Jan-Andrew Henderson and Green Light Design
Book Layout © 2017 BookDesignTemplates.com

Pilgrims of the Fall — The First World
ISBN: 978-1-7640523-0-6 (hard copy)

# Chapters


Chapters ............................................................ 3

Part One - Hell on Earth.................................... 5

Part Two - Armageddon in a Blink..................... 23

Part Three - The Price of Power......................... 33

Part Four - Los Angeles .................................... 47

Part Five - Another Revelation ........................... 63

Part Six - Casting the Dice................................ 71

Part Seven - Worlds Apart ................................. 87

Part Eight – Training and Ultimatum..................... 95

   The Council Circus ...................................... 106

Part Nine - Reunion and Regrets......................... 109

Part Ten - Dance of the Fae ............................... 121

   The Gilded Cage .......................................... 129

Part Eleven - The First World ............................ 135

   Back on Floriana ......................................... 147

   A Dark in the Park ....................................... 160

   Angels of Light ........................................... 165

Part Twelve - To Blood and to Banish................... 175

   The Mortal Realm ........................................ 191

   Dancing Hearts............................................ 195

   Rescue at a Price .......................................... 202

Exile...........................................................223

Part Thirteen - Seeking the Sonciel .......................229

Part Fourteen - James Takes the Reins...................249

Part Fifteen - A Different Earth...........................257

Part Sixteen - Race to the Three Sisters .................305

Serpent's Breath ...................................309

Seraphine's Pebble ...............................330

Part Seventeen - The Agony of Ignorance.............341

Part Eighteen - The Shores of Estrada...................357

Addendum - Time Strands...................................373

Acknowledgements ............................................377

About The Author.............................................379


For Ian

# Part One - Hell on Earth

Sam and Rose shimmered in the erratic light of a waning moon that occasionally peaked out from behind a turbulent blanket of smoke. Casting the pair repeatedly into gloomy, red-tinged shadow.

The world they knew had changed, utterly. During their pilgrimage to the Light, many months ago, they had travelled this country, through living forests, fed by a wide, life-giving river. Now… it was welcome to Armageddon, the world of the Dark. The old, familiar world had gone.

Rose was in tears. "Sam, it's all gone, shit. Everything. The forests! Where are the bloody trees? We drowned a Legion of Dark warriors in that river and now look at it. How could the Dark do so much damage so quickly?" Appalled, they both looked out at the wasteland before them.

"The Dark are drying out the world," Sam theorised. "They're removing the one thing that can destroy them, water!"

Rose nodded in agreement, but she was still in shock. Tears hidden by the gloom distorted her vision. She and Sam were wearing Dark disguises that shimmered and modulated in and out of focus. They looked just as evil, corrupting and unsettling as the Dark warriors they planned to infiltrate.

Marion, a late arrival to their recent pilgrimage, and a rare survivor of the Dark abductions, had been training the thousands of infiltrators needed to watch conditions across the Earth — the Mortal Realm.

She had taught the Light how the Dark warriors thought, their customs and traditions, there speech, how they behaved toward other warriors, their Lieutenants, and the Dark Lords. She had taught them the laws that governed the Dark Realm, wielded without favour or mercy.

Failure to use traditional sayings and colloquialisms, or to observe proper behaviour would mark them as intruders and might even be fatal, or worse. They might become warriors of the Dark, addicted to the flames, as Marion had almost been.

Sam and Rose, like the other infiltrators, had trained to wield *shaping swords* and each wore a sword concealed under their cloaks. These swords, limited in number, were relics of a time when God and the Angels ruled The Light, the way of making them now lost, as God was lost to The Light — water shaped as the sharpest of blades, deadly to the Dark but harmless to The Light and energised in a way that science could not replicate. They glowed brilliant white as they cut through the air and the living ash of the Dark.

The swords were a precaution since Sam and Rose were mere observers and would soon return to The Light.

Rose regained her composure and began studying the barren land around them. Suddenly, she grabbed Sam's arm and drew his attention to an area of barely discernible movement in the distance. Occasional sparks of light flared for a moment and then died just as quickly.

"My God Sam, the Dark are here. What could they be doing? There's nothing left to burn or destroy."

Sam begged to differ. Remembering the resilience of the Australian bush, Sam knew exactly what the Dark were doing. "Think about what used to happen after a bushfire," he explained to Rose, "the way the gum trees would sprout new growth and native seeds would burst out of the earth in a matter of days.

"Life is resilient. The Dark are intent upon destroying any signs of new life that may appear. They'll be burning every vestige of green they find."

Sam looked down at his feet and knew that he was right. "Look down Rose. There are green shoots sprouting all around us."

Sam stood up and walked out into the open. "Come on. We have to test our training sometime and it may as well be now." Rose, reluctantly, followed Sam into the open and walked away from the place of the portal.

"I'll leave the speaking to you, Sam. My language skills are still too weak." Sam nodded, and strode off toward the river, now reduced to a string of muddy pools along its length. They had no difficulty crossing it.

A stretch of desiccated earth separated each pool, showing that it had not rained for some time. Sam made a note for future reference, wondering how the Dark had reduced or stopped the rainfall and whether the Light could restore the rain to use as a weapon. It would not destroy the Dark, but it would bloody well annoy them.

At last, Sam and Rose arrived at the place where the Dark were moving about, spreading the ground with a poisonous powder that smoked as it touched the soil; and burning green shoots wherever they found them. Sam and Rose joined a large group of warriors and pretended to search for new plant growth.

One of the warriors, who had some measure of authority, called them over. Sam translated the words into English in his head. "Who're you two? Where'd you come from? Your answer better be good, or I'll take you to the Dark Lord and he can ask the questions. You wouldn't like that. Oh no, you wouldn't." Sam began reciting the explanation he had committed to memory, and hoped desperately his accent would not give him away. He activated the voice box hidden in his disguise. He sounded just like a Dark warrior, *creepy*.

"Beggin' yer pardon, mi Lord. But we's been travellin' for days and felt in need o' good company. We be on an errand for the Dark Master, exalted be 'is name, and travellin' north to the next region."

The Dark officer looked at Sam closely, and said with suspicion in his voice, "an errand for the Dark Master, exalted be his name? That don't sound right. Why would he use the likes of you? The Master's errands is for the Dark Lords, not snivelling worms that squirm on the ground."

Sam replied hurriedly, "Mi Lord, that's why we's be chosen, travellin' secret like. It be an urgent errand. The Master wouldn't be happy with anyone who upset our mission. All we wants is a few hours company and rest. And then we'll be off again."

The Dark warrior, muttered to himself for a moment and then said, "alright. Keep to your own business and don't make any trouble. I wants you gone afore the sun come up."

The warrior walked away, and Sam breathed a long sigh of relief. He whispered to Rose, "that went better than I expected. I thought he would be much more suspicious. Let's wander around a bit and see if we can pick up any useful gossip."

Rose winced. "Could you turn off the voice box, your voice is making my skin crawl."

For the next two hours, Sam and Rose wandered around the area, keeping their heads down and noting various tidbits of information that might prove useful. The most significant thing they learnt was that the Dark Master would be visiting the Mortal Realm to inspect progress. Such a visit was unheard of. Was this the reason that Sam got away with his deception so easily?

Sam was not sure whether The Light could respond to the visit and disrupt it in some way, but he and Rose would report the event when they returned to The Light.

Although smoke still churned in the sky, Sam could detect a gradual brightening of the gloom. It was time to go. He and Rose slipped away unseen and headed back across the river and to the nearby portal.

Their first clandestine visit to Earth had been a success.

*****

Travel through the Light portal is instantaneous and was becoming less disorienting with each passage. Sam and Rose arrived in The Light awake this time but still ruffled by the experience. The first occasion that Sam and Rose had entered the Light, they arrived unconscious, even though they arrived by different means; Rose by way of the Veil of Light, a grandiose version of the portal, and Sam by more 'natural' means — a death of sorts in the Mortal Realm.

They each waited a couple of minutes in silence to get their minds back into gear. "Everything okay, Rose?" Sam asked.

"All present and correct, as far as I can tell. Nothing missing anyway," Rose replied with a weary smile as she started to remove the disguise.

The portal entrance was situated within the main Government Complex. It allowed for some privacy as they changed into their robes. They stowed the swords and disguises in their packs and left hastily after Sam noticed the time on a distant clock tower. If they hurried, they would arrive at the meeting with several minutes to spare.

Sam and Rose walked quickly through the colourful, formal gardens that surrounded the Advisory Council building and entered the vast foyer. They each passed through security scanners and walked towards a bank of lifts on their left. You could only reach one floor with these lifts — the Council Assembly Chamber on the third floor.

Sam and Rose finally entered a lift, the doors closing smoothly and seconds later they stepped out from silence into a hubbub of chattering voices and closely mingled bodies.

As they were both members of the planning committee for the Great Battle to Come, they found the correct doorway marked with an impressive plaque that read, unsurprisingly, *GBTC Planning Committee*.

They entered and had to pass through another layer of security.

There was a much smaller group gathered inside, and Sam spotted Gerald and John on the periphery. John saw them arrive and waved them over. The four embraced and entered the Assembly Chamber onto a raised podium at the front of the room.

Finding their places at the table, they sat and waited for the audience to take their seats in the body of the Chamber. The new Fae, seated on a higher podium, would Chair the meeting.

Around the walls large screens enabled delegates who could not attend in person to participate in the proceedings. Many were from distant lands and other worlds of Light. No one in living memory had attended such a significant meeting.

The idle chatter slowly subsided, as the last delegates took their seats. Attendants sealed the doors. The Fae stood. "I call this meeting to order. Welcome ladies and gentlemen. You are here because of your skills in sciences and engineering and for you experience coordinating Dark related research and response. The issue before us today could not be more grave or more potent — the loss of the Mortal Realm.

"We need the means to overcome the power of the Dark, with guile and stealth and intellect; with our greatest minds solving four persistent problems: the limitations of portal travel which only allows passage by organic matter; the means to heal the Earth so that new organic life can flourish; to permanently deny entry of the Dark into the Mortal Realm.

More than anything else, we need to harness the mighty, cleansing strength of water. The art of control, wielded so powerfully long ago, is now reduced to simple organic weapons and a trickle of magic tricks for children. We must recreate the knowledge and skills we have lost.

"That is why you are here today. To learn what we are up against and consider how to shape our response.

"We will hear reports from those operatives who conduct surveillance in the Mortal Realm to assess the activities and purposes of the Dark. They returned through the Light this morning. I call on Immanuel, the Chair of the GBTC Planning Committee, to introduce the operatives who are now to report. The first operatives to speak hold positions on the Committee. I will then receive the reports from other operatives around the globe.

"Please, only report back to this meeting, verbally, if you have something new or enlightening to relate. Otherwise, your reports will be received in writing. Immanuel?"

"Thank you, Honourable Fae," John replied as he stood at the speakers' lectern, having been introduced by his Light name. "I, along with several other Committee Members, took part in the surveillance operation conducted during the hours prior to this meeting.

Everything reported is the most current information available. I ask that all reports be brief as there is a lot to discuss today.

"I and fellow member, Gerald, seated to my left, visited a coastal area near Sydney Australia. One of our purposes was to infiltrate the Dark forces and test the strength of our training and disguises. That aspect of the job was highly successful.

"Our other purpose was to see what the Dark were up to. The landscape was unrecognisable. Smoke blanketed the sky in every direction, including the east, which of course means the oceans are blanketed as well. The air was hot and extremely dry. All signs of human civilisation were burnt and trampled to rubble. The Dark have destroyed all vegetation. Those we met, and there were many, were busy destroying any new growth or signs of life. Whatever they were meant to achieve, they were achieving it.

I would now like to call Sam Pilgrim to the lectern to give his report."

Sam stood and walked to the lectern. He bowed politely to the Fae. "Good morning, delegates. My friend Rose and I returned this morning to the inland forests through which we forged our pilgrimage so many months ago.

"The place was unrecognisable. As Immanuel found during his visit to the coast, everything was burnt, dead, and any signs of new growth were being systematically obliterated.

"The Dark were intent upon recreating Hell on Earth, a sick form of terraforming, more appropriately called Hellaforming.

"It had not rained for many months. The wide river we saw on our pilgrimage is now a series of muddy stagnant pools. Red tinged smoke obliterated the stars. I suspect that every person who reports today will have seen the same things, or worse.

"The only conclusion we have been able to reach is that the Dark are using the overheated Climate to transform the Earth and make it safe for habitation."

There was an audible gasp from the audience at this last statement. A buzz of excited conversation filled the Chamber. The Fae called for order. "Sam's last statement gives us real pause for thought, but we are yet to hear the global situation so should not jump to any premature conclusions. Sam, please refrain from wild surmises at this time. It is not helpful. Do you have anything else to tell us?"

"Yes, Honourable Fae. While speaking with a junior officer of the Dark I learnt that the Dark Master is shortly to visit the Mortal Realm and inspect the rate and quality of progress; for what other purpose he did not say. The officer was excited but bemused by his visit as such had never occurred before, at least in living memory. I could not find out exactly when this visit would occur. That is all I can report."

Sam returned to his chair and sat with a sigh of relief. He had detected irritation and annoyance in the Fae's tone. Our new Fae is a politician, Sam thought.

Reports from across the globe filled the rest of the morning. And with every report the situation became clearer. Sam was right. There could be no other purpose for the Dark to rid the Earth of all mortal life, to pollute the seas and prevent all precipitation. Lakes, rivers, seas and oceans would eventually die. The land would become a dry and dusty wasteland.

No one reported any signs of recent rain. Everywhere, a thick, churning layer of smoke hid the skies.

Heated discussion ensued through what remained of the afternoon, as scientists considered the ramifications of the Dark's actions. One concern was the impact upon global oxygen levels. The Light did not know whether the Dark could live without oxygen. The Light certainly could not. Another concern was the impact of a dense cloud of smoke and dust enshrouding the mortal world. Without sunlight, would the world become colder, so that all water might freeze? A *snowball Earth* - it had happened before.

The meeting ended in some disarray, although various tasks were assigned to separate groups to provide responses to the Darks' actions. Each group was to report back to the Planning Committee within one month. As the delegates filed out and the screens went dark, the Committee remained behind to discuss the day's events. Sam was feeling a little deflated by the experience and the other members seemed similarly affected.

Napoleon Barnes, the committee representative for all military matters, was livid. "It's intolerable," he said. "To have the Dark living just next door to us, with a whole universe to search for a way into The Light. We have just one month to receive responses and one more to complete our planning. We cannot afford to take any longer. It's too urgent."

The man looked stricken at the prospect of solving so many insurmountable problems in so short a time.

Sam noted that there was not a shred of remorse or embarrassment in his words, no acceptance of responsibility for the recent failings in military planning and execution.

John had also noticed these deficiencies. He tried to end the discussion with an uplifting message.

"We are not going to do nothing while we are waiting for the responses. We are going to begin a guerrilla campaign for the ages. We are going to frustrate, destroy, and annoy the enemy at every turn. So, start thinking about how best to do this. I will inform our fellow operatives of any plans we draw up. Let us make this global, people. We have got work to do."

*****

Sam, Gerald, and John were chatting after the fiery meeting. Their chosen café was situated within the Government Complex in the heart of Floriana City, the capital of this Earth-like world inhabited by successive generations from Earth's 21st century. Their table overlooked a glorious expanse of gardens, woodland, and lakes, alive with creatures of all descriptions, including tourists and locals enjoying the bucolic surroundings and balmy late afternoon air.

They were drinking espresso, rich, dark, and evocatively pungent. The conversation took on a general philosophical bent. They needed to forget about the dramatic meeting for a while.

Gerald asked quite innocently why Armageddon had occurred and how it was achieved. The three had already agreed on the use of the Christian word for the End of Days, as they were all from a culture where the word was traditionally understood.

Sam had been wanting to ask this very question himself, given the immensity of the loss, and the power needed to bodily remove every human soul from the Earth.

He had also been wondering whether The Light or the Dark had instigated it. John was the only soul around the table able to shed any light on the matter, and Sam and Gerald looked at him enquiringly.

John sipped from his cup and then lowered it to the table. "I asked a similar question when first interviewed for an operative's position by the Fae's Advisory Council. I arrived in The Light before Armageddon occurred, because I died some years before. It was a matter of some general debate and popular discussion. Most people saw Armageddon as a threat, but in theoretical and nebulous terms.

"The Council suggested I do some research myself, as there exists an extensive literature on the subject in electronic and paper format. And I did so. Although I'm not a scientist, I think I can give you an insight into the current understanding and research.

"As to how the event occurred in the way it did, the scientists have clearly found a genetic link. The human soul is linked genetically with the rest of the body. Genetic memory in the soul controls the autonomic response to an event such as individual death, or Armageddon, and the response is different for each. With death, the soul involuntarily goes through either The Light or the Darkway, carrying the memory of genes into the next dimension. In an event such as Armageddon, the whole body is retrieved and then transformed into the bodies you see today.

"In some cases, the soul is unsure which realm to aim for and is on the cusp of both Light and Dark.

"After death, these lost souls hang around in the Mortal Realm and, over millennia, they became the source of stories about ghosts and demons. These souls are often susceptible to kidnapping by the Dark, but not all kidnapped souls are on the cusp. Marion was unlucky — in the wrong place at the wrong time.

"I'm sorry if this is all a bit heavy, but you did ask." John raised his cup and sipped his coffee, while Sam and Gerald contemplated John's explanation.

Sam chuckled at the irony of it and said as much. "To think, the soul and the body are linked genetically and living researchers had not even found the soul, let alone any genetic link. The soul is genetic memory. Who would have thought it?"

The three friends fell silent for a few minutes and sipped their coffees, while watching the sun swiftly slip into the west, the violet-tinged shadows of dusk gathering in diverse places, muting the colours of the gardens into soft silhouettes. Becky would love this, Sam thought wistfully.

He then broke the silence and felt guilty for doing so but asked his question anyway. "Would it be indelicate to ask who started it, Armageddon I mean. It must be the Dark, right?"

John laughed heartily. "It's not an indelicate question at all, dear friend. They did, as you suggest. It's their interference in the Mortal Realm that has kept our war going, unabated for countless years. If the Dark had kept to themselves, The Light would never have intervened in human affairs.

"And now we are having to deal with their most audacious and dangerous play yet. We had to act very quickly to retrieve the souls destined for The Light. Even so, we lost many to kidnapping by the Dark. Those Children of The Light with long memories will be feeling extremely nervous right now."

John looked at Sam meaningfully. "You might also have a chat with Becky. She may be feeling superfluous right now. No one goes from Fae to civilian life without consequence. She will need something constructive to do, and why shouldn't she do it with you and Rose and the rest of the insurgent operatives.

"I think she'll make a fine insurgent if she has the right training. Marion could help with that. Come to think of it, Becky and Marion would make a wonderful team."

Sam considered John's words and realised that he had been blind to the subtle changes in Becky's demeanour. She had lost that vital spark that Sam so loved in her. He thanked John for the advice and promised to raise John's concerns with Becky, at the right time.

Sam had one more thing to say. "After today's reports, and the evidence of our own eyes, I don't think we have a hope in Hell of meeting the one-month deadline set by the Council. One, month, six months, five years, I don't think we're currently capable of beating the Dark. And relying on science to produce magical answers so quickly is fantasy." John nodded his agreement with Sam's assessment.

"You're right of course. That's not the way. There is another way, but I need to think about it more deeply before suggesting it."

With this enigmatic last statement, the three friends finished their coffees and bid each other goodnight. Today had been tiring and momentous. And tomorrow, the universe of Light would be buzzing with sensational stories of Dark intentions. Sam called Becky and told her he was on his way and then he ordered an autocab. The autonomous, svelte, and silent electric vehicle arrived within minutes and whisked Sam home to the arms of his wife.

Becky, the Fae who had led the Light at the time of Armageddon, had only recently resigned after the burden of that loss and the associated guilt became too much for her to bear. It would take all of Sam's skills as husband, friend, and lover, to lift these heaviest of burdens from her shoulders and to share the load. And given enough time, heal and grow stronger together. John's idea for Becky's future employment might just be the key to unlock that healing.

# Part Two - Armageddon in a Blink

The Dark Master was both like, and yet unlike, the monster created in the human imagination over many thousands of troubled years. He wielded neither the tail of a scorpion, nor the great wings of a bat. No horns dripping blood protruded from atop his head.

He looked much like the Dark Lords that knelt before him, exuding the same auras of malice and Dark foreboding. Unlike the Dark Lords, however, he wore a mask of beastly features, from which shining, red eyes looked out balefully into the Dark Realm; and into beyond, to another Realm, teeming with mortal life ripe for harvest.

None had ever seen the Master's true features, and it was a matter of Dark conviction that to view his likeness would mean instant obliteration. Some thought that the Master's face was so horrible to behold, that he hid it to protect those who feared and worshipped him.

"Is all in readiness?" The Master asked his chief advisor, Lord Kallorgan. "Yes, my Master Louseefa, we only await your word," Kallorgan replied. "We have expanded the paths of access to the Mortal Realm to accommodate the passage of large numbers of warriors. The Legions are waiting along the border-lands, ready to strike every inch of the Mortal Realm with force and terrible purpose."

"After I speak to the Dark Lords," Louseefa ordered, "I wish to return to my chambers and prepare myself for what is to come."

Kallorgan answered in an awed, obsequious voice, "yes, my Master. I will have the chambers prepared for your arrival." He backed away and left to fulfil this task assigned.

The Dark Master turned and faced the tens of thousands of Dark Lords kneeling before him. "Rise my Dark Lords," the Master's voice boomed unnaturally through the vast Dark Realm. "You have much work to do. Return to your Legions and order them to take their positions for battle. We make the crossing into the Mortal Realm in four Earth hours. Prepare your troops. We strike swiftly and with force. Capture whatever wayward souls you come across, whether destined for us or for the enemy. Destroy everything made and un-made by human hands.

"Burn the world — to the glory of the Dark."

"TO THE GLORY OF THE DARK," many thousands of Lords shouted in unison. They bowed as one to their Master and then dispersed to return to their troops, many disappearing in whirling vortexes of fire.

When all had disappeared, the Master sat down upon his throne of authority. He seemed weary and, somehow, smaller; seated there, the back of the throne towering above his grotesque mask. His red eyes looked out upon nothing, for the mind behind them was pondering unseen things, past things, the passage of years beyond number, the Downfall, the rise of a new and darker king, the profound unhappiness that had festered in the dark hours of his every single day.

Complete victory over the Mortal Realm would be his justice; and his great victory over the Light, those incompetent, arrogant and happy fools that had shamed and dishonoured him.

Why should not Louseefa be happy? Why should he not be free to explore endless worlds of Dark and Light. First, the Mortal Realm and then, somehow, it will be forth to the Light. The Universes would be his.

If vengeance had a name, it would be Louseefa!

The Dark Master stood and walked the short distance to his chambers. As he entered, the attendants milling about bowed submissively and waited for the Master to task them. Finally, he said in a commanding, but not, unattractive voice, "Leave me. Leave me and do not return until I call you." The attendants rushed away as if the waters of death were at their heels.

Louseefa ascended a flight of stone stairs to his private rooms and removed his cloak of state, a heavy, scarlet monstrosity that he loathed.

He sat down at a side table and removed a framed tapestry from the wall in front of him. Behind the tapestry hung a large mirror. Louseefa stared at the grotesque reflection and his body began to change. The scaly blackness of Dark ashen flesh disappeared, along with the mask, finally to reveal the luminous, translucent body of an Angel of Light. An oversized human face looked back, no not just human, a face as of a Lord, a Prince of Light! Though fire was dangerous for The Light, Louseefa did not fear its touch. His powers protected him always. He could even make fire as the Dark did. He could stand in the flames as they did, protected by his God-given powers.

Louseefa did not look much older than a youth, though his startling blue eyes told a different story. The face was handsome and should have been beguiling in the right circumstances. But the years had stripped that face of any vestige of innocence and goodness. Hate and pathos battled for supremacy, and this was the source of his anxiety and unhappiness — the enormity of what he had lost, and the unfulfilling nature of what he had gained were constantly at war in his head.

This invasion of the Mortal Realm would redeem his honour and his station. He would be a Lord of Light and Dark and no one would dare oppose him. Not even… He could not bear to say it, so short a word, and yet so maddeningly significant. Louseefa remembered the injustice of his casting out into the Mortal Realm, doomed to wander like a wraith amongst mortals; the bitterness that grew to encompass both the Light and the Living, so that his dark passing disturbed all who suffered in his wake.

With every year, the bitterness grew, the evil strengthened, the need for vengeance festered in his very soul, with a desperate pain that was beyond soothing.

And then Louseefa crossed over into the Dark Realm. How could that realm bar his entry, so filled with thoughts of vengeance had he become. He saw them, the black creatures that existed there, pathetic, and led by too many Lords who squabbled and fought over trifles. Yet the Dark were vast in numbers.

And Louseefa hatched a plan. He transformed himself into a Dark Lord. Shape shifting was one of the great benefits of being an Angel of Light.

But he needed something, some distinctive feature that set him apart to create a mystique. His head transformed into the semblance of a grotesque mask.

He spread rumours of a mighty warrior whose face was death. Rumour built upon rumour, upon myth, upon legend, upon song, and then passed finally into accepted Lore.

That was the time to strike, and Louseefa struck. And all who could oppose him fell away like fine ash through a sieve.

And now he sat, staring at his reflection; and at the hollowness of a Leadership he had wielded for so long. The years of meddling in human affairs, hardening the hearts of men and women, making new warriors for the Dark; it all seemed so pointless now. If he did not hold the Light in his grasp, he held nothing.

Louseefa stood and entered another room where he created a doorway with a wave of his hand, a secret door that concealed a hidden chamber. Louseefa heard water falling into a basin. He took a mug from a shelf and filled it with some water. And Louseefa drank, savouring the life-giving lubrication of his body. He was not Dark. He needed water to survive.

This spring he had tapped was the source of the feared waters that burn but do not destroy. He transformed the clean water into that terrible substance, and he wielded it like a weapon. The Dark would rather die by the immediate agony of pure water, than bathe in the eternal embrace of that foul liquid.

Far beneath Louseefa's living quarters, and deep within great caverns of eternal suffering, the pools of endless death echoed their agonising song. The cries of those thus bound to never die, forever in those sleepless waters lie.

Louseefa washed himself clean of the grime and waste that he could not avoid in the dirty air of the Dark Realm. Louseefa could not bear to wait much longer to be rid of this horrible place. Let the Dark have the Dark and Mortal Realms. He will have the Light.

As always, mortals had never been more than a means to an end.

*****

At the appointed hour, warriors blew the mighty horns of war along the length of the borderlands. Billions of Dark warriors stormed through the pathways into the Mortal Realm. The storm broke upon every shore, every mountain, forest and plain, all at once, entire.

And the foul breath of so many Dark warriors did poison the air so that mortal souls might be released. Many souls welcomed the Dark and clung to them for safety, whilst others, fewer in number, fled before the horror and sought the Light.

Tremendous fires consumed the world and bathed everything in an eerie light the colour of blood. Cities, towns, villages, and farms were torn to shattered ruins by the weight of evil numbers.

The mighty works of human civilisation, the well springs of art and learning, the hubris of a species born to rule the world with bombastic and tragic statements of authority, in steel, and stone, silicon and glass, all swept away in a blink.

Warriors of The Light at last came forth to meet the Dark, but they were vastly outnumbered. They were the better warriors, better trained and better equipped, yet they could not turn the black tide.

On violated plains of burning, midst arid wastes and forests primeval, on icy mountain tops and tropical shores, Light and Dark danced an age-old ritual. And everywhere, The Light fell back, consumed by fire and loss; fell back before the armies of Louseefa.

As the Light warriors retreated, they secured as many lost souls as they were able, freed many captives and passed them into The Light. These warriors wielded blades of shaped water, that dazzled as they cut through the ranks of shrieking Dark. But there were too few warriors and too few blades. It was merely a rearguard action, played out in every corner of the Realm, as they retreated to The Light. Taken by surprise, overwhelmed by Dark numbers, The Light lost the Mortal Realm.

Louseefa received the news of complete victory as he knew he would. Meticulous planning had secured the victory. He basked in the adulation of his warriors, and would, in time, take ownership of the Mortal

Realm for the Dark, for himself. Until then he would direct the progress of assimilation and transformation, designed to make the world fit and safe for the Dark to inhabit.

But victory was not total. The Light had known that the Dark invasion would come, though they did not know exactly when it would be. They could not know the numbers ranged against them. So, they hatched their own plan. They took precautions, they found candidates through skilful surveillance; candidate souls to protect and nurture through the storm of invasion, to grow and to learn on the difficult journey to The Light.

These candidates, if they succeeded, would carry their hard-won experience into The Light and form the basis of counter strike and guerrilla warfare, to harry the Dark at every turn, and win back the Mortal Realm forever, and for all times.

And thus, it was that Sam Pilgrim woke up.

Sam woke to storm and destruction, not to fire. He woke into a world already lost, a world he knew and loved, now gone with the winds of consuming fire — though he did not know it. The fickle fortune of weather saved him from the worst of invasion. But, unbeknown to him, eyes guarded, protected, and encouraged him. And in this way, Sam set out on pilgrimage to find a place of rest and redemption, where his mourning might resolve into solace and wistful memory. A place like The Light.

# Part Three - The Price of Power

Sam awoke in the early hours of the morning. He remembered falling into bed, exhausted by the day's events, making gentle love to Becky, and then holding her with a desperation he did not understand.

I'll never lose you again, was the last thought he remembered as he drifted off to sleep. And now, he had awakened with a start, because Becky was not lying with him. Sam threw aside the bedclothes and put on a robe before venturing out of the bedroom to find his wife.

He found her sitting on top of the back steps that led down from the veranda to the garden. Making a little noise to let Becky know he was behind her, Sam sat down awkwardly in the dim light and looked out at the world before them.

The air was clear. The stars in myriad array filled the dark sky with treasure immersed in wispy clouds of starlight, like sparkling dreams; seeming so close that Sam might pluck one jewel from the sky to adorn the woman he loved, sitting silently beside him. There was only a sliver of moon to reveal silhouettes in the beauty before them.

Sam had never been so happy, and unhappy, at the same time.

"It's beautiful isn't it," Sam clasped Becky's nearest hand and held it with a firm but gentle passion. Becky remained silent. Sam turned and looked at her face, so classically beautiful, softly glowing in the dim light. The moonlight found a glistening tear balancing there, exquisite, upon the point of falling.

"Oh Becky, I know you want to sit here to grieve alone in the darkness. But you don't have to grieve alone. Your loss is my loss. Your grief can be my grief, if you will share it with me. Please, let me fight this with you."

Becky turned her head and looked at Sam. She could see the concern and love fighting for supremacy upon his face and the sight stabbed her heart.

"Sam, I'm sorry. You don't deserve to be part of this. What an awful mess." She lay her head on Sam's shoulder and wept.

She was weeping for a dream turned to nightmare. Barely two months in The Light, elected Fae, though she did not want the title. Her beauty, grace and goodness had captivated the Realm, and none could see beyond the vision they had created, to the real woman given such a task.

Initially, Becky felt like Cinderella going to the ball in her golden carriage. How quickly then her carriage transformed into a pumpkin rotting at the core.

Although the role of Fae had become little more than figurehead over the past few thousand years, she retained legal, constitutional powers to govern. Her every attempt to assert those governing powers was subverted by her Advisory Council.

She could have used her powers to dominate the Council, but she did not, fearing the consequences of using them against The Light.

Her dreams of doing good turned very quickly into the cold reality of ineffectiveness. She was a lame duck - and don't let her forget it. She had no say in the government's preparations for, or response to, Armageddon. The Advisory Council saw to that.

And when Armageddon proved such a monumental disaster, the people with the real power scurried away and hid themselves in their office towers and left the Fae to face the consequences alone.

They deflected all public criticism directly to her door. She could not mount an informed defence of the Government's position because she was never, ever informed.


With John's support, Becky asked the Advisory Council to use her powers to aid the Testing Program. The Council's agreement freed Becky to try and regain some sense of worth and to save what little could be saved from the ravaged Mortal Realm.

She transformed into Guardian, and with the powers she still held as Fae, flew to Pilgrims Rest, and watched over Sam.

If she couldn't influence events as Fae in The Light, then she would do so as Guardian, the faithful hawk. She could protect and guide the soul of the man she loved, and of those who travelled with him.

Through her tears, Becky told Sam the parts of her story that she had kept from him. She left nothing out. The relief she felt in the telling was profound. When she fell silent, and her tears had stopped falling, Sam held Becky in his arms and said, "You did good, Becky. We wouldn't have reached The Light without you. Guardian gave you a sense of purpose. You raised your finger at your betrayers and went out on your own. And you were good at it.

"And you can do it again. I've been wondering if you would like to join me and the other operatives, working in the Mortal Realm. As Guardian, you've already proved a fine operative. I'm sure Marion would be delighted to train you in Dark etiquette, what little there is of it. And Rose and I can give you some pointers on the insurgency/infiltration side of things. There are many students training to be operatives at the Training School."

Becky was intrigued by the idea. She wiped her eyes and thought for a moment. "It would give me something to do. The alternative - moping around here all day, by myself - doesn't thrill me. Yes Sam. I think getting back to real work will be good. But, if we're both away at the same time, who'll look after Barney and Marge?"

Sam gave Becky an enquiring smile. "We could invite the Foremans to move in here for a while. The house is large enough. It would be like a holiday for them, and Barney and Marge would love it as well. What do you think?" Sam asked.

"I think, Mr Pilgrim, you have been thinking about this for some time." Her recent tears, subsumed by the growing excitement, and Sam was glad of it.

He didn't correct her misguided belief that his suggestion was the product of long deliberation since John had only mentioned it last night. He assured himself that there was no need to over-complicate matters.

Decision made, Sam and Becky went back to bed and slept soundly in each other's arms, until morning light blazed into their bedroom.

*****

Over a light breakfast, Sam, and Becky planned their day. The Foremans were expecting them first thing, and then Sam would deliver Becky to the Training Centre, where Marion was expecting to take charge of her new pupil.

Sam called John and asked if he could meet him there. John twigged as to why he would be meeting

Sam at the Training Centre. Sam could almost hear the whoop of joy in John's voice. "I'll see you there after lunch. Well done, Sam," John said happily.

The morning progressed as planned. They took an autocab to the Foreman's place. They were overjoyed by the invitation to look after Barney and Marge. Becky gave them a genetic pass key so that their house would give the Foremans entry. Security was one of the perks given to retired Faes, although Sam could not fathom why. Crime was non-existent in The Light. *A perk is a perk, I guess...*

They took another autocab to the Training Centre. Once they arrived, Becky scanned her genetic code into the cab's payment system, and they exited without having to make any kind of payment. *Now that is a perk I can appreciate.*

The Light did not use cash. They used electronic credits, but Sam still didn't understand how it worked. Debits and credits based upon the receipt and giving of kindnesses and good works, or services toward the well-being of The Light, or something along those lines. Credits could be spent on one's own needs, no need of money to complete the transaction.

Sam wondered what would happen if his account went into the red. *Keeping accounts here must be daunting.*

Marion was waiting in the foyer when Sam and Becky arrived. They hugged her warmly and she led them into a side room where they could sit and chat for a few minutes. Sam thought Marion looked a different woman. Gone was the frightened and scarred refugee that the pilgrims had rescued on their way to the Veil.

She was a pivotal part of the small team, formed to plan the overthrow of the Dark. An educator and administrator during her life on Earth, she managed the new Training School. Here, operatives and infiltrators learnt the skills needed to disrupt the Dark's operations in the Mortal Realm. They learnt the language of the Dark. They learnt how to wield shaping blades and practised throwing water bombs at moving targets. Those Light warriors who participated in the battles for the Mortal Realm assisted with the training.

Thus, many of their teachers were the veterans of Armageddon, the brave Light warriors that fought a rear-guard action to save the souls that might otherwise have fallen to the Dark. Their base of operations was next to the Training Centre. They formed the nucleus of a Light Defence Force that might one-day defeat the Dark.

Marion's was a big job, and Sam was in awe of this woman's resilience and ability. So recently healed from her time in the Dark and now central to The Light's fortunes.

Marion was Sam's height and a little taller than Becky, exuding a confidence that matched her elegance and fitness. Her fame travelled swiftly throughout The Light Realm. Students flocked to the school from all over Floriana and from several other worlds of Light.

"It's quite remarkable. So many off-world applications, even though these applicants have no obligation to help clean up our mess."

"One thing that does bother me however," Marion added, "is the one-month planning schedule set by the Council. It's unrealistic. We can't train the people we'll need in so short a time."

Sam replied decisively, "I agree, but don't despair just yet. The inner circle will take care of the politicians." Becky chose this moment to enter the conversation.

"Sam's right, Marion. We more than most, know what it will take to defeat the Dark. And the powers of a Fae are nowhere near sufficient to do it." This statement silenced the group as they contemplated the implications.

Finally, Becky continued. "We have to convince the Fae to relinquish his powers and return them to the Universal Consciousness, the Sonciel. Only the natural bestowal of powers by the cosmos, the primordial spirit, will give us a God of Light worthy of the task."

Marion looked dubious. "I wish you luck with that; I really do. The political faction will fight you all the way. They will put their own power and ambition ahead of defeating the Dark."

"Then we must convince them," Sam concluded. "We need the rest of The Light Realm to support the change, to make it clear that the Fae cannot refuse the wish of his people.

"Someone will have to take this message directly to the inhabited worlds. We need a powerful and persuasive speaker and someone who carries authority and reputation with them."

It was at this fortuitous moment that John knocked and entered the room.

"Hi everyone. The front desk said I'd find you here." Marion, Becky, and Sam looked meaningfully at each other and then looked directly at John and smiled.

"What? Why are you looking at me like that? Has something happened?" John, perplexed, stared back at them. "Should I be part of this, this, whatever it is?"

Sam stood and welcomed John warmly. "Thanks for meeting me here, John. We're all just delighted to see you.

"You're wondering what this is," Sam spread his hands wide, "this is exactly what it looks like. Three friends chatting amiably in a private room and planning a bloodless change of power."

John, taken aback, said in a much more serious voice, "a bloodless what? A coup? You're joking." The three friends continued to stare at John and burst into laughter.

Becky could not help herself. She stood and walked over to John and kissed him on the cheek. "We're sorry John, Sam is teasing you. We were, in fact, discussing our Fae problem."

Becky brought John up to date with the discussion thus far, finally revealing the need to capture and redirect public opinion across The Light Realm.

"The limited powers of the Fae won't be enough to defeat the Dark. We need to convince him and the Advisory Council to relinquish their authority. The natural order can then prevail to restore the God of Light and retrieve the Mortal Realm. "Someone needs to convince The Light to support us."

John's expression shifted markedly as if some great revelation had sprung to mind. "And you believe the someone should be me." John was thinking deeply. "I have already been thinking upon these lines myself and have come to the same conclusion. I understand why you might feel that I'm qualified to lead the delegation. But there are complications. The Fae appointed me to Chair the Planning Committee. The expectation being that I develop plans to defeat the Dark. I don't think the

Fae envisaged that my duties would extend to forcing him out of office."

"I can see why you would find that awkward," Marion commented drily. "I suggest a delegation from the Planning Committee meet with the Fae and reveal our intentions up front. No secret conspiracies, no deceptions. A simple request that he and the Advisory Council put the interests of The Light ahead of their own political interests and ambitions."

"And if we manage to secure the support of all the worlds of Light, and the Fae and Advisory Council still refuse to step down, what then? Must the bloodless coup become something more, something much darker. Such a thing has never occurred in The Light."

An ominous silence reigned. John's latest complication killed the conversation. Sam finally spoke.

"If The Light can't convince the politicians to see reason, then perhaps we need the Sonciel to do it for us. How we achieve this I can't even guess but it may be the only way."

"If I hadn't resigned as Fae, we wouldn't be in this position," Becky's small voice interrupted.

Sam stood quickly and took Becky into his arms. Staring into her eyes he said, "No Becky. That isn't true. Even if you as Fae willingly relinquished your powers, to whom would you relinquish them? The Advisory Council. The Council is as bad as the Fae." Sam turned toward the group, staring at them with conviction.

"The Fae is not the whole of the problem. I see it clearly now. The Advisory Council controls the power. These diminished Lords of Light, no longer Angelic, these politicians, will not submit to reason or overwhelming opinion." Sam took a deep breath as the vision drove him. "We'll be wasting our time and energy pursuing such a change of heart.

"Our appeal must be to the Sonciel. We need direct access. How do we achieve this? Where do we find the Consciousness of the Light Universe? How do we travel there? How do we speak with it? Can we even speak with the Consciousness?

"No one living knows these answers. We need to find those answers. And where will we find them? We need to study the earliest Archives, right back to the rebellion and the creation of the Fae. We'll find our answers there."

John stood abruptly. "Sam's right. The heart of the issue is our relationship with the Sonciel. We must restore the ancient ways. I know just the person to lead the exploration."

"Gerald!" Everyone said at once. It was obvious. Gerald would be able to speak with the philosophers and academics who had spent many years studying the Archives.

Sam asked innocently, "where are the earliest Archives kept?"

"There are a few copies here in the Central Library, but all of the original documents are on the First World of Light," John answered. "Travelling there needs multiple journeys by StarLight portal. The First World is similar, but alien to our modern eyes and thinking. The Angels of Light live there. They eschewed the later worlds of Light because of the changes wrought by the rebellion, the rejection of God and the withdrawal of the Sonciel. They will be suspicious and unfriendly when we arrive seeking their support and permission to study the Archives.

"And who can blame them. Their bitterness has festered in isolation for thousands of years." John took a breather as the others digested the difficult road to restoration.

Marion finally and decisively curtailed the discussion. "None of us expected to be speaking about these things this morning. Right now, I need to introduce Becky to her fellow students and teachers. Why don't you have lunch and discuss these weighty matters of State elsewhere. Our priority must be the mundane task of defeating the Dark and teaching the skills needed to do it." Sam thought he detected the tone of an impatient CEO.

John looked abashed by Marion's little speech. "Of course, Marion. I'm sorry our discussion delayed your plans. Sam, why don't we leave and get ourselves a late lunch and then find Gerald?"

Sam kissed Becky goodbye and agreed a time to collect her later in the day. He and John took their leave and left the room. At the same time Marion ushered Becky into the hallway, and they walked briskly into the bowels of the building.

# Part Four - Los Angeles

Rose and her partner hid themselves in the shattered rubble of the Getty Museum's South Pavilion, atop a slope overlooking the eastern end of the ravaged city. "Los Angeles, what a joke. Los Diablos, more like!" Rose said quietly, disgust in her tone. This was not a city any longer. As far as their eyes could see through the red-tinged gloom, there was destruction — smoke, flame, and an aura of death.

The nearby tiny portal, secreted within the rubble of another building through which they had travelled offered little comfort. There was always danger, always hordes of Dark wherever they ventured.

Rose's partner, Ayana, crouched beside her, trembling.

"The first time is always a shock. So are the second and third. You never get used to it. This is the way the Earth looks now, wherever you go," Rose explained in a kindly voice meant to calm the new insurgent.

Ayana was weeping. A Japanese born American in her old life, quietly spoken and gracious, with impeccable English, she replied with despair in her voice. "This was my home once and it's their home now. How can we change anything? Look at it. The Dark Realm must be just like this."

Rose was starting to think along the same lines, though not from despair. She had used many portals, seen many places on every continent over the past few weeks, and everywhere, the same destruction and gloom. She had seen St Peter's in Rome as ruined as the ancient Roman Forum; the Eiffel Tower a melted heap of iron; the Louvre Museum burnt and smashed; the Renaissance swept away; the highest aspirations of human artistic endeavour all gone.

*How can the Dark do this. They were once human. Surely, they felt some twinge of conscience as they pillaged the world.* Rose remembered thinking this when she first set eyes on smashed pieces of fresco near St Peter's. Was this heap of debris Michelangelo's masterpiece, the ceiling of the Sistine Chapel? A larger piece of fresco, a painted index finger pointing now at nothing save the ghost of Adam's outstretched hand, lost somewhere in the ruins.

The savagery and excess of the destruction wrought by these once-humans spoke otherwise. The Dark had no conscience, no memory of ever being human.

The water bombs and shaping swords Rose and her party carried were laughably inadequate. Millions of water bombs could not change what she had seen and her reports to the Planning Committee were, invariably, pessimistic.

So, why were they here? Here where hope had no place to be. They and several other teams of insurgents were here because the Dark Master would be making an appearance later today. Intelligence received from operatives said as much.

Rose as Leader of the observation teams on either side of the Pavilion where she hid, gave the pre-determined signal and the teams moved stealthily down the hillside, seeking scant cover amongst the mounds of scattered rubble from the Museum. It was slow going, but Rose was no risk-taker. Their objective was the Los Angeles National Cemetery.

This was where Intelligence told them the Dark Master would first appear before his tour of the devastated city. *Sacrilegious* was the only word that came to Rose's mind, to describe the choice of that place. More than 90,000 war veterans, from the Mexican American War to Afghanistan and beyond, lay there in neat rows, each marked by near-identical headstones. Rose knew from personal experience that death was the great leveller.

The way to the cemetery grew increasingly dangerous, the further they travelled. Rose had already seen large numbers of Dark warriors in the distance, travelling east. *They're going to the same place we are,* Rose thought glumly.

To reach the cemetery, they had to cross the San Diego Freeway via the Sunset Boulevard overpass, assuming it was still there. Whether they could do so without being seen was another matter. At some point, the teams would have to merge into the crowds of warriors and trust in their training and disguises.

After another couple of kilometres of slow but steady progress, the teams reached Sunset Boulevard and took shelter in the ruins of a large hotel. They could go no further. Fallen warriors crammed the boulevard. The teams converged on Rose's position, hidden by the broken remains of a masonry wall.

"Okay people, time to do our jobs." Rose was speaking in the language of the Dark, telling the operatives to spread out along the side of the boulevard and to merge with the flood of Dark warriors as surreptitiously as they could. "The virgins among you," this statement accompanied by a few nervous titters, "first timers, keep close to your partners and don't draw attention to yourselves. Everyone, turn on your voice boxes.

"All of you, your job is to listen, to pick up gossip and any information about future planning. Is that understood?" Each of the gathered operatives raised their left arms, confirming that they did.

"The Dark Master will say a few words. It won't want to miss this opportunity. Listen to what it says. Once it finishes speaking, withdraw through the crowd and meet at our rendezvous point.

"And people, don't get caught. Leave your water bombs and swords hidden behind the wall. They must not be used under any circumstances. We will regroup here in four hours. Dismissed."

The operatives each removed several water bombs and their swords from beneath their cloaks and stacked them in a pile behind the wall, hidden by a sheet of broken particle board. This was no place to use them. Yes, in an isolated skirmish with obvious escape routes, but not in the middle of an excitable, hostile crowd of enemies.

They fanned out along the extent of the wall, and one-by-one disappeared through the broken masonry into the dense crowd of disturbing Dark warriors.

"Ayana, are you ready?" The frightened girl nodded. "Keep close to me and remember your training. Don't look at the warriors. If a warrior speaks to you, mumble a reply. The disguise will protect you."

Rose chose her moment and stepped through the wall, Ayana following close behind. They walked alongside the warriors and merged naturally into the flow. Ayana quailed at the sight of these black things; things that flickered and roared. She kept her head down, not wanting to see the monstrosities. As she marched, Ayana repeated her mantra, *remember your training, remember your training,* over and over, the words commanding her rapt attention, diverting her from fear and flight.

They marched on and as they marched, racing hearts slowed, and confidence grew. For half of the operatives, this was their first encounter with the Dark, an encounter with so many, many Dark. Rose had endured a much slower introduction on the pilgrimage with Sam and was thankful for it. Even she felt the confounding, emotional pressure of so many vile creatures.

They were now marching down Sepulveda Boulevard which ran parallel to the San Diego Freeway. The freeway provided no clear passage, clogged as it was by burnt wreckage.

The closer they got to the cemetery, the gloomier the daylight became. Even so, Rose could see hordes of Dark warriors converging from every direction. This will be a mighty crowd indeed. Getting close to the Dark Master was the goal, *achieving it a challenge,* she thought.

Rose marched and sang along with the warriors confidently and brashly. And Ayana took heart from this display of courage and conviction.

In the distance, Rose saw a stage set up closer to the western end of the cemetery, and they were marching toward it. This was a stroke of luck. The space was nowhere near filled. They would be able to get quite close to the Master, the architect of the devastation all around them, without much difficulty.

As they entered the cemetery, she saw thousands of toppled and broken headstones trampled into the ground, none left standing. The large space was devoid of the trees and lush lawns that once graced that solemn and peaceful place — before the Dark.

Rose and Ayana stopped when they reached the periphery of the crowd, about 50 metres from the stage. Rose wanted to be closer so she could hear every word and study every nuance of the Master's demeanour and behaviour.

The crowd was milling about allowing easy movement forward. The inevitable crush would come later when the Master appeared. Their fire-resistant cloaks should prevent them from being burned.

After several minutes of slow and impeded progress through milling warriors, they reached an ideal position, less than 20 metres from the stage.

Now, they waited. Two hours they waited. The crowd and excitement grew, banners flew, and raucous singing and chanting broke out throughout the crowd, finally combining into one monstrous density of sound. It was like the biggest, nastiest football crowd ever assembled, and the home team was winning.

Something was happening on the stage. Rose stared at the place where whirling colours appeared in a storm of spinning madness, slowly drawing inward to coalesce into a massive black figure — the Dark Master. The noise of the crowd reached a painful crescendo as the Dark warriors celebrated their Master's appearance.

The Master raised its right hand, and instantly, the crowd grew silent. Rose assessed that the figure was as tall as the two Dark Lords that had appeared with him. It was wearing a hideous coat and, stranger still, a mask that covered the head, as of some demon, red eyes staring into the distance. *Why does it need to wear a mask, was it a flair for the dramatic, or was the Master hiding something?* These and other thoughts passed through her mind, and she looked at the Master with increased intensity. *Why, why?*

And then, the Master spoke. The language was ugly but, surprisingly, the voice was not. And what a voice! Somehow, it filled the world with words. The warriors at the back of the crowd could hear it. Rose thought it remarkable.

She noted other things. The Master was not brutish, not like the Dark Lords. Physically, it looked the part, but, in every other way, it was so much more. The voice was eloquent, cultured, and hypnotically persuasive. The stance of the body, and the fluidity of movement spoke of nobility, not corruption.

This was wrong. This thing, this Master, should exude evil, should feel evil. Instead, Rose felt comforted, accepted and — and *loved*. This thing felt *human*. Rose did not believe it was a trick or deception. Why bother with such niceties? To impress the Dark warriors? No. They neither had the wit nor the learning to appreciate good manners. What Rose was seeing and hearing was not an act. It was weird, unexpected, and frightening.

The incongruity did not make any sense. The incongruity persisted as she listened to the words projected from behind the mask. The words were exactly what she expected to hear.

"Brothers, sisters, my children. We are victorious. You have won the Mortal Realm for the Dark. A new world to inhabit and make our second home. Victory rewards your loyalty.

"I honour you, my children, but the victory is not yet complete. Today I tell you, we will conquer The Light."

These last words delivered with audacity and panache yielded a mighty roar from the assembled crowd. Ayana covered her ears, overwhelmed by the tremendous wave of sound. Rose, who was yelling along with the rest of the crowd, saw Ayana's alarming reaction and nudged her hard in the ribs. Ayana quickly dropped her arms and mimicked Rose's behaviour.

The girl had forgotten her training. She had put herself in danger. A cold sweat formed on her brow as she waited for savage, burning, grasping arms and discovery. Slow seconds passed. Nothing. Relief. No warrior had seen her.

"The Light have become weak," sneered the Master. "They cannot defeat us.

"We. Will. Find. A. Way. We will enter and conquer The Light!" The crowd of Dark roared their approval.

Rose whispered to Ayana. "We've heard enough. It's time to go." Just as she said this, there was a disturbance in the crowd about 10 metres away from their position. Grappling and high-pitched screams, both Dark *and* human drew the attention of the crowd. The warriors moved toward the action, and this provided the diversion that Rose and Ayana needed to withdraw.

It took a few minutes of patient withdrawal for them to finally stand on the periphery of the crowd. As yet, no one else was leaving. From their distant vantage point, Rose saw a figure dragged on to the stage, smoke rising from the charred flesh where he was held. The Master held the black figure up by its legs for all to see and stripped it of a disguise. Then, bending down, he picked up a small spherical object from the floor of the stage. "Water, *foul be its substance,* this spy has brought water into our midst," the Master said indignantly. "How dare he. What shall we do with this thing?"

The crowd roared a rage-filled reply, "burn it. Burn it."

"So be it," answered the Master. He turned to the Dark Lords, said something Rose could not hear, and threw the man towards them. The doomed man, grasped in the mighty hand of one Dark Lord, disappeared in a whirlwind of flame.

"We have lost one of ours," Rose whispered. "He brought a water bomb and has paid a terrible price. Ayana, learn from this."

The Master had finished speaking and he too disappeared, albeit in a grander, more colourful whirlwind.

*A flair for the dramatic. This Master is a consummate performer.*

The crowd started to disperse. Most were heading toward the east. Only a few warriors were travelling in their direction. Rose whispered again, "Ayana, this will be extremely dangerous. The Dark will be searching for other intruders. If we're questioned, let me do the talking." Ayana nodded her understanding.

They walked back along Sepulveda Boulevard confidently, pretending to chat as they went. They reached the Sunset Boulevard overpass. So far, so good. No Dark warrior had shown an interest in them. As they turned left to cross the overpass, their luck changed. Another warrior turned left and walked closer seeming to want to talk with them.

Many other warriors walked about 20 metres behind them.

"Where's you two off to then? Bloody marvellous, weren't it, the Master gave that Light thing what for. He be God to us."

Rose put her language skills to the test. "God he be, no doubtin' that. What a great show it were. You's goin' far?"

"Me? Nah. Just along this ways a bit and then into the hills. Me and me mates is huntin' see. There be more of them Light bastards about, no doubtin' it. We's-ll find 'em."

"Good huntin' friend. We got to leave you now." Rose and Ayana turned in the direction of the derelict hotel.

"Wait a minute, where's you goin'? There be nothin up there for the likes of you."

"We's got friends waitin' up the hill a ways," Rose said, hoping that this creature would leave them be. Rose stepped through the broken wall. Several other operatives were waiting. "Quick, arm yourselves," she ordered in a faint voice. "We've got trouble."

Just as Rose picked up her sword, the Dark warrior poked its head through the wall. The head disappeared in a cloud of steam as Rose cut it off. "Spread out and guard the openings in the wall. Take plenty of bombs with you. There are more of them."

Yelling erupted on the other side of the wall as the Dark saw the Warrior's body fall.

Rose and Ayana armed themselves and watched their opening in the wall. Another head, another dazzling blade. Five more heads went the same way. And then, all went quiet until a battle horn blew.

"Okay people we move now. Up the hill as fast as you can. More of these bastards will be coming."

The group ran, fanning out to create multiple targets. As they ran up the hillside Rose shouted for all to hear. "They will chase us. Watch out for firebombs. Zig zag if you can." Everyone followed Rose's example, and they kept running. Rose developed a painful stitch in her side, but it would pass. Breathing became laboured and Rose could see that Ayana was in trouble. She stumbled up the hillside, fighting for every breath. If the Dark caught her, she would die in flames. *Not on my watch,* Rose thought as she ran to Ayana and encouraged her to keep going.

Dark warriors appeared at the bottom of the hill and gave chase. They were fast. The portal was not more than 200 metres away, but Rose thought it might be too far.

*Catching up, catching up*, they were within throwing range and the first firebombs fell. Rose dropped behind the others to watch over Ayana, who was running on adrenalin alone, now, at the end of the race. A firebomb fell just to Rose's side. She grabbed Ayana and pulled her up the hill out of danger. The last few steps, and into the broken masonry. She stole a peak behind. A warrior was reaching out to grab Ayana. She pulled her into the portal entrance, then turned to face the warrior. "You can't have her you steaming heap of shit." She took out her last water bomb from under her cloak and threw it directly into the head of the warrior.

*Steaming shit, an accurate description,* Rose thought as she passed with Ayana through the portal to safety.

When she emerged from the portal on the other side, Rose saw that there were only three operatives waiting for she and Ayana. They had lost half their number. *What a debacle.*

"We'll wait here for one hour in case the others arrive. While we're waiting, get your tablets out and enter your memories and impressions of this operation. Anything may be important, no matter how trivial it might seem." The five exhausted survivors retrieved their tablets from the hidden pocket in their cloaks; collapsed where they stood and began their reports.

Rose was downcast. So many lost, two of them newer recruits. Given the number of Dark that chased them up the hillside, she was not hopeful that anyone else would be coming through the portal.

After a fruitless hour of waiting, Rose spoke. "Listen up. We've lost friends today and there'll be time to grieve, but the time is not now. Now, we must complete the job we set out to do. We'll meet at the Training Centre in one hour to compare notes and debrief. Then those of you who live elsewhere on Floriana may leave by your chosen portal. You are dismissed."

Before dispersing, the operatives removed their disguises and swords and handed them to Rose.

Ayana stayed behind after the others had left. She looked distraught. "I'm sorry Rose. It's all my fault. If you didn't have to look after me, the others might have survived."

Rose held Ayana at arm's length and looked the girl squarely in the eyes. "That's rubbish Ayana. We all knew the risks, particularly the seasoned operatives. You did good today. You survived the toughest introduction to the Dark I've ever seen. With more experience, you'll make a fine operative. Well done.

"Now, go, review your report, and we'll meet again at the Training Centre to debrief in one hour." Ayana smiled thankfully and walked off. Rose bent down and collected the disguises, cloaks, and swords. She gave a resigned sigh and said to herself, "I'm getting too old for all this stuff. My aching back…"

# Part Five - Another Revelation

Sam, John, and Gerald were sitting in the Training Centre Coffee Shop when Rose walked in, looking deflated and tired. Her eyes lit up when she saw her friends. There was no one else in the place save serving and service bots. It was early evening, and most people had gone home to their families.

Walking over to their table she was lacking her typical swagger and vitality. "May I?" Rose asked as she retrieved a chair from a nearby table and sat down before they could answer.

John looked amused, but there was concern in his voice. "Of course, Rose. Please join us. You look terrible?"

"Thanks for that," she said wearily. "You wouldn't look so flash either, if you'd been chased up a steep hillside by dozens of Dark warriors, with firebombs falling on your head.

"Sorry guys," Rose shrugged and stretched her shoulders, "it's been a tough day. I lost five operatives today, and all things being considered, it was — my fault."

John took Rose's hand and held it tightly, but with obvious affection. "I don't believe that for a minute Rose. You're the best operative we have. I'll get you a coffee and then you can tell us about it." Rose nodded and looked down at the table while John placed the order through his tablet. Rose had a beaten look about her, and the three friends could see how badly today's events had affected her.

After a minute, an autonomous trolleybot arrived at their table. A pleasant voice said, "good afternoon, I have a coffee for Rose. Please take the cup from the serving tray." Rose sat glum, silent, and unmoving. "I'm sorry. I have a coffee for Rose." Rose sat, lost in her own world of pain. "Is there something wrong with the coffee? I can replace it at once."

John reached over and took the coffee from the tray. "No thank you, the coffee is fine."

"Is there anything else I can get you?" The trolley asked politely.

"No thank you — mmm — Zelda," John said, searching for the name card on the trolley.

With a cheery "have a nice evening" the trolley left as quietly as it arrived. John thought the customary cliché unfortunate given Rose's emotional state. He continued to hold Rose's hand, stroking it gently with his thumb. After a few more minutes, Rose's mind returned to the table.

She looked up and blinked several times, then saw John's hand gripping her own. She stared at him and gave him a thankful smile. Then, addressing the whole table, said wearily, "can we rewind and start again. Pretend I just arrived. Hi guys, what's new?" Rose looked down. "Oh, is this coffee for me, thanks."

Sam was happy to start again. "Lots actually. We've been discussing plans for handling the Advisory Council and the Fae and have settled on a course of action. After discussing it with you, Becky and Marion, of course. Before we tell you is there anything that happened today that might affect our planning?"

Rose took a sip of her coffee. "Oh, that's good.

"I don't really know. Why don't I fill you in on today's events and you can decide."

Sam realised how silly his question was. "Umm, that seems logical," he answered, sheepishly.

Rose spent the next ten minutes telling them about the day's events. "So, I've just left a very solemn debriefing session with the four surviving team members. They're cut up about losing their friends but today has taught them a lot more than a classroom or training ground could. Particularly about the value of obeying orders."

John, still holding Rose's hand interrupted, "and that's why what happened today is not your fault, Rose. One operative disobeyed your orders, deliberately. He knew what he was doing, and he was prepared to die for it. You had a right to expect obedience, not deliberate disobedience which put everyone else in danger."

"I guess," Rose said in a small voice, not sounding convinced. She took another sip of her coffee and decided to change the subject. "I've given you the facts — John, I've sent you a copy of the Report being sent to the Advisory Council — but I haven't told you the best part.

"Based on my discussions with the other operatives, and my own observations, I can tell you that the Dark Master is not Dark!"

It was as if a firebomb had hit the centre of the table. Shock on every face, profound silence. Then Gerald spluttered, "not Dark? What is he? Who is he? That is extraordinary. He has been the Dark Master for several thousand years. The Archives say as much. If he is not Dark, how has he managed to keep the job so long?"

No one answered immediately, preferring to think about the question. Gerald answered it himself. "I could hazard a guess, but first I need to know what led you to believe this."

Rose told them, laying out the tell-tale signs that had confirmed her belief. "More than anything else, it was the voice. That was not the voice of a Dark. Sure, he looked the part, except for that horrible mask, but he certainly didn't sound it."

Gerald pondered Rose's evidence for a while then said, "I'm convinced, and if other reports from around the mortal world agree, that will only make the evidence incontrovertible.

"If he is not Dark then several things follow, firstly, he is susceptible to fire but is able to protect himself. Secondly, he needs water to survive. All other living creatures do. And thirdly, his hold over the Dark must be powerful indeed.

"Let us consider the timeline. Several thousand years ago, Louseefa rebelled against God leading to his exile to the Mortal Realm. Copies of the earliest Archives held in the Central Reference Library tell us that shortly after the exile, the Dark Master appeared, as if from nowhere.

"What if... the Dark Master is an Angel of Light, the Fallen Angel of Light?"

It was John's turn to splutter. "Louseefa? You're saying the Dark Master is Louseefa?" John stopped talking and slowly looked around the table. "It's a lot to take in, but — it makes sense. Terrible sense. The Dark Master is one of us, and he must hate us with a passion. Rose, you told us that his endgame is to conquer The Light. This revelation explains why.

"Friends, we are in trouble. Rose might have other, more basic words to describe the situation," looking at her with smiling mischief in his eyes. Rose looked back with hope in hers.

"I'll leave those words for dealing with the Dark. They don't belong here."

John ordered a fresh round of coffees, and the group settled in for a serious and fateful discussion. Sam told

Rose about the earlier discussion with John, Becky, and Marion. After speaking for several minutes, he finished with a summary of there thinking. "So, you see Rose, there's really no point appealing to the Fae alone. It's the Advisory Council that has always pulled the strings and controlled the power. Becky knows from personal experience just how much control they can exert upon the Fae.

"Once we get our thinking in order, we'll need to send a delegation to meet with the Council. We must do this out in the open. They'll hear about our activities anyway. So why not cut out the middleman and go straight to the top.

"We can politely ask the politicians to relinquish their authority and return it to the Consciousness — the Sonciel; in other words, ask them to restore the old order. And we all know what they'll say." Nodding heads around the table greeted Sam's assertion.

"Once we have their refusal there is only one path open to us. We must complete another pilgrimage, this time to the First World, and convince the Consciousness, God, and the Angels of Light to take back what was taken from them."

"Our suspicion that Louseefa is the Dark Master might be the key to gaining their support," Rose suggested.

Gerald raised an issue that no one else had yet mentioned. "What if the Advisory Council tries to prevent us from using the StarLight Portal Network to travel to the First World. Would it not be wiser to keep that part of our planning from them? There is no telling what they might do to protect their power. They might even shut down the network altogether."

"Worse still," John said, gravely, "they might decide to cut their losses and destroy the portals to the Mortal Realm. Once they receive further reports, from operatives around the Earth spying on the Master's victory tour, they'll know just how badly they have bungled things and decide to raise the drawbridges. There would never be a Great Battle to Come. Unless the Dark find a way into The Light."

Everyone started speaking at once and Sam banged the table. "Please, everyone. I know how much we have invested in rescuing the Mortal Realm from the Dark, but we won't achieve our goal without careful planning; and talking over each other won't help.

"Before we plan anything else, we need to bring Becky and Marion up to date; assign specific tasks to those best able to research and organise them; and, most important of all, keep our planning secret until we reveal our hand to the Council. Do you all agree?"

No one sitting at that table objected to Sam's assessment. "Rose, could you speak to Marion about our latest thinking? Sam asked. "I'll speak with Becky."

"Speak with us about what?" A familiar voice cut into the conversation. Marion and Becky entered the coffee shop and walked over to the table.

Rose was crestfallen. She would have to break the news of today's losses to Marion. Please God, not tonight. Rose was barely keeping herself together. How could she possibly handle Marion's grief as well?

Rose projected the most natural smile she could manage and said, "hi Marion. Oh, it's nothing that can't keep until tomorrow. I'm kind of beat after today's adventure and just need to collapse into bed. Perhaps we can chat in the morning?"

"Okay with me Rose," Marion answered cheerily. Becky and Sam embraced, and Sam could see that today had been good for her. Sam said to everyone, "it's getting late so why don't we call it a night and reconvene our conversation tomorrow? I could do with a good night's sleep myself." And so, the discussion ended. John said good night and left holding Rose's hand, Marion and Gerald walked out talking quietly together, leaving Sam and Becky alone. "I can see you had a fun day. You seem excited about it," Sam said, "I don't want to spoil the moment by having a deep discussion with you now. We need to keep you abreast of our thinking, but we can have that chat in the morning. Becky embraced Sam and with her head resting on Sam's shoulder, they walked out to call an autocab.

# Part Six - Casting the Dice

The weeks passed by, and with every report received from the Mortal Realm, the news grew worse. The Advisory Council could be in no doubt about conditions in the Realm, and yet they had done nothing. They had sat on their hands. Made no announcements. Not a word to the people. The Fae was equally absent and silent.

The Foremans had settled into their new accommodation and were perfect house guests. The home was big enough to allow each couple privacy, and, on most days, the Foremans had the place to themselves.

On the first morning after their arrival, Gwen, and Dave, for these were their names, said how thrilled they were to be with Barney and Marge again. "How did you manage to get Marge here?" Gwen asked, "and why-ever would you think to bring a cow?" Sam laughed at this, remembering how insistent Marge had been to travel with he and Barney after they left that hidden paradise in the valley. "I had no say at all. Marge would not be left behind. You can thank Becky. She rescued Marge from the bush and led her to us. Oh, and Becky was a hawk at the time. Did I mention that?" Sam asked with a grin, which led to further hilarious discussion over breakfast; including how to milk a cow, a revelation about Marge that astonished the Foremans. After breakfast, Sam and Becky gave their horses and Barney some exercise and Sam conveyed the latest information to Becky. She looked most concerned by Sam's words.

That was then, and this was now. Today was crunch day. The group were to meet with the Advisory Council this afternoon. Every member had done their homework, and they were ready. John had asked Sam to do the speaking for the group, and he agreed, although reluctantly. He was inexperienced at public speaking and felt the weight of responsibility keenly. None of them knew how the meeting would go. They had no idea at all whether the Council would accept their arguments.

If the group could not persuade the Council to see reason, they had planned what would follow, meticulously; bags packed, and every member of the pilgrimage ready to leave at a moment's notice. Marion and Becky would remain behind to oversee things on the home world, Floriana, while they were away.

At 2 o'clock in the afternoon, the group sat, assembled, waiting for admittance to the Advisory Council's Tribunal Chamber. Sam flicked nervously through his notes, staring every so often at the door that would admit them, either to success or to ruin. It was that clear cut. Placing their arguments on the record would mark them for the rest of their journey in The Light. There would be no turning back. They would forever be heroes or villains.

The Council kept them waiting for 30 minutes. The delay only increased Sam's determination. This petty exercise in power left the rest of the group unmoved as well. Political games would not deter them.

At 2.30 the doors opened, and the group walked confidently into the Chamber. Sam saw at once that the room was organised as if for a trial.

There was a raised dais at one end of the Chamber. There were eleven seats. The central seat was larger and more impressive. For a judge, Sam thought. The realisation hit the group. This would not be a meeting of equals in The Light. This was a Tribunal, and they were here to be judged.

Ten senior members of the Advisory Council filed into the Chamber and sat. The next person to enter was the Fae. He took his place in the judge's seat.

"This Tribunal is called to order," the Fae announced. "Will the defendants please name themselves for the Record."

John spoke, barely keeping his rage in check. "Defendants? Is this a lawsuit or judicial assembly? We requested a meeting, not a trial."

The Fae looked imperiously at John, "that may have been your wish, but I and the Advisory Council have decided otherwise. Once we have your names on the record, we will inform you of the charges brought against you. Now please, identify yourselves." Sam spoke quietly with John, and they agreed that there was no point in antagonising the Tribunal.

"Sam Pilgrim, spokesperson for this delegation." Each member of the group read their names into the Record.

The Fae read from a gilded book placed on the tribunal bench. "You are all hereby charged with the following crimes: One, subversion of the State. Two, plotting to seize power lawfully vested in the Fae and Advisory Council. And three, spreading false rumours and encouraging dissent amongst the populace. How do you plead?"

John spoke for the group. "We cannot plead because there are no such crimes legislated in The Light."

The Fae smiled, "Ah, there you are wrong. As Fae, I signed these crimes into law yesterday. You will now plead. If you refuse to do so, we will hold you in contempt and enter Not Guilty pleas on your behalf."

The group, shocked by the turn of events, remained silent.

"So be it. We will record pleas of Not Guilty."

Sam, Becky, John, Rose, Gerald, and Marion stood before the Tribunal. There was no place for them to sit. Psychological warfare, dirty tactics, Sam thought.

Sam spoke for the group. "Let the Record show that we do not recognise the legality of this Tribunal as there exist no precedents. Never before, has The Light

Realm seen such an abuse of power. We came to you openly and willingly to discuss matters of great consequence for the future of two Realms, both Mortal and Light. We respectfully ask that you listen to our arguments with open minds. We came to petition you in good conscience."

"Or, have you already decided our guilt?" Questioned John. "Is this so-called Tribunal, nothing more than a charade, a kangaroo court?"

The Fae looked sternly upon the group. "No. This is not a kangaroo court, as you so colourfully describe it. We will hear your petition and your arguments. If or when we find you guilty, you will all be banished from The Light."

Banishment from The Light meant one thing only. They would walk in Louseefa's shoes, banished to the Mortal Realm. Louseefa became the Dark Master. The group's banishment was a death sentence.

The Fae concluded, "we will confiscate your genetic identity discs for the duration of these proceedings. I urge you to seek legal counsel. This Tribunal is adjourned. We will reconvene at 11 o'clock on Friday morning.

Two days to turn the tide. Sam feared the worst.

The judge and jury filed out of the room, leaving the group alone, shocked and confused by the audacity of the Council's actions.

*****

Sam and Becky were sitting on the back veranda with the Foremans, sipping their drinks of choice and staring into the evening darkness. That darkness was a fitting metaphor for how Sam was feeling. Everything felt surreal. The Advisory Council's pre-emptive strike left Sam bereft of answers. Was this what defeat felt like? Defeat, before the fight had even begun.

Gwen and Dave Foreman were aware of the situation. Sam and Becky had spent an hour explaining the group's evidence and arguments and the proposals they had hoped to put before the Council. "We're accused of crimes that do not mirror our activities or intentions," Sam explained.

"To consolidate their power, the Council has arbitrarily created the means to protect their political ends. They have picked crimes out of the ether and legislated them. We're condemned before the hearing even begins. It's a terrible precedent, and I fear for the future of The Light." Sam was on the verge of tears at the injustice of their situation.

Now, the four friends looked into the Darkness, three of them seeing nothing but the void. One of them, however, saw something more. Becky held Sam's trembling hand, and said, "Sam, there is still hope. I must tell you all something in confidence. Gwen, Dave, please don't tell anyone what I am about to say, including your family. The fewer people who know, the safer we will all be.

"Over the past few months, since I resigned as Fae, my supporters have been active throughout The Light; on every world they have spread the group's message. Even now, news of this afternoon's hearing is flashing around The Light. There is a groundswell of active support for our desire to restore the old ways. Billions have signed petitions, and my supporters are ready to present them to the Council. My supporters and I have foreseen the likelihood of today's indictments.

"Several of my supporters work in the Government Registry and are this minute preparing genuine, replacement, genetic identity discs. They are also providing false, but also genuine, identity discs, should the pilgrims need to travel anonymously. These discs will be delivered tomorrow.

"Legal practitioners amongst my supporters will prepare papers seeking a two-month Adjournment of Proceedings on the ground that we need sufficient time to consult legal counsel and prepare a proper defence. They will present the Adjournment documents to the Council tomorrow.

"So, you see Sam, there is hope. We can still pursue our plans."

Sam spent some time absorbing Becky's information, his black pit of despair slowly transforming into renewed purpose. The relief of this release was dizzying and Sam grabbed Becky and kissed her, as much with thanks as with passion.

"Becky, this is marvellous. I knew that you had supporters, but I never dreamed, I never suspected. They've done so much while we've just been talking."

"Wait Sam. Our plans depend upon a successful two-month adjournment. I and Marion must stay behind and cover for you as much as possible. The Council will notice your absence, despite our best efforts."

Sam saw the implication. If they did not return to Floriana within two-months, Becky and Marion may find themselves in front of the Tribunal, fighting for their lives.

"Becky, no. We can't leave you behind. The Tribunal may reconvene at any time and try you. You know they will find you guilty. Banish you to the Mortal Realm. I can't risk that happening. Please, you mustn't stay behind."

"Sam, it must be this way. My supporters here will need me should they come under suspicion. I can't abandon them.

"In any case, the actions of the Fae and the Council will generate outrage around Floriana. My supporters will encourage the population to besiege the Council Assembly Building should the Tribunal reconvene. Given the public outcry, they would not dare to banish us."

"But the danger. There are no police or military or weapons to use against The Light. But what about the Fae? You know how much damage his powers can inflict. This will change The Light forever. People may die!"

Becky hugged Sam tightly, willing him to understand. "Sam, please. My supporters know the risks. They and the populous will do what needs to be done because they believe in our cause. They call themselves the God Movement. They know the risks. We've spoken about these possibilities often. I can't leave the people to face this future alone."

Sam was not convinced, but he saw her dilemma. She was determined to stay, and nothing Sam could say, would dissuade her. He nodded sadly, acknowledging the reality of Becky's position. "Then it's up to us to return within two months. I'm not happy about this at all. We're taking such a risk; with your life and with the future of The Light."

"Sam, ever since we began our quest to restore the old order, we have been taking risks. Our quest was always a risk. Yet we carried on because it was the right thing to do. We owe our supporters the courtesy of pushing our quest to the end, whatever that end may be."

Sam had nothing else to say. And even if he did, he hadn't the strength to say it. He marvelled that this brave, resourceful, intelligent, and beautiful woman could care for him so much. All he could do was hold her in his arms and pray that the unknown God would protect her.

They held each other, there on the edge of darkness, for what seemed a lifetime, finding strength in the passion that they shared. It was only much later that they realised the Foremans had quietly left the table and gone to bed. They were so involved in their conversation, that they had not even noticed. Sam and Becky rose from the table and went to their room seeking the welcome oblivion of sleep.

*****

The wait felt interminable. It always does when you are waiting for water to boil. Or when you are waiting for an answer that brings the judgement of life or death.

The group gathered in a Lecture Hall at the Training Centre were not waiting for water to boil. John was speaking quietly with a junior member of their legal team; the others were nervously eyeing the door through which the answer would come.

The Group of Six, the popular name for these anxious pilgrims, knew that their fate lay in the hands of a hostile Tribunal, this very minute hearing their legal arguments. Leading Counsel, an impressive man who worked as a Barrister before the Fall, considered they had a good chance of receiving the Adjournment they looked for. The assessment was comforting. But that assessment was not certainty, hence the nervous wait.

Sam left the hall and went to get some food for the group. Upon his return he uncovered a tray of mixed sandwiches and left it where everyone could help themselves. Some eagerly sated their hunger, others, like Sam, were too nervous to eat. Sam noticed that the junior counsel waiting with them did not take a sandwich. Hardly encouraging, if one of the legal team is so nervous he can't eat, what does that say about our chances? Sam did not believe in omens, but this one stuck in his brain and increased his anxiety.

Two hours later the Group of Six learnt their fate. The Leading Counsel walked in with his two clerks and wasted no time delivering the Tribunal's ruling. "There is good news and there is less than good news," he said. "The Tribunal has allowed the Adjournment, but they have halved the time we were looking for. The Adjournment is for one month, not two." The Counsel handed the Adjournment document to Becky, as she was to stay in Floriana City, along with Marion.

"One month. Can we do it all in one month?" Sam asked, a note of desperation in his voice. "Everything will have to run like clockwork; any delay would be disastrous." Sam looked at Becky with pleading in his eyes. Come with us, come with us they were saying.

"We'll bloody-well have to," Rose said, in her usual way of getting to the nub of the matter. "The sooner we leave, the sooner we get back."

"On that note," the Special Counsel advised, "I suggest you leave tonight and travel using your alternative identity discs. That way, the Advisory Council will not know where you have gone. I intend to disappear as well, to work on your defence. Becky will deflect any questions by saying you are with me at a hidden retreat, somewhere on Floriana.

"You are fortunate that your supporters filled the Tribunal room. They did not hide their hostility toward those on the Tribunal Bench. Without their influence, you would not have received an Adjournment at all.

"We will leave you now. Good luck on your travels; and please return with God and the Angels, and the blessing of the Consciousness. The Light needs them." He shook hands with each of the group and quickly walked out of the Lecture Hall with his assistants.

"The race is on, it seems," Sam said with a weak smile. "We must leave tonight. John, you know how the StarLight portals operate. Could you tell us what to expect?"

"Of course. I was intending to do just that before you asked. The portals are always open. When you arrive, you will pass through security and then wait in line to walk individually through the portal to the world of your choice, except there is no choice. All StarLight Portals on Floriana, travel to the same world — a security feature, I suspect. The portals look like a mini version of the Veil of Light. Imagine in front of you an octagonal hole in the wall, the circumference large enough to accommodate a train carriage. All you can see is a featureless curtain of white light.

"You wait in line and when it's your turn, the Portal Attendant will wave you through. I suggest you split up and mingle with the other Portaleers. When you arrive on the next world, wait for each other. Don't wander or split up. It may look like Floriana, but it isn't. The populations of the 20th century live there. The name of their world is Piaf, after Edith Piaf, the French singer of torch songs."

"Piaf?" Why Piaf?" Sam asked. John looked at him knowingly.

"Poignant isn't it. The name refers to the inherent sadness and longing of a century that demanded so much from itself but never earned it. As with Edith Piaf, every loss was enfolded in tragedy."

Gerald interrupted, "that is the 20th century. The description is so very apt. I wish I had the chance to use it in the last book I wrote on Earth."

"I'm not saying that Piaf is an unhappy planet. Far from it. Piaf in The Light is just as comfortable, peaceful, and happy as Floriana is — was, and, hopefully, will be again. The name reminds them from whence they came.

"Be warned. The Group of Six is famous on the world of Piaf. If anyone recognises us, the Advisory Council is sure to hear about it. They will issue Extradition Papers all the way to the First World. Members of the Council will pursue us and then, it becomes a race. The Tribunal's Adjournment decision would be overturned and the trial — for that's what it is — will begin without us.

"We travel through three portals to reach the First World. The second group of portals go to various worlds, but not the First World. To make it harder to find us, I'll select the world we will travel to shortly before we enter the StarLight Departure Centre in Piaf City. That decision will dictate which portal we will use to journey to the First World.

"Should we disguise ourselves?" Sam asked. John answered immediately.

"The style of the robes we wear, marks us out as citizens of Floriana. This will not be a problem travelling to Piaf City. The amount of two-way travel and commerce between Floriana and Piaf means our robes would not stand out. We should, however, wear our cloaks and hoods to shield our faces from prying eyes.

"Once we leave Piaf our robes will be a liability. We'll need to take additional clothing with us — nondescript, middle-of-the-road clothing that won't draw the eye. Although the Group of Six is known and admired on the other worlds of Light, our faces will be less known, but we should still use our cloaks and hoods, just in case.

"One final thing, there is no paperwork to complete when travelling between worlds. The only thing we need for travel is our identity disc. So, keep it safe.

Without it, you become Worldless. You won't be able to prove who you are until lengthy genetic testing is completed. You aren't permitted to stay, and another world will not accept you. Things get very messy indeed — genetic testing, paperwork, intervention by the authorities — lengthy delays we can't afford.

"I think that's it. I suggest we travel separately to the StarLight Centre. Get there about 9 tonight. Use your alternative identity disc to access an autocab and the portal. We don't acknowledge each other or link up, until we all arrive on Piaf."

John gave Becky and Marion supportive hugs. He grasped Rose's hand, and with a cheery smile and a wave he and Rose walked out of the Hall.

Gerald approached Marion and said a few words that Sam could not hear. Such a brave woman, he thought. Once they had said goodbye to Gerald, he and Becky walked over to Marion. "Please look after each other while I'm gone," Sam said, "I know how capable and strong you both are, but I'll worry like hell all the same. He and Becky gave Marion a parting kiss and hug and they walked out, leaving Marion standing alone in the large Lecture Hall. She surveyed her domain and smiled wistfully. As the last to leave, she said Lights off, and her world went dark.

# Part Seven - Worlds Apart

Nine o'clock on a Sunday night was a busy time at the StarLight Centre. People of all descriptions coming and going, some wearing clothing that marked them out as off-worlders. Sam inserted his pseudo identity disc into the cab's transaction slot. Anxiously, he waited for the beep that would tell him all was well. Beep — So far so good. He picked up his travel bag and stepped out of the cab which said have a nice evening Sir as it pulled away to a nearby autocab rank.

Sam was wearing a clean white robe, well-worn walking shoes and a hooded cloak that partially shrouded his face. He walked casually into the Star-Light Centre, which was buzzing with activity, even at this hour. He did not realise how much commerce took place. Travellers crowded several shops, some of them obviously tourists, if their strange taste in clothing was any guide.

Before him, he saw a large, striking sign announcing the No Nos of StarLight travel: no foodstuffs, no explosive materials, no animals, or birds, living or dead. Under the brief list was an illuminated, animated sign pointing the way to the Portals.

Sam looked around discreetly. So far, he had not recognised anyone. No. Wait. That man over by the coffee stand. I know him, but from where? Then Sam remembered. This man was an attendant at the Advisory Council Building. What's he doing here? And then he saw another person, this time a woman, over by the far wall, talking into her tablet device and staring at the people passing by. She, too, was an attendant. Did the Council always keep surveillance at the Centre, or was this something different, more special, more sinister.

It occurred to Sam that they may be looking for the Group of Six. The Council could be targeting all transport routes out of the city. Typical bureaucrats. They don't trust anyone. Sam laughed inwardly at this ludicrous thought. Of course they don't trust us. The Council wants us dead and people do desperate things when their lives are hanging in the balance.

Sam walked by casually, averting his face, slightly hunched over to appear smaller and unthreatening. He walked in the direction the arrow was pointing and began following a shining golden line sunk into the floor. The hall he walked curved like a meandering river, shops and delights becoming visible at every turn. These shops and attractions didn't take money. Every transaction using a customer's identity disc provided the owners and staff with credit towards their own transactions.

Quite a neat system. Money may, indeed, be the root of all evil. And we can't have that in The Light, Sam thought. He bent as if to fiddle with his bag and took a quick glance behind to ensure no one followed him. No one; Sam's relief coloured, however, by the knowledge that anyone could be hiding in the dense crowd.

Each world of Light had a tourism kiosk here or so it seemed; at which eager travellers sampled native delicacies and gathered information about famous attractions.

Sam had so much to learn about The Light; so complex and various.

After walking another 200 metres Sam came to a stationary crowd, waiting in several lines for their turn to pass through Security. Sam joined a queue at random and waited. He grasped his identity disc tightly in hand. As he drew closer to the security machines, he saw four people he recognised. Three of them, attendants from the Council, were sitting at screens, presumably looking for anomalies and watching the names of the travellers passing through the system.

The fourth person he recognised was Rose. Dressed similarly to himself, Rose waited in another line. Despite her disguised features, Sam would know Rose anywhere. He looked away and waited patiently, creeping forward as each traveller used their disc and passed through a scanner of some sort. *Probably looking for forbidden fruit.*

Sam's turn came. He inserted his disc into the slot to record his passage. A barrier moved aside to let him pass and he entered the scanner, a large metal gateway that buzzed and beeped disconcertingly as he walked through. No one accosted him as he reached a line of tables upon which baggage was searched at random, or so it seemed. No one asked him to open his bag, which was a relief.

As he passed the tables, he saw Rose standing there with her bag open, a stranger rifling through her belongings. Sam gulped, praying that she had packed discretely. He continued walking and finally stepped through an archway into the Departures Portal Gallery. And then, it was another wait in line as travellers walked individually into the portals. While he was waiting, Sam saw Rose standing on another line. She had her face hidden as she studied the people around her. She looked in Sam's direction, then her eyes moved on. No flicker of recognition; either staggering control, or she didn't know him as well as he knew her.

Sam reached the Portal attendant who checked a machine in front of him and then waved him through. He hefted his bag and passed into the light. Sam was surprised when he emerged instantly into bright sunshine, no ill effects or dizziness. An attendant waved him forward and another traveller emerged behind him.

Light years travelled instantly! Quite extraordinary. Sam was more than impressed. It beat sitting in a hypersonic plane for two or three hours. As he walked further from the Portals the crowd dispersed in all directions, although some lingered to admire the impressive cityscape on the other side of a wide river. He stopped, lowered his travel bag to the ground and waited. The air was chill, but not uncomfortably so.

It was not long before a hooded figure walked up to him and whispered follow me. Sam hoped it was John, and not some local mugger. *Stupid! That's mortal thinking.*

He followed casually at a distance for about fifteen minutes and entered a diner after the man. The diner looked remarkably like something out of 1950s America. Sam felt comfortable here; this was welcoming nostalgia. He walked toward a table in an alcove partially shielded by potted plants. He could just see several people seated around the table. As he approached, he counted three seated figures sipping coffee and chatting softly.

There was a free chair for Sam. He sat down and placed his bag against the wall.

"Last again. Sorry I kept you waiting." Sam said. "Hi Rose, Gerald, John. How did you get here before me Rose? I nearly fainted when I saw that security guy searching your bag."

Rose laughed and said, "Yeah, I was expecting to put on clean underwear, until I saw his eyes staring at my breasts. His search of my bag was nothing compared to the time he spent undressing me with his eyes. Isn't lust a no-no in The Light?"

The three men laughed uncomfortably, and Sam changed the subject. "We're a little obvious, aren't we? Four people huddled round a secluded table dressed in cloaks, with hoods concealing their faces."

John chuckled. "Don't worry Sam. I've already explained to the others that I chose this place deliberately. I know the owner well. Anna is a longtime friend and an avid supporter of our cause. She's a friend of Becky's and has organised the movement that has travelled around Piaf like wildfire; billions of signatures collected for the Petition which will be presented to the Advisory Council, along with the other Petitions, when the time is right."

Sam ordered a coffee from the table tablet. It was delivered by polite trolley within seconds. "How do they do that so quickly and produce such great coffee?" Sam suspected magic was involved. "Did anyone else notice the attendants from the Council checking the crowds in the StarLight Centre?" Everyone had.

"They made themselves obvious. We couldn't miss them," John said. "The Council don't usually watch the transportation hubs, so we can assume they were watching out for us. None of the attendants followed us. We're safe for now."

"Okay. Now that we're all settled, I'll tell you what's happening next. In about an hour, the diner is going to close temporarily. While it's closed, we're going to change out of our Floriana robes and put on the street clothes in our luggage. Keep your hooded cloaks handy.

"To leave Piaf, we must travel into the city. The Starlight Departure Portals are there. Here's the bad news. I had planned for us to leave tomorrow morning. But that won't be possible. The city is going to be jammed with tourists and locals taking part in the Remembrance Festival of Culture."

"Now we know why it was so crowded at Floriana's portal centre," Sam interrupted.

"The festival lasts for two days," John continued, nodding agreement with Sam's statement. "There'll be stewards and monitors everywhere controlling the crowds.

"I'm certain that the Council will have sent our descriptions to the city authorities. It's too great a risk. So, I propose that we sleep here for the next three nights and leave for the city-centre the following morning. We need accommodation, and staying here is much safer than finding it in a strange city. The food's good as well. I'll introduce you to Anna when the diner closes."

Sam was disheartened at the delay. Two days lost and the trip had barely begun.

# Part Eight – Training and Ultimatum

Their parting had been emotional. Sam and Becky had stood together at the front of their house. Sam had not yet called the autocab. He couldn't do it. Not yet. He looked at his wife with longing in his eyes. Even now he wanted her to come with them to the First World.

"I don't trust the Council one bit." Sam spoke with venom in his voice. "Please be careful dear heart. In a few days, when they can't find us, they'll want to speak with you, and they won't be gentle. They'll question you, ask where we are. When they can't find us, they may even rescind the, the…"

"Don't worry Sam. Marion and I have a credible story, and we'll tell it with conviction. I won't know where you are, and that will be the truth. You're with the Legal Counsel somewhere on Floriana, finalising our defence strategy. That last bit may not be the truth but needs must. Now call the autocab before I burst into tears."

Sam hugged Becky as if he could never let her go, but he had to. Sam ordered the cab and stared at his wife, his face filled with love and misgiving. The thought that their travel might be delayed tortured him. Just as he was considering calling the whole thing off, the cab pulled up silently beside them.

They kissed and Sam got quickly into the car before he lost his nerve. As the cab pulled away, Sam blew Becky a kiss and she waved silently back. In the end, the parting had been quick. But it was no less painful for that.

The next day, Becky arrived at the Training Centre as expected and walked straight to her first lecture. When she arrived and entered, she saw that the Hall was almost full. Marion was standing behind the lectern. She saw Becky arrive and gave her a brief smile before turning back to the audience.

"Good morning boys and girls. This is your first language class. We are going to learn the Dark language. It's a vital skill to take with you into the Mortal Realm. Without it you will not last long.

"On the tablet table in front of you is a strange, little contraption that we call the voice box. It will transform the sound of your voice. You will sound like them. As a practice pick up the box and switch it on. Now say anything you like, so that you can hear your voice as the Dark will hear it."

A cacophony of strangled voices filled the Hall. Marion waved for their attention, and the students stopped talking. "Okay, perhaps doing it all together was not such a great idea. You'll have a chance to practice one-on-one later in the class…"

Becky had zoned out. This all seemed so surreal. If Sam and the others were successful, The Light won't need trained operatives at all, she was thinking. Then she realised that getting on with what the Council expected her to be doing, was critical to delaying their inevitable suspicion. She cleared her head of uncertainties and gave the class her full attention.

She found the training fascinating and threw herself into the set tasks with enthusiasm. This enthusiasm persisted for a week. And then she received a 'request' to appear before the Tribunal. Marion and Becky were to front the Tribunal together, tomorrow afternoon. They both knew what questions they would be asked.

After the lessons had finished for the day, Becky and Marion sat down together to discuss how they would approach tomorrow's grilling. "I wish we could discuss it with Sam and the others," Becky said. "I know why they left their tablets behind, but it doesn't make the waiting any easier."

Marion had heard Becky say this earlier in the week and tried to calm her student. "If they took their tablets with them, the Council would know straight away that they'd left the planet. It's for their safety, Becky. And ours." Becky nodded, slowly, half-heartedly.

"I know it's hard, not knowing what's happening to them, where they are and what they're doing. But we must trust them, and, more importantly, we must have faith in ourselves. The Council may think they hold all the cards now, but it's amazing what you can do when you have a few extra cards up your sleeve. They may threaten to banish us, but they won't intimidate us. If they play dirty, we'll play dirtier. I for one am looking forward to tomorrow's confrontation. In any case, we'll have our junior Counsel with us."

In her heart, Becky knew that they would say the right things tomorrow. But her heart would be elsewhere, and it was her feelings that so distressed her. She missed Sam. Simple as that.

*****

Becky and Marion were sitting in the antechamber to the Tribunal. It felt like déja vu, but it wasn't. Same time, same place, same wait, but not the same group. Becky and Marion had arrived with their junior Counsel just before 2 o'clock. They expected a long wait. The Tribunal would not miss this opportunity to make the occasion as uncomfortable and inconvenient as they could. And thus it proved to be. This time, the wait was longer.

The junior Counsel had told the women that the Tribunal could not, under normal legal procedure, call them before it, unless the Adjournment had either expired, or there was evidence of a breach. Since the Adjournment decision did not compel the litigants to stay in Floriana City or provide contact details, The Tribunal was exceeding its powers in calling Becky and Marion before it.

This advice did not ease the women's concerns. The Fae and the Advisory Council had shown they were a law unto themselves and would do what they liked. There was not a higher court to which Becky and Marion could appeal.


At 3.30, the women and their Counsel walked into the Tribunal Chamber. As before there was nowhere to sit for any of them. As before the ten-member Tribunal jury filed in, followed by the Fae. The Fae called the session to order.

He smiled, graciously, at each of them. Smiles can be deceptive. Becky felt this man was enjoying the humiliation of his predecessor. The defendants and Counsel remained stony-faced.

"We wanted to call you both in for a chat. I see you have brought Counsel with you, and he is welcome to participate."

The Counsel spoke up at once. "Honourable Fae. If you have called us in for a chat, as you call it, then where are the seats for comfort and bar table, for consultation with my clients? It is customary and well-mannered to provide such things.

"Further, I am the appointed junior Counsel for my clients. I need no welcome. By law and convention, I must be in attendance when my clients are summoned in this irregular way."

"The conventions of the Mortal Realm do not apply here," the Fae replied. "There are no precedents. These proceedings will set the precedents.

"Counsel, you are here under sufferance. We wish to ask questions of your clients, only two of which are here.

"As for seating, there are no seats available so we will have to make do. We will not keep you long. We have been trying to locate your other clients but have not yet found them.

"Becky Pilgrim, is your husband in Floriana City."

"I have no idea where my husband is at present," Becky spoke up confidently. "I have no way to contact him. I am in the same position as you, Honourable Fae."

"But that is most irregular; you are his wife. Surely you must know where he is," The Fae smiled benignly.

"No, I do not. Our Senior Counsel and fellow defendants are preparing our defence arguments and wanted no interruptions. They knew you would try to interfere, so they deliberately chose to disappear. Under the terms of the Adjournment, they do not have to speak or meet with you, and neither do we." Becky was trying hard to keep calm. She breathed deeply and stood tall, staring at the Fae, defiance manifest in her stance.

The Fae went red in the face, shocked by the realisation that Becky was right. They did not have to speak with the Tribunal at all. He cleared his throat and was about to speak when the Counsel interrupted. "Honourable Fae, my clients have done you the courtesy of attending this chat, and since there is no reason for them to stay, I will instruct them to leave and hereafter remain silent until the Tribunal is legally reconvened."

The Fae leapt to his feet in a fury. "You will not leave until we are finished.

"We do not believe your clients, Counsel. This Tribunal rules the following. Should all your clients not contact us and provide contact details within 14 days, the Tribunal will reconvene and try them in their absence. Is that clear?"

The Counsel approached the Fae. Becky had never seen him so angry. "This is an outrageous abuse of power. This is not a Tribunal. This is a witch-hunt!" Becky, placed her hand on his arm, willing him to calm down.

"Fae, we all know what this is," Becky said. "You are frightened of us. You and the Council will do anything to keep your power. It has corrupted you. There is no place for corruption in the Light Realm.

"Billions of your children will oppose you, You know this is true. They yearn for the return of God and the Angelic Light. Do you think that the Sonciel Consciousness will not hear them? You failed the Mortal

Realm. And now, Louseefa will look to return and take The Light from your grasp. You have started a confrontation you cannot win."

Becky turned away and walked out of the Chamber. Marion and the Counsel, surprised by Becky's heated remarks and by her sudden disappearance, froze for a moment. Then they too followed Becky.

As the three left the Chamber, they heard the Fae scream after them, "Louseefa? What do you mean? Louseefa?"

*****

Thirty minutes later, Becky was still trembling with emotion. The three sat in a shaded part of the beautiful gardens surrounding the Government precinct. Nearby, children played under the watchful eyes of parents and carers. It was all so normal, so peaceful.

The tranquil, rose scented air and the exuberant cries of children, clashed with the turmoil in Becky's heart.

The world moves on, oblivious, and I've just defied the Fae. I did exactly the opposite of what I intended. These thoughts and others clashed in her head. *Sam, I need you.*

Marion sat on one side of her, the Counsel on the other, each holding a hand and trying to calm her. "Becky, you said what must be said. If you hadn't said it, I probably would have," Marion spoke gently. The Counsel nodded.

"What Marion says is true. You have not worsened your situation, Becky." The Counsel's unspoken words were glaringly obvious, however.

"I know that! Our situation couldn't get any worse no matter what we say. But I'm sorry I lost control like that." Becky began to regain control, the trembling in her limbs decreasing and her quivering voice returning to normal. "I just wish I hadn't mentioned Louseefa. It just came out. It was stupid."

After a brief period of silence, Becky said, "can we walk through the gardens for a while? A bit of exercise in the real world, might help us see things more clearly." The others did not object, so Becky stood, and sauntered off toward the Rose Garden. The others walked a few paces behind talking together.

"The Council and the Fae had already decided to cut short the adjournment. I'm sure of it," Marion said. "The chat was just an excuse for them to tell us. Nothing we said or could say had any bearing on the outcome. Although, I think mentioning Louseefa may have unintended consequences." Becky winced at the comment.

The Counsel replied resignedly, "what's done is done, I think that's the saying. The words can't be taken back, so we will live with the consequences, unintended or otherwise.

"Let's hope the others get back in time and bring the Angels with them. I don't want to contemplate the opposite situation, although as your Counsel, I should be doing just that."

The walk brought them closer to the children's play area. Becky stopped walking and the others, immersed in conversation, almost bumped into her. Something had caught Becky's attention. Marion followed her eyes. She was looking at the children. What has captured her attention, Marion thought. And then she saw the reason. Midst a whirlwind of playing children stood Phil and Kate. Amongst the playing children, she saw Jack and Josie, chattering happily with their friends. Becky hurried off, Marion and the Counsel, following in her wake.

As Becky drew much closer, Phil looked up and grabbed Kate's shoulder, pointing out the approaching visitors. Kate put her hand to her mouth and ran toward Becky. She flung her arms around her friend and they both burst into tears at the unexpected reunion.

"It's so good to see you, Becky," Kate gushed. "I've been meaning to catch up but, you know, life gets in the way. Where is that wonderful husband of yours?" Kate's eyes looked around and fell on Marion. "Oh, hi Marion. How extraordinary to meet you both here."

She started to ask about the things they had been doing, and Becky placed her fingertips upon Kate's lips. "It's a very long story, Kate. Too long to tell here. Perhaps when you're free, we can go somewhere quiet and have our long-overdue chat." Becky suggested.

"Phil and I are taking some of the children for Sports Afternoon. As you can see, somewhat less structured than usual. You do know that we're both teachers now. We work at the nearby primary school. Jack and Josie will shortly return to classes and both Phil and I are free, if later would suit you?"

Marion interposed. "Hello Kate. It's been a long time. I must get back to the Training Centre but there's no reason, why you can't catch up," she said to Becky.

"At the top of the rise behind us is a coffee shop. Why don't we saunter up there and get you settled, while you wait for Kate and Phil."

"That's fine with us. We'll be less than an hour. Promise," said Kate. Becky agreed, giving Kate a friendly smile. Then, remembering the Counsel standing awkwardly behind her, belatedly introduced him to her friend. "Kate, I'd like you to meet our Legal Counsel…" before Becky could say his name Kate blurted out, "Legal Counsel. Why ever would you need a legal representative?"

"That's the long story," Becky advised, enigmatically. "I'll see you both soon then."

## The Council Circus

The Fae was livid, his face afire with anger and frustration. "How dare she? I am the Fae, and she speaks to me in that fashion. It's outrageous. We will legislate to make this behaviour a crime. No one should be able to disrespect the Fae without legal consequence. She and her cronies will regret pushing me."

The other Council members in the Tribunal Chamber looked at each other with alarm. Contrary to the common belief, this Fae was no figurehead. He ruled the Council without constraint. The legislation the Fae was proposing would not only affect the populace. It would also hamper their aspirations for advancement. This Fae might even refuse to stand down at the end of his term. What would that mean? Autocracy? A police-state? It didn't bear thinking about.

Trust and harmony amongst the Councillors were in limited supply and arguments arose concerning how best to respond. The Fae sat fuming amidst the tumult.

"Silence!" He screamed. "If you cannot discuss our course of action without fighting amongst each other, I will make the decisions without your advice." He stared at each of the ten Councillors and his stare froze them into nervous silence.

"Should we not find the missing members of the Group of Six within seven days, I will rescind the Adjournment and resume the Tribunal. The missing criminals will be found guilty in their absence."

An audible, sharp intake of breath filled the Chamber. One Councillor, braver or more foolish than the others, spoke up.

"Is that wise, Honourable Fae? The people will not stand for it. You know it. No telling what they may do."

"Let them do it. My powers will be more than sufficient to deal with them."

That statement brought a storm of protest. "You can't use your powers against The Light. You can't."

"You convinced us to forbid your predecessor to use her powers against the Dark during Armageddon, yet you think our people deserve harsher treatment. I cannot condone it."

"Will you place yourself above everyone else in the Light Realm? You would no longer be First Among Equals. You would be a, a dictator." Such comments left the Fae even more irate.

"I will have silence," he screamed again.

"Does any one of you know what the Pilgrim woman meant when she spoke of Louseefa? Anyone? No? then may I suggest that you find out? You have an army of attendants at your disposal. Use them. Ruthlessly, if necessary."

"Those of you who value your positions on the Council, listen very carefully. Discover the whereabouts of the missing criminals and the situation regarding Louseefa. Those who bring me useful and credible information will keep their jobs on the Council. Those who do not, will resign. Now, get out of my sight." The other members of the Tribunal scurried out of the Chamber.

There he was. The real Fae revealed at last. A political predator hungry for more. Corrupted by the politics he lived. Hungry for the whole of Light. Hungry for the stars. Yearning, even to devour God.

# Part Nine - Reunion and Regrets

Becky's wait was no longer than 30-minutes. She didn't realise she was sitting at the same table, in the same café where Sam had sat with John all that time ago, after the first great meeting of the GBTC Planning Committee, post Armageddon.

How innocent those times seemed now. Then, the sole thought was rescuing the Mortal Realm from the Dark; all energies directed toward that one purpose, a heroic and moral purpose.

Becky reflected that the present had become — complicated. There existed so many forces at play, any one of which could throw the Group of Six into disarray. Her head span, just thinking about it all.

She was sipping a fruit juice concoction when she spied Kate and Phil striding up the rise to the café. They walked in and spied Becky sitting at the table overlooking the gardens. The reunion was effusive and genuine on all sides.

"Becky, it's been far too long, and it's my fault," Kate said, as she hugged her saviour from the first pilgrimage.

Phil likewise hugged the person who, as Guardian, had brought his wife home to The Light.

Becky's eyes glistened as she spoke. "No. It's not anyone's fault. A wise woman said quite recently, life gets in the way." Becky smiled warmly at Kate. "Would you both like a coffee or something cooler?"

"Actually, a coffee would be good. We could both use a pep me up after a long day at school," Phil suggested. Kate nodded her agreement. Becky scanned their orders and continued talking.

"Josie and Jack seem to be doing well," Becky ventured, "lots of new friends that I could see. It must be quite a novelty for them."

"There's no shortage of new friends," Phil nodded. "I'm amazed how well they have both adapted to school life."

Kate struggled to say what came next. "I suppose, with two young children and the new jobs at the school, we've become a bit obsessed. We've tried to ignore or avoid other things happening in the world. And we've ignored our friends. I'm sorry for that."

"One of the less prominent by-products of Armageddon has been the number of orphaned children needing accommodation and care," Phil added. "There are millions of orphaned children around Floriana, many of them still suffering from shock. Many others have only one parent. It's a terrible situation and we've been trying to fix it, here, in our little part of the world."

Stunned, Becky said she had no idea. "But, of course, there would be orphans. How stupid of me not to realise it. It's me that should be sorry. I've been so bound up with the fate of Floriana and the wider Light that I've forgotten about the everyday lives of people."

Becky looked wistfully at her friends. "You know Sam and I never had a chance to have children, although that may change now, if The Light gives us the opportunity. Our minds never thought of children once we came here. They seemed so distant from our lives. It must seem awful to you."

Kate hugged Becky again. "Not awful at all. You were Fae, and Sam has been so busy with the Planning Committee. Oh yes, I do hear some of the news. And of course, there's always gossip. Most people seem very tense at present. Rumours of invasions and coups and Government corruption. Discontent seems to be spreading. We try to keep our heads down as the kids take up so much of our energy."

"I know about the Group of Six," Phil offered. "I was stunned when we heard that the Fae and Council had charged you with such ludicrous crimes…"

Kate looked accusingly at Phil, "God, Phil, why didn't you tell me? I'm sorry Becky for not knowing — I should have known," she cried.

Phil tried to explain, but his words sounded hollow in his ears. "Kate, the needs of our children and the welfare of so many others, already overburden you. I couldn't add to your worries. I didn't have the courage, and I see now that I made the wrong decision. I'm sorry Kate."

At that moment, the trolley arrived. Kate and Phil took their coffees and with its obligatory have a nice day, the bot withdrew.

"Whether it was right or wrong doesn't matter any more," Becky said firmly. "We're here, now, and I'm so happy that chance has brought us together. To be honest with you, it was lonely at the top, and it's even lonelier at the bottom. There is so much happening that I can't speak about. Telling you would put you in danger."

Kate was shocked. "Is it that bad? We know about the Petition calling for the return of the old ways, we've even signed it. I suppose our signatures have already marked us as suspect."

"You and many billions of others on every world of Light," Becky said with a weary smile. I can tell you a few things, but not everything. The Fae and Council are determined to banish the Group of Six to the Mortal Realm. They see us as a threat to their power. They will do anything to keep control, and by charging us, they are setting a precedent that places everyone in peril. They don't care about regaining the Mortal Realm. I suspect that once we are banished, the portals will be destroyed."

"But that's a death sentence, Becky," Kate cried, rather louder than she intended. More quietly she added, "we can't let this happen. Please tell us if we can do anything to help."

"You have the safety of Josie and Jack to consider. I don't want you caught up in this mess. All I can say is that when the trial begins, the people of Floriana City, and further afield, will peacefully besiege the Council Tribunal Building. It will be the largest crowd ever assembled in The Light."

"Won't that be dangerous, Becky?" Phil asked.

"I can't imagine how. There are no police or military to oppose the crowd. And I can't imagine the Fae using his powers against his own people. I wasn't allowed to use them against the Dark, and the new Fae hasn't used them at all, to my knowledge.

"No Fae has ever done anything so extreme. It's unthinkable."

Phil suggested something ominous. "Becky, you are a talented, compassionate soul. Of course you wouldn't do it. But this Fae is a politician. He has power and he will use it. I didn't trust politicians in the Mortal Realm and I'm not going to start trusting them here in The Light." Becky went white.

"My God, you're right, Phil. I must let our supporter network know. The crowd should not get anywhere near the Tribunal Building. We'll need a new strategy."

"Maybe the crowd should surround the building at a distance," Kate suggested, "just to let the Fae and

Council know that the people are there to support you, but not in a threatening way."

Becky thought a moment and said, "that would work! I'll suggest it.

"There's one other thing that I've now realised. This Fae isn't me. He's not subservient to the Council as I and earlier Faes have been. This Fae is exerting control over the Council. He holds the power. He'll use it against anyone who opposes him, even the Council. Dear God, I hope Sam and the others get back in time."

Kate and Phil looked mystified. "Sam is away? Where is he?" Becky, horrified, realised her error.

"Please forget I said that last bit. I can't tell you. I mustn't. Please don't mention this conversation with anyone." Becky looked seriously at Phil and Kate. "I mean it. Anyone may be an informer for the Fae."

"It's really that bad?" Kate asked, concern in her voice.

"Oh yes. It's that bad. Your coffee is getting cold. Let's talk about something else, casually, as three friends enjoying the view of the gardens. I just need to feel normal again. I feel like my life is part of a spy thriller. How are Josie and Jack, tell me all about them."

Parents like nothing more than speaking about their children, and Becky relished the next hour as they spoke lovingly of their family.

*****

Sam sat by himself on a bench overlooking the river, and the city skyline in the distance. He stared at a large party boat sailing by, ablaze with a kaleidoscope of coloured lights, strains of music drifting across the water. Sam listened, entranced by the familiar tune and that magical, ghostly voice rising above it. Edith Piaf singing her defiance to the evening skies and the world about. Non, je ne regrette rien. No, I regret nothing.

No regrets. Sam was not so sure. As he sat and watched the boat disappear round a curve in the river, he thought of Becky, alone and vulnerable in Floriana City.

He had left her to the whims of a hostile ruling Council; a Council capable of anything, particularly with the powers of the Fae to call upon.

The chill evening air seemed suddenly colder, and Sam pulled his cloak tightly around his body as much for protection as for warmth. He shivered.

Yes, he did regret leaving Becky behind. How could he not. At the same time, he accepted that he had no choice. The pilgrimage to the First World was necessary for the survival of both The Light and Mortal Realms. He had started this, many months ago in

Pilgrims Rest. The Group of Six had a responsibility to see it through to the end.

With duty and regret fighting for supremacy in his thoughts, Sam stood and walked the short distance back to the diner.

It was the last night of the Cultural Festival. Anna had given the group a program to read. And it read like no Festival ever created in the Mortal Realm. The highlight was a spectacular concert of works by Mozart — conducted by Mozart. Say no more, Wow.

Artists, musicians, composers, and actors, singers, and poets of historical renown, drawn together from all times and places to lend their love to the nurture of remembrance. Sam's heart raced when he saw that Shakespeare's King Lear was on the program, performed by timeless actors, and directed by Shakespeare himself.

He was dizzy with amazement. Oh, how he wished he and Becky could have attended. Impossible he realised. Not with the future of the Light Realm hanging in the balance.

Sam arrived at the diner and entered. He climbed a flight of stairs to his room which he shared with John and Gerald — three single, bunk beds in a tiny room, a bit squeezy, but comfortable enough. John was lying on his bed when Sam walked in.

"A bit cold out there?" John asked by way of conversation. Sam removed his cloak and boots and sat on the only chair.

"Cold, indeed, but dazzling," Sam replied. "There was a party boat sailing up the river; Edith Piaf singing her heart out. I could almost believe it was a live performance."

"Perhaps it was," John said. "The Light never fails to surprise. Now that you're back, I'll get Rose and Gerald, and the four of us can talk about tomorrow." John stood from his bed and went to knock on Rose's door. A few minutes later the four friends were chatting quietly together.

A break in the chatter gave John the opportunity to take charge. "Okay, you know we're leaving tomorrow for the StarLight Departure Portals. The procedure will be the same as in Floriana City. Separate autocabs, no acknowledgement of each other until we reach the next destination, use your pseudo identity discs.

"The portal we need will take us to Renaissance, a world that's home to the populations of the fifteenth, sixteenth, and seventeenth centuries. It's there that we'll find the portal for the First World. We'll leave separately tomorrow morning after breakfast. As before, don't let your guard down. If any of us is recognised, stealth will no longer help us. The Council and Fae will pursue us. So please, keep your faces hidden."

After they finished speaking, Rose, Sam, and John went downstairs to get something to eat before retiring for the night. Gerald opted out, blaming tiredness, and feeling a little unwell.

As the group found their secluded table at the rear of the near empty diner, Rose said quietly, "I'm worried about Gerald. He doesn't look well, and have you noticed how quiet he's been lately? I hope he'll be all right travelling alone tomorrow. Perhaps one of us should travel with him. I'd be happy to keep a watch."

"That will add to the risk Rose," John answered, "but we may have no alternative. If Gerald is no better in the morning, Rose will keep a close watch over him. Are we agreed?"

Sam nodded his agreement and added, "Gerald's learning and skills will be crucial for us on the First World. We need to look after him. And, in any case, he's a friend. We help."

Anna, the owner of the diner, came over and sat with them at the table. "You three look as though you need something to eat. Where's Gerald?" Rose explained his absence.

"As you can see," Anna surveyed the room, "it's a slow night — usually is during the festival — so I can whip you up something quick. Vegetable burgers, fries, salads, soup, whatever you like."

"Soup sounds good," Sam and Rose said at the same time. John laughed and added, "yes, soup does sound good. Thanks Anna."

"Soup is easy. And I've got some fresh bread as well. Back in a jiffy." Anna rushed off.

The friends sat silently pondering their situation. A few minutes later, Anna returned with the bread and soup. "Wow, that was quick," Rose said. "Smells good too." There were four bowls on the tray.

"I had some hot on the hob," Anna announced. "Do you mind if I join you? I've closed the diner and would appreciate a final chat with you."

"Please, please join us," John said. He stood and helped Anna with the tray. "You've given us sanctuary, even knowing how dangerous our situation is. I, for one, could never repay you for your kindness."

"John, we've been friends for a long time," Anna replied. "There's nothing I wouldn't do to help you bring back the old ways. Our petition is ready — billions of signatures, 90 per cent of the population is behind us. The Fae knows that someone must be organising these partitions and I know he has spies everywhere. Having you here cannot increase the risk I am already taking. And even if it did, you would still be welcome. Now, let's eat our soup before it gets cold."

The group ate in silence for a while, then Anna said ominously, "my network of supporters informs me that large numbers of visitors have besieged the city. They're here ostensibly for the festival, but they don't attend anything. These are the spies and informers I mentioned. They will be everywhere. Please take great care tomorrow, especially at the StarLight Portals. One misstep and we may lose everything. The Fae will suspend the Adjournment and continue with the trial.

"He will know where you are and where you are going. And he will hunt you down."

Saying it bluntly like that left the table speechless. So much depended upon staying hidden. For Sam, the price of failure would be the death of his wife. For John and Rose, they feared for each other and for a future they might never get to share.

Tomorrow would tell.

# Part Ten - Dance of the Fae

The Fae fumed. He sat on the faux leather chair behind his massive desk and stared out at his vibrant city beyond the office windows. He should be basking in the love and respect of his people. Not cowering from them.

He knew. He knew how they plotted against him. The petitions, the vicious accusations, the disrespect. It was intolerable.

And he knew who the ringleaders were, oh yes, he knew. His army of operatives, his spies, and informers rounded them up this very minute across all the worlds of Light, save one.

The Angels of Light had refused them admittance to the First World. Why, if not to show themselves supporters of the festering rebellion? How dare they get in his way. He was God now. He ruled the Light. He would have their respect!

The Fae's Personal Assistant begged entry, nervously standing at the door. The Fae turned towards the intrusion. "Yes, what is it?"

"Honourable Fae, I have news. May I inform you of the latest reports?"

"Get in here and tell me. And it better be favourable. If I'm displeased, I may just strike you dead on the spot. Now tell me," He shouted.

"Hon…Honourable Fae," he stammered. "Y… your supporters have rounded up hundreds of the ringleaders, as you ordered. The w… warriors' barracks are now a prison, and many are already in detention."

"So why are you so nervous? That is good news… I sense a but coming. But what! Tell me." The Fae was rapidly losing his patience.

The Assistant found a modicum of courage, cleared his throat, and spoke plainly. "The missing members of the Group of Six are still at large. There has been no sign of them."

"I knew it!" The Fae screamed. "Order them to search harder. If these criminals are still free by midnight tonight, I'll need a new Personal Assistant. Now, get out!" The PA scurried away, thankful that he still breathed.

Alone again, the Fae stood and walked towards his office windows. He looked down and saw the crowd gathering several hundred metres back from the Government Building, surrounding it in an ever-growing ring of Light. He could not guess how many there were. They still arrived in a flood of disloyalty.

Thousands, millions, he did not care. He could handle them. Make an example of a few. The rest would bow to his authority. If he could not have their devotion, he would have their obedience.

*****

The Fae sat, brooding, and indecisive, for several hours. As dusk gathered, tiny patches of flame and many tents appeared throughout the crowd. This was organised. The rabble were prepared for a long wait. Were they intent upon laying siege to the building? Would he run out of food and water? He did not know.

He could not decide what to do. Put that Becky woman and her fellow criminals on trial straight away? Make a public example of them? The indecision was maddening. The Fae screamed for his PA. The man timidly poked his head around the door.

"Yes, Honourable Fae, how may I assist you?"

"Call an urgent meeting of the Advisory Council. Tell the Advisors to be present in the Council Assembly Chamber in two hours."

"But, Honourable Fae, many of them have already left for the day. How will they pass back through the crowd unseen?"

"Do not dare to be insolent with me," the Fae warned. "Tell them to disguise themselves. I don't care how they do it, but they will do it. If any fail to arrive for the meeting, order them arrested and detained, like the rest of these criminals." The PA stood transfixed.

This was unheard of. The shock was too much. He grabbed hold of the door frame to keep his balance.

"Why are you still here? Go! Now!" The PA wobbled off, relief and despair at war upon his stricken face.

The calls went out and many of the Fae's advisors quailed at the call. They had seen the gathering crowd when they left the Council Assembly Building, adjacent to the Government Building and the Fae's office and living quarters. Somehow, they would need to get back through that hostile ring.

Some gathered their families and fled. Others, dressed in heavy, hooded cloaks, some wearing wigs, hoped that their disguise would see them safely to the meeting.

Unfortunately, for the Council members who braved the crowd, most of the disguises were inadequate. Who, in their right mind would wear a heavy cloak on a warm night? The disguise was obvious for all to see. Many unfortunate Councillors found themselves detained in a tent, under armed guard; guards carrying heavy implements capable of breaking bones.

The Fae strode into the Assembly Chamber, confident that his Council would respect his stern call. He stopped walking. Only six Advisors were waiting there for him. Six. Six. The Fae demanded, "where are the rest of you?" He turned to his defeated PA. "Did the call go out to all the Councillors?" The PA looked miserable. "Yes, Honourable Fae," the PA replied in a small voice. "All were informed."

"Then. Why. Aren't. They. Here?" The Fae screamed.

The PA fell back in alarm. "I do not know," and quieter still, "I do not know. Please Honourable Fae, I did what you asked."

The Fae lashed out, wanting someone, anyone to pay for the effrontery he suffered. With a wave of his hand, a blast of wind tossed the PA heavily to the wall. He fell to the floor.

Two Councillors ran forward to his aid. They knelt and checked the PA for injuries, for vital signs. There were none.

"You have killed him," one of them said. He looked aghast at the Fae. "You have killed him. Why? Why do this? He did you no wrong."

The Fae smiled evilly at the Councillors. "Because I can. Get someone to move the body, hide him somewhere, anywhere, I don't care. Just get him out of my sight. If I can't have obedience, there will be other bodies to join him."


One of the Councillors rushed out and returned with two attendants. They looked at the crumpled body. "What happened here then?" One of them asked. "Is he dead? No one has ever died here, not unnatural like; and this don't look natural."

The Councillors nearest to the attendants shushed them and one whispered, "please, if you value your lives, don't ask any questions. Find somewhere to hide the body, until we can deal with it."

The attendants looked undecided, until they saw the fearful glare from the Fae. That decided them and they quickly lifted the body and carried it out of the Chamber.

A line had been crossed. For the first time ever in The Light, murder had been committed. And these Councillors were witnesses. With horror, they realised that the next bodies could be theirs.

The six councillors waited for the Fae to speak. "If news of this unfortunate 'accident' gets out, I will know who to blame. Do you understand me?" The Fae smiled benignly upon his subjects. They understood. Their lips would remain sealed. One of them thought despairingly, I won't talk, but I can't vouch for the attendants… oh, dear God, I'm dead.

The six Councillors in attendance were not particularly loyal to the Fae. They just happened to be in the building when the meeting call went out. They all realised the significance of this. The other Councillors had either fled, or the crowd had caught them.

They were alone, unarmed, and at the mercy of a powerful man who had just committed murder. The only thing they could do in such circumstances was to prostrate themselves at the feet of the man who held the cards. They did so, trying to hide their humiliation.

"Please rise my children. I note your loyalty. For my purposes, six of you will have to do. So, I ask you, how do we proceed? Do I act swiftly to crush this insignificant rebellion, or do I wait and see what happens over the next few days. Advisors, please advise me."

The six looked at each other. They stared into each other's eyes and asked the questions, what do we do, what can we say? Somehow, without speaking they came to a decision.

"Honourable Fae," one of them said, "lest we intensify the situation by being too aggressive, should we not show forbearance and let emotions subside for a few days. At least until the adjournment period ends. Then, we can proceed with a lawful trial of the defendants, currently in detention." The other Councillors nodded their agreement with this advice.

The Fae considered what was advised. "My instinct is to crush them now. And I could do so, but I respect your advice and will wait the few days until we can go ahead with the trial of the six criminals.

In the meantime, the rabble outside will suffer discomfort and anxiety, wondering whether, or when I will attack them. Let them wonder. Let them squirm. They can't hurt me. I am their Fae, and they will obey me."

The six Councillors dared not look upon the face of this man whose eyes gleamed with a manic intensity. They had seen the madness in those eyes. The power has overcome him. He will kill us all.

The Fae looked up at the ceiling, looking at nothing the Councillors could see. The Fae saw something else, perhaps a wild and turbulent place his heated brain had concocted. Quietly the six withdrew. The Fae did not notice, lost as he was in that vision spawned by his lustful imaginings.

Outside the Chamber, the Councillors briefly discussed their options. Stay, and remain in thrall to a madman, or leave and surrender to the crowd surrounding the building. They had no options. Only one path made sense.

Together the six exited the building and walked quickly toward the crowd. They raised their hands in surrender, and several members of the crowd led them to the place of detention.

"The Fae's gone mad," one of them said to his captor. "Be careful. He's capable of anything now. He's already killed once. He will do it again. Warn your leaders. Please."

The captor was amazed. "Killed? Murdered? In The Light?" The man's shock was palpable.

Slowly, the captor regained his senses and led them to the makeshift prison. "You'll find a lot of your friends inside. Tell them what you've told me. Once you've had your discussion, you might even consider joining us."

The Councillors nodded their agreement. "Yes, we have access to information that you might find useful," one of them said. "Thank you." They entered the tent and were surprised to see that half the Council were inside. This would be an interesting discussion indeed.

The captor, whose name was James, walked over to the Leaders' tent and entered. In a loud voice he asked, "has anyone seen Anna? I need to speak with her now."

## The Gilded Cage

Becky and Marion had a bird's eye view of the massive crowd gathering outside the building. They had been in this sumptuous cage all day, watching the part of the crowd they could see, arriving in vast numbers. By the time dusk settled over the city, the rear of the crowd was lost to the gathering gloom.

Small fires sprang up midst the many tents and lights gave the scene a festive touch. But there was nothing festive about it.

A team of aggressive Council attendants had arrived to detain the women at the Training Centre. Many students confronted the team, shouting threats and insults, and chanting Bring Back God, the adopted slogan of the God Movement. They tried to shield their teacher and fellow student from the team, linking arms and glaring at the brazen intruders.

The team members raised massive metal truncheons, shouting get back, get back. Their leader cried, "we will injure you if you get in our way." He waved the truncheon. "You see this? We will break your bones, don't tempt us. Move aside now!"

The students froze. They had never experienced such aggression before. The team misinterpreted the lack of movement and rushed the students, their truncheons flying back and forth and clearing a path to Becky and Marion.

The leader declared, "by order of the Fae you are both under arrest. Come with us peacefully, otherwise…" the leader looked down at the students writhing in agony on the floor. He stared at the women. "Get moving."

Becky sat on her bed and cried as she recalled the confrontation. So brave. So brave. She was proud of her friends. But that pride was tempered by a real fear of violence festering in the hearts of participants on both sides. Their cause was peaceful and just. Yet goodness and decency in The Light had so easily succumbed to this overheated moment.

Was this the Fae's doing? Or had there always been a kernel of mortal aggression, festering in the hearts of all in The Light? In her black void of doubt and despair, Becky feared it was so.

One of the attendants guarding the front door of the gilded prison, knocked and poked his head around the door. "Are you both okay? Do you need anything?" He asked in a friendly tone. Becky looked up and saw his sheepish expression. Why is he so embarrassed? Becky smiled, wiping her eyes and collecting herself. "Thank you, we're fine... I don't know your name... wait, I do know you. You were on my personal staff when I was Fae."

"It's Phillip Ma'am. Are you sure I can't get you anything? My partner's off using the facilities and, well, I just had to say that I'm a friend." He opened the door wider and stepped into view. "Please don't weep. You have many friends outside who respect and support you, including me."

Becky regarded Phillip, her eyes still glistening. "I see you're wearing a uniform — black shirt and trousers — that uniform had an unhappy history in the Mortal Realm," she sniffed.

"I got my uniform earlier today. I hate it. It makes me feel dirty, stained in some way. We're called the Black Shield now. Our official job is to protect the Fae. But he doesn't need protecting. Our real job is to intimidate people like you. And I'm sorry for that. That's why I had to speak with you. Anything you need me to do, just ask."

The man disappeared and quickly closed the door. Becky heard discussion outside, and assumed Philip's partner had returned. And he didn't sound very friendly at all.

Becky joined Marion at the window. It was dark now and all they could see of the crowd were lights and small fires disappearing into the distance. "It's quite a turn out isn't it," Marion said, holding Becky's hand to comfort her. "Imagine, there are supporters coming here from across The Light. It's momentous. Surely the Fae can't ignore it."

Becky looked crestfallen at her friend's assessment. "I believe he will ignore it. He wields the only real power in Floriana. He could kill thousands with a wave of his hand, and I think he will do it if pushed.

"Marion, what have we started? The Light will be changed forever. And it will be our fault."

"Rubbish," Marion retorted. "If anyone is at fault, it is the Fae and the Council. Don't let them off the hook. Political ambition has corrupted them. This was always going to happen once a Fae came along who would put his own ambition and survival over the needs of everyone else.

"That is why God must return. Only God and the Angels of Light are more powerful than the Fae. And the only people who can bring God back, are Sam, John, Rose, and Gerald. Becky, we must believe they can do it."

"Do you think we can trust Phillip? He seems genuine but, I don't know…" Becky's small voice trailed off.

Marion considered the question. "Phillip may be genuine. He may not be. The Fae will have many spies, and where better to place one than outside our prison door. He would have to prove his worth before I could trust him."

Becky had to agree with this assessment, though she wanted to believe otherwise. Unfortunately, they had little time to gather that proof. In a few days, maybe less, they could be standing before the Tribunal and shortly after, pushed through a portal into the Mortal Realm where death awaited.

# Part Eleven - The First World

Sam and John were sitting downstairs in the diner, waiting for Rose and Gerald to arrive. Anna was with them.

"Thank you for the fake Identity Disc, John," Anna said. "If I used my authentic disc to get to Floriana, I would be arrested on the spot. We're both in boats it seems, albeit rowing in different directions."

"Nice metaphor, Anna," John replied with a smile that said, you're welcome.

Sam had been wondering for some time about the StarLight Portal Network. "It's so much more sophisticated than the portals we use on Floriana to enter the Mortal Realm. I started talking with Gerald about it once, but he lost me with all the big words; quantum wormholes, entanglement, space-time…

"The StarLight portals allow metallic objects to pass through, freight vehicles and such. Why hasn't the technology been adapted for use on Floriana? It would make subduing the Dark so much easier."

John sighed. "I have been wondering when you would ask that question.

"The StarLight portals are a relic. God created them untold thousands of years ago to bind the worlds of Light together. There are more than ten earth-like worlds linked by portals, several uninhabited. When God and the Angels of Light withdrew to the First World, we also lost the knowledge to create new portals."

"So modern science hasn't been able to replicate the technology?" Sam asked. John shook his head and added, "scientists can replicate some of the structure, but they can't replicate the energy source needed to run it. Frankly, I believe the portals are more than technology. There is no conventional energy source involved. The energy sources are God and the Sonciel."

Sam's face lit up. "But that means they haven't given up on us, completely. Surely this is good news. It gives us reason to hope that God can be convinced to restore the old ways. At the least he will give us a fair hearing."

Anna chipped in, "that's the reason I'm involved in this fight. God and the Sonciel do care, otherwise the StarLight Portals would not be working."

"The one benefit of this is that the Fae can't turn off the Network and strand us," John concluded.

Anna was carrying her travel bag. "I'm heading off to Floriana now. Could the last one to leave, lock the front door? Good luck, and please, don't get caught.

"Say goodbye to Rose and Gerald for me." Anna started her journey to Floriana by walking through her front door with an encouraging wave.

Sam and John sat quietly for a few minutes and then heard footfalls on the stairs leading down from their rooms. Rose appeared, and she was supporting Gerald. They slowly approached the table and sat down, Gerald more heavily than was comfortable. He did not look well. His face was ashen, and he could barely walk. "I'm sorry my friends," he said wearily. "I don't think I can do this. I am sure I can get medical care here. So please, please go on without me. I will only be a burden."

Sam looked alarmed and upset as he said, "Gerald, we need you. If Rose supported you and travelled with you through the portals, do you think you could do it? There will be healing in the First World."

"But won't that increase the risk?" He asked.

"Not if you travel as father and adopted daughter. You can explain Rose's different family name as the result of an earlier marriage. It should fool the Fae's agents for long-enough to get you through the portal to Renaissance."

Gerald looked unconvinced. "It's still a risk, but if you believe it will work then I will try." He gave a weary smile. "Don't be surprised if I fall on my face."

Thirty minutes later the travellers were ready to leave. John spoke up. "I'll leave first, then Sam, and lastly Rose and Gerald. Check carefully that there are no watchful eyes around to see you leave.

"Oh, Anna said to give you her best wishes, Rose, Gerald. She has already started her journey to Floriana. She asked the last person to leave to lock the front door."

"I think I can manage that," Rose said drily.

*****

"Okay Gerald, it's time for us to leave," Rose said as she walked to the window and checked outside. Sam had left 15 minutes before them. "I can't see anyone nearby. Are you ready to move?"

"I will try Rose, but I feel so very weak. I am sorry but you will have to support me."

"That's okay Gerald. It's not far to the autocab rank. We'll be fine. Just let me take your weight and you can focus on putting one foot in front of another. We can do it." Rose's positive tone sparked renewed purpose in Gerald.

He stood unsteadily, swaying as he held the table for support. Once he had regained his balance, Rose asked him to place one arm across her shoulders, so she could take his weight.

"How's that?" She asked. Gerald tried a few steps towards the door and answered with a smile. Rose picked up their travel bags and opened the door, checked that hoods concealed their faces, and then stepped out into the crisp early morning air, keeping Gerald upright with a firm but gentle grip.

Locking the door, Rose and Gerald headed slowly towards the autocab rank.

The StarLight Departure portals were in the centre of town on the border of an expansive park. Even at this early hour, the place was busy. Rose hoped this would aid their quest for anonymity.

"Do you have the correct identity disc ready for the scanners?" Rose whispered.

Gerald held up his fake disc. "The real one is in my pocket." Rose nodded, surprised that he had not packed it in his bag, which Rose was carrying. Deciding not to query the matter, Rose set off for the portals, carefully supporting Gerald. As in Floriana, there were retail and tourist outlets along the way, mostly closed.

Rose noted many men and women dressed in startling, black uniforms lining the walls of the entryway. Each carried a heavy metal truncheon. And all were grimly eyeing the crowd that passed back and forth.

*Not good,* Rose thought. She prayed that she and Gerald weren't stopped and questioned.

A little way ahead she saw a tourist stand for Renaissance. Closed, but there were brochures on display, near at hand. She boldly took one under the cold eye of a black-clad guard and read as she walked. Better to have an idea of local attractions *before* any questions are asked.

Ahead, Rose saw the first security point. "Okay Gerald. We're going to reach the first scanner in a few minutes. Have your disc ready and scan it. Then I'll scan mine. They walked ahead and waited at the back of the only queue, shuffling forward, until they reached the scanner. Another black uniformed Guard sat there, watching his screen, and checking travellers as they passed through.

Gerald held out his disc to scan it and dropped it on the floor. The man at the screen noticed the holdup and was starting to rise when Rose bent down, while holding Gerald upright, and retrieved the disc from the floor. She scanned it for Gerald and then scanned her own.

"You two. Wait over there. The old man don't look well. Sit him on the chair. I won't be long." He returned his attention to the screen while Rose walked Gerald over to the chair and sat him down.

I am sorry Rose. So clumsy of me," Gerald whispered.

"Don't fret, these things happen," Rose replied. "I'm sure he'll ask us some questions. Remember, I'm your adopted daughter, Annette. If he asks about our different last names, I'll explain that mine is my married name, and I'm a widow. Is that clear?" Gerald nodded, too weak to answer.

They waited ten minutes before the black-clad security Guard walked over and asked if they needed any help.

"I think we're okay," Rose answered. "My father is ill and weak but I'm managing to support him. The doctor says he's not infectious, and on the mend, which is why we are travelling now."

The Guard looked at the brochure in Rose's hand. "You're off to Renaissance then? Lovely place to visit. I've been there myself.

"Why do you have different last names?" The Guard asked, without warning. Rose told her story. "I'm sorry to hear that. You're a good daughter to look after your father like this.

"There are strict rules in place now, with all that trouble on Floriana. Your father will have to walk through the portal by himself, carrying his own luggage. Do you think he can manage it?"

Rose, not wishing to sound alarmed by this news said that she would rest her father before passing through to Renaissance. "You wouldn't have a spare wheelchair by any chance?" Rose asked hopefully. The Guard shook his head. "Oh well, worth a try."

Gerald added in a husky voice. "I'm sorry to cause all this trouble. I am sure after a rest I can do it." Despite his words, Rose *was* alarmed.

The security Guard looked dubious. "If you need help, ask for it at the next scanner. Good luck and enjoy your holiday." The Guard left them and returned to his screen.

Rose breathed out a long sigh of relief. "That could have been much worse. He was actually friendly and supportive. I wasn't expecting that. I almost feel bad about deceiving him. Almost."

Her flippant comment belied her inner turmoil. She was afraid that Gerald would not be able to continue. The short walk, alone and unaided, carrying his bag might as well have been a marathon. *He's so weak. I don't think he can do it.*

"Maybe we should delay our trip for a few days," Rose suggested, "so you can get your strength back. I'm sure Anna won't mind us staying at the diner."

Gerald looked alarmed. "But Rose, we locked the diner door, and we do not have a key."

"How stupid." Rose slapped her forehead in frustration. "Of course we don't have a bloody key. What was I thinking?" Gerald took her hand and patted it several times.

"Please let me try to do this. We must get to Renaissance. Sam and John will be worried if we don't arrive soon." Rose had so many misgivings that she could not decide which was the most pressing.

"Okay," she decided, "I don't like it, but I agree that we don't have much choice."

Rose let Gerald rest for another five minutes, then asked if he was okay to continue. Gerald answered by trying to stand. He managed to get unsteadily to his feet and smiled weakly at Rose. "I feel much better thanks, Annette. Let's go to Renaissance."

"Okay, Dad. Let's walk." Rose quipped.

A few minutes later they were waiting patiently in the next queue. The portal for Renaissance was a few steps away. The queue wasn't long, and they soon arrived at the next scanner. Rose supported Gerald while he scanned his disc, successfully this time, and passed through to the portal. The Guard called Gerald forward and Rose, still supporting him, intervened, asking whether her father could rest for a few moments as he was unwell. The Guard pointed out a nearby chair without a word and turned to the next traveller.

"Okay Dad, tell me when you feel strong enough to continue." Rose put down the bags and sat on the floor beside Gerald.

The minutes passed agonisingly slowly, and Rose was becoming quite worried. *Sam and John will be wondering where we are.* A few minutes later, Gerald said to Rose, "I think I am right to go now."

Rose stood and helped Gerald to his feet. She waited for him to regain his balance. Then lifting the bags and taking Gerald's arm, she led him slowly back to the portal. The Guard noticed them and waved Gerald forward. Rose handed Gerald his bag. He stumbled a little with the extra weight. Rose continued to support Gerald.

"Not you lady," the Guard said in a commanding voice. "Get back. He must pass through unaided. It's the law."

Gerald steadied himself, took a deep breath, and walked forward shakily. Rose held her breath. *Come on Gerald just three more steps.*

Gerald managed two, then collapsed to the floor. His bag flew from his arms; belongings strewn across the entrance to the portal. Rose and the Guard rushed forward to help him. The Guard bent down; his attention drawn to something lying amongst the belongings.

He picked up an identity disc and was about to hand it back to Gerald when he saw the other disc clutched in Gerald's hand. The Guard rushed to the scanner and read the result on his screen.

"Gerald Solipsis. Hey, you're one of those criminals we've been looking for." Rose desperately tried to drag Gerald through the portal. The Guard grabbed Gerald's legs and heaved him back. Rose pulled harder and Gerald cried out in pain.

It was no use. She couldn't do it. With tears streaming from her eyes, she abandoned Gerald and rushed through the portal.

Sam and John were standing a short distance from the portal exit. Rose rushed over and blurted out the warning. "Run, we've been discovered." Without question or comment Sam and John ran. They picked up their travel bags and ran hard, turning several corners, looking to confuse any pursuers, and seeking a place to hide and catch their breath. They needed to find a quieter place with fewer people about. Running as they were, was drawing unwelcome attention.

After many twists and turns, they found themselves lost in a maze of back streets and alleys. They stopped running and walked casually for several minutes, no longer drawing the attention of the few people about. They finally sought refuge in a narrow alleyway, a hidden place where they could regroup.

Heaving to catch his breath, Sam looked at the weeping Rose. "It's Gerald isn't it," he wheezed. "They caught him."

Rose nodded sadly, still unable to speak. Over the next few minutes, they gradually regained control over their breathing and looked at each other, Rose's tears subsiding.

"It's worse than you think," Rose said softly. "Security didn't just catch him. They know who he is."

Rose explained every detail of the fiasco. "That fucking disc. Sorry Sam. Swearing isn't going to help. But I feel so damn guilty. If I'd been more careful, Gerald wouldn't have lost his disc. It's my fault — again!"

John embraced the woman he loved. "Rose, it was Gerald's decision to try. You had no choice so don't feel guilty. There isn't time for that."

Sam said it succinctly. "They know who Gerald is. The know a woman was travelling with him. They know about Rose. They know where we are going. This is so bad.

"My God, they'll block the portal to the First World. The Fae and the Council will stop all travel on the StarLight network. They'll banish Becky before we get back. What a *bloody* mess. Rose, you've got me doing it now."

"Sam. Quieten down. Just keep quiet so I can think." Tense silence lasting many minutes, was tearing at Sam's nerves. Until John smiled.

"I've got it. I think," John cried. "What if we created a diversion? Cause a riot at the Departure Portals. Would that work?"

Sam and Rose stared at each other in confusion. "Yeah, sure. A diversion could work. But where are we going to get one of those?"

John, looking a little smug, said, "from my travel bag. I always carry one, just in case."

Rose looked at John's bag even more confused. "I don't get it."

"There's a secret partition in my bag," John explained, "where I carry things I don't want Security to find. Would a screaming, scary, black creature, terrorising the Guards cause a diversion?"

"What?" Rose said in a high-pitched voice. "You've got a Dark disguise in there? Bloody hell. It won't be a diversion, it'll be chaos."

For the next 30-minutes they planned the diversion. The plan was simple, as most good plans are. "Are we all clear about our roles, no more questions or suggestions?" Sam and Rose remained silent. "Okay, let's find a way out of this maze and head for the Portals. It's a long walk.

## Back on Floriana

The Fae was ecstatic. The news had just arrived from Piaf. "We've caught one, we've caught one," he sang, as he gambolled around his office. The Black Shield officers who delivered the news looked at each other, open-mouthed and embarrassed at the childish display.

The Fae suddenly stopped gambolling. "Men," (one of the officers was a woman), "giggle, find my Personal Assistant and order him to my office. We have work to do."

The officers fled. "Good grief. I heard he was mad, but that, that was insane," the woman opined as they walked briskly away.

Shortly afterwards, the new PA hustled into the Fae's office. "Honourable Fae, you called for me. How may I be of service?"

The Fae looked startled for a moment. "I did call for you, didn't I. Now what… oh yes, prepare an official Order requesting the Black Shield Commander to personally deliver the captured criminal, Gerald Soli…psis to my office. Bring it to me to sign when it's ready.

"I want all travel to Floriana stopped. Order the Shield to prevent travel to Floriana and to use force, if necessary.

"Lastly, we now know that Gerald's co-conspirators are trying to flee to the First World. Have the Guard prevent their escape. Blockade all First World portals if necessary.

"And finally, prepare a decree, ordering the rabble outside to disperse. And, and notify the Council that we will be reconvening the treason trial as soon as the captured conspirator has arrived."

The Fae turned around and went to the window, muttering to himself about traitors and scoundrels, staring intently at the surging mass gathered down below. He said to himself, "if that rabble don't disperse, I'll kill every one of them. Kill them dead."

The Fae's voice was loud enough for the PA to hear. He backed fearfully out of the Fae's office.

"My God," he said in a faint voice, "what have I gotten myself into? I should never have accepted this job." The PA remembered what had happened to his predecessor. "And how am I going to contact the Council — there is no bloody Council!" The PA disappeared into a side office to fulfil the mad Fae's wishes.

*****

The Black Shield Commander flung Gerald onto the floor in front of the Fae. "As you requested

Honourable Fae, I bring you the fugitive. The Commander kicked Gerald, who was groaning on the floor. "Get up and show some respect for the Fae." Gerald tried to stand, but could not, falling back to the floor. "I said, get up." The Commander kicked Gerald again. He cried out in pain and writhed, yelling piteously, "I cannot stand. Please, I am too weak. I need a doctor. I cannot do it."

The Fae intervened. "Leave him, Commander. He can stay where he belongs, grovelling at my feet." The Fae gloated at the little victory this pathetic figure represented. "Now, Gerald. May I call you Gerald? Where are the others, the criminals you were travelling with. I want to hear you say it. We know where they are going, but I want you to say it. Where are they going?"

Gerald heard the Fae speak through a surging flood of pain and despair. He knows. He knows. What have I done? There seemed no point in remaining quiet.

"First World," he mumbled softly. The Fae bent down closer to his victim.

"I didn't hear that. Say it again, loudly this time." The Fae leant closer.

Gerald gathered as much strength as he could and shouted, "The First World. God will return to destroy you."

The loud reply took the Fae by surprise. He blinked and screamed, "How dare you..." but Gerald did not hear him. He had succumbed to his illness and fallen unconscious.

"Take him away and get him ready for the trial. I'll decide who destroys who."

The Commander did as he was instructed; he half carried; half dragged the unconscious man out of the office.

The Fae's beleaguered mind saw assassins behind every curtain, poison in every morsel of food, and countless enemies on every world. He had the power, but no longer the wit and the subtlety to wield it responsibly.

God would return and take back what was no longer his. And who was making this possible? The Six, the Group of Six. Three members were still at large; capable of bringing ruin down upon his head. The people were against him; even the Council had deserted him.

But three of the Group were in his grasp. What if… what if… a tiny spark of effective action set fire to his brain.

He recalled his PA. The man nervously peaked round the door. "Yes, Honourable Fae. How may I help you?"

"Ah, yes. PA — what's your name? — No matter. I want you to prepare a Proclamation addressed to the fugitives on Renaissance. The Proclamation should say that, if they are willing to surrender, I will guarantee a pardon for the three members of the Group in detention, here on Floriana.

"Saturate all means of communication with this magnanimous offer."

"Yes, Honourable Fae, I shall do it at once. Is there anything else? Do you wish me to report on my earlier tasks on your behalf?"

"What earlier tasks? No, no. Get two officers of the Black Guard. They will escort me to the cell holding my two female captives." The Fae giggled and spoke to no one in particular, "I have a little surprise for them," he clapped his hands and giggled some more.

*****

Becky walked restlessly backwards and forwards across the width of their suite of captivity. It was getting on Marion's nerves. Hour, after hour, backwards and forwards. In desperation, Marion stood and walked to Becky. Looking startled, as if she had forgotten she had a fellow prisoner, Becky stopped and looked enquiringly at Marion.

"Becky, please, fretting and pacing backwards and forwards is not helping. It's giving me a headache. We are where we are. Wishing it were different won't make it so.

"Sam and the others have their job to do, and we have ours. Our job is to stay alive after the Fae banishes us. We should be talking about that. We should be planning an escape before the trial starts and deciding whether we can trust Phillip."

"I'm sorry Marion. I'm just so worried about Sam. I can't stand not knowing whether Sam and the others are safe. You're right, we must talk about the things that affect us. It'll give my mind something better to do. Where do we…"

There was a disturbance at the door, loud voices, and then the door flew open. Two Black Shield officers walked in and stepped aside to admit the Fae. The other two guarding the door walked in and shut the door. Phillip was not with them.

Marion smiled meekly. "Oh, Mr Fae. Are you so scared of two defenceless women that you need to bring an army to protect you? Don't worry, dear, we'll be good girls, for now." With that last statement, the smile disappeared, to be replaced by two angry and accusing eyes.

"Or have you come to gloat, to rip off our clothes and rape us? Yes? No?

"No, I didn't think so. You don't have the balls."

The Fae went red in the face, blood vessels threatening to explode all over the carpet.

"How dare you speak to me like that. It's Honourable Fae, not Mister," he hissed. "You will kneel in my presence." Becky and Marion remained standing, smiling sweetly at the shark in their room.

"Shield, teach these women some manners." The two officers grabbed the women and forced them to their knees.

"That's better. Not so difficult, was it?" The women ignored the Fae and spoke to each other about mundane matters.

"Silence. If you do not show some respect, I will ask these officers to teach you. And it will be painful."

The Fae was breathing like a bull about to charge. Becky and Marion fell silent, looking up with smiling adoration at the man who held their lives in his hands, the satire quite obvious. But not to the Fae.

"Ah, I see you have recognised my divinity at last. That is good. Because I have some happy news for you."

How quickly the Fae's demeanour changed. One minute, apoplectic with rage, the next smiling benignly on his devoted subjects. "You may rise. Please sit down at the table so I can tell you my news." The Fae giggled. Becky looked at Marion.

As they stood and walked to the table, Becky whispered. "The Fae's gone ga ga." To which Marion replied, "ga ga indeed. And much more dangerous."

They sat and stared at the Fae, lips and expressions sealed.

"I've got good news for you. We have brought one of your friends to Floriana, to keep you company. Alas, he cannot come today. He is sick, and the doctors hold out little hope for him. Like you, I wish him a speedy recovery, so he can stand beside you at the Tribunal. Aren't you pleased? Giggle."

Becky's thoughts went immediately to Sam. Please not Sam.

'Which friend are you speaking about? We have so many — billions." Marion smiled at the Fae with big fluttering blue eyes.

"Stop that," the Fae blushed. "If you must know, his name is, what was it officer, oh yes, his name is Gerald Solipsis. Funny name, don't you think? Giggle."

Marion stood and looked down at the Fae. He was much shorter than she was. "What did you do to him? Did you get you thugs to beat him up?"

"Nothing so dramatic. Sit down — now!" Marion sat. "He is genuinely sick. We will delay the Tribunal until he is well.

"There was something else." The Fae whispered to one of the Guards. "Oh yes, I am going to set you free. Isn't that nice?"

Marion and Becky looked at each other in confusion. What the hell is this nut job talking about?

"If… there's always an if isn't there. Pesky little word. Giggle."

"If, the three fugitives surrender to the Black Shield; if they do that, I have announced that I will set you free."

Becky and Marion laughed in the Fae's face. Becky said, "You're joking. I don't believe you, and they won't either."

The Fae shrugged his shoulders and giggled. "We'll see, we'll see."

The Fae turned to the senior Black Shield officer. "Withhold all food from these women, until further notice. They'll learn good manners, one way or another."

Giggle, giggle, giggle followed him out the door, which a Shield officer then closed and locked.

"Well, that was fun while it lasted," Marion concluded, with a cynical chuckle.

"Yes, I enjoyed annoying him as well," Becky replied. "Cheap fun, but it may come back to bite us. No food until further notice. Let's hope Sam and the others get back before we die of hunger."

Becky thought about what the Fae's visit had revealed. "Poor Gerald. I hope he'll be okay. Sam, John, and Rose are still alive and causing the Fae heartburn. He must be getting desperate if he thinks they will fall for his ludicrous bargain. No wonder he's gone ga ga." The two women had a hearty laugh at the Fae's expense.

"To top it off, he thinks he's God," Marion added more seriously. "A divine Fae is one thing; an insane Fae who thinks he's God is something else altogether.

"Our Fae has gone Dark!"

*****

Anna and James were in deep discussion, having just heard about the closure of the StarLight portals. "The Fae is trying to stop the flow of supporters to Floriana," Anna said. 'How many of the delegations with their petitions are already here?"

James referred to his tablet, "Umm, all but one Anna." Anna breathed a deep sigh of relief. The blockade had come too late.

"That's good." Anna replied. "We now have tangible evidence of overwhelming support. But it won't be of much use when the Fae has gone mad and is capable of murder, or worse. Petitions won't mean anything to him. Only people here and now, have the power to influence him."

"You think? I'm not so sure," James offered. "If, as we're told, he believes he is God, then even people power may not shift him. He could kill us all with the flick of a finger.

"Anna, the situation is extremely dangerous. The people here have a right to know what's at stake. We should call a meeting of the delegations and give them the facts." Anna considered James's suggestion. "Do it. You're right; they need to know."

At this point, a woman entered the tent. "Anna, someone has just arrived and wishes to speak with you. He seems genuine enough."

"Let him in," Anna said, "he can't add any more complexity to the situation.'

A man, dressed as a Black Shield entered the tent. "You're an officer of the Shield," James said belligerently, "you have no business here. You're either a spy, a pretty stupid spy, or a fool. Your kind aren't popular with the people."

"I know, I know, I'm taking a risk but I'm willing to risk my life so that I can speak with you. My name is Phillip." Anna was impressed by the man's audacity.

"James, let him speak. I'll decide whether he's genuine, or not. Come in Phillip and take a seat. James, why don't you go and organise the meeting of delegations while I have a chat with Phillip."

"But Anna, for all we know he may be an assassin." James cried. Anna looked at Phillip intensely.

"No James, he's not an assassin. If he were, he would be dressed as a sheep and not as a wolf. Please do what I ask. I'll be fine." James did not look happy, but he followed Anna's wishes.

Once they were alone, Anna asked why she should trust what Phillip said.

"If I were you, I wouldn't trust my words," Phillip agreed. "But I hope to win your trust by my actions. I'm a member of the Shield but not because I volunteered. Previously, I was on Becky's staff when she was Fae. All attendants in Government service are draftees into the Shield by default. Carrying a lethal truncheon to intimidate and injure people makes me sick to the stomach.

"But these are just words — easily said. I came because I can be of practical use. I'm a member of the detail tasked with securing Becky and Marion. Becky and…"

"I know who Becky and Marion are," Anna interrupted, a note of excitement in her voice. "You have seen them recently? Are they okay?"

"They are two gutsy ladies, and they're both well, physically. But their confinement is emotionally destructive, not knowing what's happening. Even so, they have risen above all that and taken the fight to the Fae. My God, they defy him at every turn, and he doesn't know how to handle them.

"He's gone mad, you know, and he's liable to get rid of them at any time. They need to be freed before the Fae can reconvene the Tribunal. I'd like to try to do that."

Anna was astonished. "You would risk that for them, and us? If anything went wrong, it could cost you your life."

"I know the risk. Just coming in uniform to see you was a risk. But I had to come. I can't stand by and do nothing."

Anna went quiet. After several minutes of deep thought, she made her decision. "Phillip, you're a brave man. I gladly accept your offer.

"Freeing Becky and Marion would be momentous. It would change the dynamics of our situation. It will be dangerous. Have you thought about how you might get them out?"

"I've done little else for days," Phillip explained. "I have a shift coming up in two days. I'm going to obtain Shield uniforms for two of your people, and one each for Becky and Marion. I'll incapacitate my partner, who's a brute, and replace him with one of your people. I'll give uniforms to Becky and Marion.

"Suitably dressed and armed, the five of us will casually walk out of the Government Building."

"You make it sound so easy." Anna said. "But it won't be easy, will it? You can't plan for everything. I'll need to get two volunteers to assist you. That's my problem and I'll do what I can. In the end, however, I can't order anyone to risk their lives. If no one is willing to volunteer, I'll have to volunteer myself. I'm sure I can convince one other to join us.

"You'll need to get the two uniforms and truncheons to us before your shift." Anna advised.

"I can do that," Phillip said with a broad smile on his face. "I'll get the uniforms to you on the morning before my shift. Thank you for believing in me."

"Well, that's decided. Come with me and I'll escort you to a safe place where you can cross the frontline, back to the Government sector." Anna shook Phillip's hand warmly and they both left the tent to make the short walk to the frontline. As they walked, Anna was already thinking about the things she needed to do.

## A Dark in the Park

Finding the Portal to the First World was proving maddeningly difficult. Lost in a maze of backstreets and alleys, they had no sense of direction. They tried walking in a straight line, but the confusing streets made it impossible.

More than once, Rose cried, "not again. Bugger… We walked past that building an hour ago... We're going round in circles... Why didn't anyone think to bring a compass."

John called a halt. "We need to try a different approach. Instead of trying to walk in a straight line, and failing every time, why not walk in circles and increase the radius each time. Eventually we should reach a major street. See a street sign, or something. We're wasting time. The longer we take, the more prepared Security at the Portal will be.

Rose liked the idea. "One of the first things I learnt in the army, was to work with the terrain, not against it. Let's try it. We can judge our direction by our shadows. It's after midday so our shadows should give us an idea of the direction we're going.

And so, they tried John's suggestion, gradually increasing the radius of their circular movement. After two tiring hours of steady walking, they stumbled upon a busier, wider street, and a sign that pointed to the City Centre.

"The portal we need is in the City Centre, within a park," John advised. "Do you need a rest, or should we rest when we find the park?" Rose and Sam were eager to keep going.

Half an hour, and three kilometres later, the three fugitives staggered into a large park, and knew the portal could not be far away.

"We'll rest for a few minutes," John said. "No time to think about food and drink. Let's hope they eat and drink in the First World," he added with a wry and weary smile, "Otherwise, we're stuffed." Sam and Rose were too tired to think of a witty reply.

Half an hour later, Sam was ready to scout ahead.

"Sam are you clear on what you need to do inside the Portal Centre?" John enquired.

"Sure. Ready to go now my heart has stopped racing. What a morning. I'll have nightmares about that bloody maze for the rest of my life.

"Shouldn't we separate a little?" Sam added. "Three people together might attract uncomfortable questions. There's sure to be enemies patrolling the park and they'll be looking for three fugitives — us. I'll return to this spot after I've checked out conditions inside the Portal Centre. It shouldn't take too long to find out what we're up against. I'm ready to go now. I'll be quick, promise."

Sam adjusted his cloak against the strengthening breeze, picked up his travel bag and walked off, giving the plants intense scrutiny as he passed them by.

He saw several characters ahead in black uniforms, carrying their lethal truncheons. He disappeared discretely into the shrubbery until they walked by. These were the enemy. It was a strange feeling, knowing that they were patrolling the park looking for him.

A few minutes later he was standing just outside the entrance of the StarLight Departure Centre where he had managed to hide himself in a milling crowd. The Fae had closed the Floriana Portal. People were angry. Most of these travellers were bound for Floriana. He realised the anger might help them to create further chaos. Several black clad Guards were eyeing the boisterous crowd with obvious disdain. This place is going to explode if the crowd keeps getting bigger.

Sam walked casually into the Centre and followed the signs to the portals. There were many Guards inside, although some were moving toward the entrance to help control the threatening crowd.

He took his opportunity to approach as close to the portals as he dared, standing at a general tourist information booth and leafing through several brochures. Sam could see the closed and heavily guarded Floriana portal.

At the end of the row was the First World portal. There were a couple of Guards there looking bored, but the portal seemed to be open.

An order from Floriana to close the portal hadn't yet reached Renaissance. Sloppy, very sloppy, but fortunate for us, Sam thought.

He reversed course and headed back toward the entrance where the crowd had continued to grow. Some in the angry crowd held clubs and he saw several lethal looking knives as well.

Sam walked out of the crowd and back toward John and Rose. He realised that they needed to hurry to put their diversion into effect before an uncontrollable crowd made entering the StarLight Centre impossible.

Sam saw John and Rose sitting on separate park benches in the shade of several massive trees. He approached casually and while studying a nearby plant, told Rose about the situation at the Centre. She was delighted. "What a bonus. An angry crowd fleeing a monster and attacking the Guards is just what we need." Rose stood and went over to John and told him Sam's news. He also was delighted. "We better hurry. Let's go and create mayhem."

The three friends walked through the vegetation trying to keep hidden. They reached a place that was as close as they were going to get without walking into the open. John put on his Dark disguise. The sight still made Sam's skin crawl. John lit a torch he had prepared, and Sam carrying John's cloak and travel bag approached the entrance and lost himself in the crowd. Rose did the same from a different direction.

Sam entered the StarLight Centre and walked along the corridor so that the Guards minding the portals would be able to hear him when he started to scream.

Rose was outside on the periphery of the crowd angrily berating the Guards when she stopped suddenly and started to scream. The crowd was galvanised. A monstrous sound, a snarling and screeching in a language the crowd had not heard before. Sam heard Rose scream, "dear God, what is that thing oh, it's coming this way, help." She pushed through the crowd screaming as she went.

The Guards were bewildered, that is until they saw the hideous flickering creature rushing toward them, wielding a flaming torch. The crowd started screaming and running in all directions, knocking the Guards down in their rush to escape. The Guards started beating the crowd and the crowd fought back. It was mayhem. Sam cried out "to the portals, to the portals, escape through the portals." And the crowd near him obliged, running down to the portal station, and overwhelming the Guards on duty.

While all this was going on, John found a spot behind an advertising screen where he took off his disguise and rolled it up into a tight bundle. He set fire to waste bins nearby and threw the torch into the midst of the crowd. He ran into the Centre looking like one of the travellers. He kept the voice box operative and every so often reminded the crowd that the monster was still in their midst.

Separately, the three fugitives converged on the First World portal. One Guard remained there whilst the other was trying to stem the flow of angry travellers to Floriana. John gave him a blood-curdling screech and the Guard all but fainted. He was terrified. Another Guard saw what was happening and rushed over, swinging his truncheon in wild arcs.

Unfortunately for him, he chose Rose to attack. He aimed a wild blow at her head, missed, and Rose finished him off with a sliding kick to his legs, which put him on the floor. A forceful blow to his stomach left him fighting for breath and out of the game.

Sam, John, and Rose ignored the other terrified Guard, and, one by one, passed through the portal to the First World.

## Angels of Light

It was dark. Not nighttime dark, but the deepest, densest darkness the travellers had ever experienced. They walked into black nothingness, the only sense providing information being the pressure of a floor under their feet.

"Gees… at least they've got gravity and breathable air here," Rose quipped. "Everything else is a toss-up."

She heard fumbling in the black and without warning a strong beam of light shone directly into her eyes. "Shit, watch where you're putting that thing. If I wasn't blind before..."

"Sorry Rose." John's contrite voice spoke from somewhere in the darkness. "Stupid. I should have pointed the torch at the ground." As the soft voice spoke, it moved closer to Rose. The beam's side glow illuminated John's hand reaching out to grasp Rose's arm and pulling her into a tight embrace. She lowered her travel bag and responded by saying in a provocative voice, "you're forgiven," and held John tighter still.

"Ahem," Sam cleared his throat melodramatically, "not alone. Just saying," he chuckled and added, "we're here at last. Where is here exactly? I can't see anything but you two making out."

John and Rose let go of each other, the beam of light flashing erratically around wherever they were.

John settled the light ahead of him to reveal a solid stone wall. He moved it slowly left and right, as far as the light could reach, to reveal a semi-circular space, about 5 metres in diameter, enclosed by a wall devoid of mortar or linear breaks, indicating that the space was hewn from solid rock. The ceiling was likewise solid stone.

The only means of exit seemed to be to return through the portal to Renaissance, an exit they could not take.

"I'm glad I'm not claustrophobic," Rose said. "This would be a great place to set a horror movie, the ceiling slowly descending, grinding away in the darkness…"

An agitated voice spoke up. "Stop it Rose, just because you're okay in confined spaces doesn't mean everyone is." John took a deep breath and let it out slowly.

Sam had had enough. "Okay guys, settle down. We've arrived in the First World and it's not what we expected. But we're here now and we must play by the rules that apply here.

"We had no right to expect a welcome with open arms. The rest of The Light rejected them all those years ago, so now they take precautions. I would, in the same circumstances.

"They must allow some people in, researchers and historians, otherwise we would have heard that the First World was off limits. We didn't, so it isn't.

"I think, this is a test, a vetting process. We must earn the right to enter."

"A shame then that the Fae has captured Gerald, the one person whose training and qualifications might have granted us access," John said sadly.

"Then we'll have to earn the right ourselves," Rose declared. "The Angels must know who we are and why we're here. They must know how determined we've been to get here.

"Just as we have operatives that watch conditions in the Mortal Realm, why shouldn't the First World have their own operatives at work throughout The Light?"

Sam spoke up. "You're right Rose. They know how dangerous the Fae has become. They know he's willing, and able, to kill whoever gets in his way, and that includes the Angels of Light. If they choose not to help us, then the Fae has effectively killed them. The Fae will become God, and billions of good people will suffer.

"Worse, he'll abandon the Mortal Realm to The Dark and the Dark Master, Louseefa. And we know, with certainty that Louseefa's real goal is to rule The Light.

"If the Angels don't speak with us, The Light is lost and Louseefa will win."

A voice boomed in the darkness. "Louseefa is the Dark Master? This is something we only suspected. But you have proof? I will speak with my brothers and sisters. This may take some time."

"I hope they don't take too long, I'm starving," Rose complained. "And a glass of water would be good," she shouted into the void. No one answered her directly but a sound to their left prompted John to switch the torch back on. A short search with the light revealed the source of the sound. A low table had mysteriously appeared, crammed with a variety of fruits and nuts, and red wine and crusty bread and olives. Three voluminous cushions provided the seating.

"Wow," Rose cried with delight. "That's what I call service. Thank you," Rose added, just in case they were still listening.

Driven by hunger and thirst, the three travellers chose one of the cushions and sat down. The torch provided light in the centre of the table as they attacked the food with gusto. Fortunately for Sam there was juice provided, so he could satisfy his thirst like the others.

"So how did you know?" John asked Sam. Sam looked innocently confused. "That they were listening. How did you know?" John repeated his question.

Sam explained, "I didn't know. But I suspected they had to be listening. How else could they vet new arrivals?"

"Whatever the case, well done Sam. Mentioning Louseefa was a masterstroke," John added.

The sound of eating dominated all else for the next twenty minutes. Later, lying back on their comfortable cushions, the three travellers succumbed to their interstellar 'jet lag' and drifted off to sleep, their bodies seeking respite from the hectic schedule they had set themselves since leaving Piaf.

Many hours of deep sleep later, the three woke up slowly, as if from a gentle dream. There was now a soft glow emanating from the walls and ceiling, pushing back the darkness. To reveal a table that had, mysteriously, been relaid, this time with hot water and soap and fluffy towels.

"These Angels think of everything," Rose declared. "A bath would be good, but, in the circumstances…"

"Sorry to spoil your fun," Sam laughed. Sam couldn't see it in the dim light, but John blushed. "Does everyone else feel as refreshed as I do?" Sam enquired. "I feel like I've been relaxing at a beach resort for a week."

The others agreed with Sam. There was something different, almost magical, about the sleep they had all experienced.

They each had a separate bowl of hot water, and set about cleaning themselves up, grabbing toiletries as they needed them from their bags. Three clean white robes appeared mysteriously from out of the air and settled slowly down to rest on each of the cushions. Three pairs of sandals, likewise, settled beside each cushion.

"I guess we're meant to wear these," John saying the obvious. "This is a positive sign. Perhaps they will meet with us after all."

The three quickly changed into the clothes provided and repacked their bags, slipping on the sandals — each a perfect fit. They waited in the hope that the walls would instantly slide apart to reveal an idyllic landscape.

They stood and waited, and waited, but nothing happened. "Perhaps they're still discussing whether to let us in," Rose suggested. There was nothing more they could do, so they sat down on their cushions and waited some more.

Three hours later the walls slid apart to reveal, not an idyllic landscape, but another wall.

"Well, it's an improvement, I think," Rose said. They picked up their bags and walked forward into the next, much larger room. Still no doors or windows. Looking up they saw that there was a parapet topping the walls, the ceiling much higher still. The reason for the enormous height of the ceiling became obvious as five supersized figures filed onto the walkway behind the parapet. They arranged themselves around the walkway so that the three figures below them had to turn toward whichever of the Light Angels was speaking.

"This is an uncomfortable way for us to converse," John said confidently; not liking the unequal arrangement one bit.

'It must be this way, for now. My name is Zadkiel, to my right are Seraphine and Aurora, and to my left are Haniel and Anael. I have to tell you that we are, as yet, undecided, about admitting you to the First World.

"Your arrival is as a mountain tossed into a tranquil sea. You bring change and unpredictability with you. The waves you make will impact the shores of every world in the Light. And not least of all, The First World."

"Where there has been tranquillity and certainty for so long, you offer us new challenge and uncertainty. And most of all, new relevance. We are yet to decide whether we want or need relevance any longer."

"All of that is true, Lord Zadkiel." Sam said. "We came to offer you The Light. The Light is yours, always has been. Louseefa planted and reaped the storm that carried God and the Angels far away from us." Sam lowered his head in particular deference to Seraphine and Aurora.

"And now the *Last World of Light* is calling to the First World for aid. The populations of every world yearn for your return. They oppose the Fae who has fallen to the corruption of undeserved power. He will kill billions, if necessary, to preserve that power."

Zadkiel interrupted John, "we know all this. Our indecision does not come from disbelief in the rightness of the cause. We admire your vision, tenacity, and sacrifice.

"Our indecision is born of inertia. It is hard to move, when for thousands of years, nothing has moved at all. Nothing, except the inevitable loss of our numbers. Immortality is not forever. Our God left us many ages ago and the Lords have declined as well. We are all that remain."

The travellers were shocked. "All? God is dead and the angels are dying?" Sam found it hard to believe. "But why haven't the Sonciel invested a new God and raised more of you to Angelic Light?"

"The Sonciel have withdrawn from The Light, and from us," said Seraphine, "though not completely. We have an idea to where the Consciousness has withdrawn, but we don't know how to get there. The Archives may help but we gave up the search long ago."

"But there must be a God," Sam cried. "Without the power of God, The Light will be at the mercy of the Fae, the Dark and Louseefa. And they have no mercy." Sam was near distraught. "If you allow us, we will help you find the Consciousness. Locking yourselves away, here, cut off from The Light, will not save you when Louseefa comes for revenge."

"We know," said Zadkiel. "Yet the quest seems hopeless, from our perspective. We accepted the inevitable long ago."

"Nothing is inevitable." Sam spoke boldly. "If you will not help us search for the Consciousness, then let us search for you. We may seem insignificant and weak in your eyes, but we have endured much to get here; I have left my wife behind, banished to The Mortal Realm by the Fae. A death sentence. Yet still I came, and you cannot deny our help."

Zadkiel sighed and looked at his brothers and sisters. Unspoken words passed between them. Then, resignedly, Zadkiel said, "You have given us much to think on. We will open the wall and let you into The First World. You will be given lodgings, until we make our decision."

The wall behind Sam, John, and Rose slid closed and the wall in front of them opened to a vista they had been longing to see. Rolling green hills faded into a bluish horizon, the sun shining down upon the verdant life beneath. A few simple houses were in the near distance.

The three travellers walked into The First World, captivated by the life and beauty of the place. "Paradise at last," Sam said softly.

# Part Twelve - To Blood and to Banish

Becky and Marion had not eaten since yesterday. Phillip had promised to smuggle some food in for them, but his shift had changed. He would not be on duty until later tonight.

"What a nuisance," Marion declared. "I still dream about meat you know; steak and sausages and bacon and…"

"Oh, Marion don't torture yourself. The Fae is doing nicely on his own without you helping him." Becky always got testy when she was hungry. *Something to do with hormones I expect.*

"I'm sorry, Marion. It's the waiting, the not knowing, I can't stand it. And hunger doesn't help." Becky looked out of the window at the massive crowd. "So many people, I never saw such a crowd when I was Fae, but now that we're prisoners, the Light have come to Floriana to support our cause. It's ironic, and wonderful, and crazy, and humbling, all at the same time."

Marion walked over and stood beside Becky, enthralled by the number and variety of the crowd. It was a melting pot of Light. "Their faith in us, and the God

Movement is humbling, I agree. We must believe that the complex unravelling of our times will lead to a better future. We can do nothing else. We can't promise or predict the outcome. We can only believe in it and keep the faith."

"Why, Marion, you are a real philosopher. I can see it now, an astounding book, a bestseller, written by Gerald Solipsis and Marion Smith."

Marion smiled wickedly; troubles forgotten in the moment, "why, Honourable Former Fae Rebecca Pilgrim, don't you mean Marion Smith and Gerald Solipsis? And what would we call this book, mmm?"

"Oh, I don't know. The Return of God, Battle for The Light?" Becky stopped speaking and a pained expression replaced the smile upon her face. "Who are we kidding?

"We're kidding ourselves, Marion. We can't keep delaying the discussion. We both know it's unlikely that Sam and the others will return with God in time to save us. That doesn't happen in real life. The book we're imagining will just be a work of fiction." Becky lowered her eyes, turned around and sat down on her bed.

Marion walked over and sat on her own bed. "We've been putting it off haven't we. Avoiding the future. Thinking it will all go away if we ignore it. But it won't.

"So, let's have that talk now. How do we avoid banishment? What do we do if the Fae attacks the crowd? What do we do when we're pushed through that portal into the Mortal Realm? How do we survive?"

The conversation was lengthy, hours in fact, only interrupted after dark, when Phillip tapped on the door and poked his head into the room. "Sorry to interrupt. I must be quick. My partner will be back soon. I've been to see Anna and we've organised an escape for you in the early hours of tomorrow morning, during my next shift."

The news stunned Becky and Marion. "You've seen Anna? My God Phillip. You took that risk for us?" Becky cried.

"Shhh. I'm going to give you two Shield uniforms and truncheons. Hide them somewhere safe." he stopped talking. "My partner's coming back. I must go. Here's the food I promised." Marion took a bag and the uniforms from Phillip, and he quickly locked the door.

Becky was dazed. "Unless this is a dream, or a very clever deception, I think we can trust Phillip now. What do you think?"

"What do I think? Wow! Food, and an escape plan. What's not to like? Phillip is honourable and decent. And I believe he's honest. Yes, I trust him. I'll trust him with my life." Marion got a faraway look in her eyes as if her mind had drifted off to somewhere else, to sometime else. Becky saw the signs right away.

"You're smitten aren't you. I can see it in your eyes. He is handsome. And your character judgement is correct as well. I hope you and Phillip have a chance to get to know each other better. Becky started humming a familiar tune. Love will find a way."

Marion blushed. "Stop it, Becky. We have serious things to do. For a start, let's eat." And so, they ate and drank; and laughed together without reservation or misgiving.

Now, they had hope.

*****

"No food?" The Fae screamed at his PA. "No food for God; no food for the God who holds the power of life and death over everyone on this planet? It's outrageous. Whose fault is it?" The PA could hardly say it was the Fae's fault; that the people hated him so much that they had blocked all deliveries to the Government sector; not if he wished to keep breathing.

"Honourable Fae. For untold years there has only ever been two days supply of food in storage here. We depend upon regular fresh deliveries. Those deliveries have been — delayed."

"Delayed? What do you mean by delayed?" The Fae questioned.

"There are too many people outside blocking the way. The crowd is so dense, they cannot get out of the way, even if they want to." The PA hoped, desperately that the Fae would accept his explanation.

The Fae didn't. "Send out the Shield to clear a way for the deliveries. I don't care how they do it. Just get it done."

"But Honourable Fae, there are too many people. If the Shield use force, the crowd will fight back. You will lose your protective shield." The Fae did not listen to reason, could not listen to reason. He had lost his reason and had no need for it anymore.

He spoke through clenched teeth. "If you don't follow my orders, now, I'll send you out there to face the mob. Get it done and ensure I can see what is happening from my window. Go!" The PA stood, immobile. "I said GO!" The Fae screamed. The PA fled from the office.

One hour later, the Fae watched the first ever Battle for Floriana. A group of 100 Shield stood a short distance from the crowd. Phillip was not among them.

An emissary walked forth from the crowd and spoke with the Shield Commander on duty. The Fae imagined what they might be saying… the emissary might say, "why have you come here?" The Commander will say, "two vehicles carrying supplies for the Government Complex will arrive on the other side of the crowd. You will let them through." The emissary might say, "and if we don't?" The Commander will say, "We have orders to force you to do this. People may die. Is that what you want?" The emissary turned on his heels and walked back into the crowd.

The Fae clapped his hands with delight. "Oh, this will be good. Giggle, giggle."

The Fae watching from on high, saw the Shield force form a solid square of armed officers, ten rows deep. In the far distance, he saw two large vehicles driving slowly through the crowd. The mob is letting them pass. The Fae knew the people would not dare to defy him.

He was giggling away happily as the vehicles moved forward. Then, about 200 metres from the other side, the vehicles stopped. One million, two million or more voices started chanting bring back God, bring back God. Even from far above, the Fae could hear the chanting, the defiance, the betrayal. And to top it off, the drivers got out of the vehicles and joined the crowd.

The Fae would put a stop to this rebellion. He rushed out of his office and took his private portal to the roof. He walked to the edge of the building facing the crowd and the stalled food supplies. He stepped into the air and approached the crowd, floated there above their heads and raised his hands. The trucks started moving, without their drivers. Who needs drivers when we have God.

The crowd panicked and tried to get out of the way. But the trucks were picking up speed, crushing unfortunate people who could not move in time. Enraged, the crowd swarmed over the trucks, trying to stop them. At the same time the square of Shield officers crashed into the crowd, wielding truncheons, and breaking bones. It was chaotic. The square advanced and then slowed as the weight of numbers overwhelmed them.

The Fae could yet win his prize. The trucks advanced. All the doors were open people hanging off each side.

Then as the trucks reached the road below where the Fae stood, the crowd jumped off and the trucks rumbled up the slope and stopped. The Fae lowered to the ground and accepted his prize, circling around the trucks to inspect his food supplies.

Except, there weren't any. The cupboards were bare. The crowd had taken everything. All he had succeeded in doing was feeding the mob.

Then the crowd started laughing at him. Louder and louder, the laughter mingling with chanting. The Fae covered his ears, which only encouraged the crowd more.

He could not stand it. He willed a mighty storm to form above the crowd. Hundreds of lightning bolts flashed amongst the crowd, setting fire to tents and striking people dead. There was no escape. The crying and the screaming reached a crescendo and then stopped, turning to screams of outrage.

The front ranks of the crowd ran up the slope as one and sought to capture the Fae. A mighty wind of flame was born with a flick of the Fae's hands. It burnt and flung the people, sending their stricken bodies flying back into the crowd.

The Fae smiled contentedly. They could not harm him. He turned and walked up the steps and back into the Government Building.

The First Battle for Floriana was over. Many hundreds of people had died. The Fae went hungry, and the people mourned their dead and dying.

The flame of the Dark, had come to The Light.

*****

Anna and James met with their surviving advisors, one of whom was James's partner, Charles. Their eyes met and each smiled briefly.

Everyone looked shattered. Many had lost friends and loved ones. There would be no volunteers now; no volunteers to aid them with Becky's release. None would risk the power of the Fae again.

Anna's advisors counselled her to wait, to continue the siege and starve the Fae into submission. She saw right away that this would not work. Where the trucks had failed, the Fae would use his powers to get food in other ways.

"Do we know how many of us have died?" She asked an advisor.

He consulted his tablet. "Almost one thousand dead, and many more gravely wounded. They will not last the night. The wounds are terrible. The doctors do what they can but there are just too many people needing urgent care."

Anna grieved the loss. But they had learnt one important lesson. "The Fae will do anything to keep his power," she said. "He will kill us all, without hesitation, if we push him. So, we won't push.

"Order the crowd to move further back. Take the pressure off. If any trucks arrive carrying food, stop and strip them, before they enter the crowd. Check for booby traps. I wouldn't be surprised if we found concealed explosives."

Anna's last statement shocked those within hearing. The Light had no need for explosives and projectile weapons; never seen as necessary before, never accepted as part of the culture. Expressly forbidden in the oldest Archives.

This Fae, this murderer, was different, neither Light nor Dark, but something else altogether; something in between. The worst excesses of the Mortal Realm in The Light? Unthinkable, monstrous. Could it be possible?

"But Anna, none of us have experience with explosives and booby traps," Charles said. "Are you sure?"

"Oh yes, I'm sure. This Fae is capable of anything. In many ways, he's worse than the Dark. At least with the Dark we know what to expect. This Fae will continue to surprise and shock us. Always expect and prepare for the worst.

"There must be explosive and projectile weapons experts amongst our supporters. Find them and use them. Have you noted all that I have said?"

"Yes Anna, I'll spread the word." Charles left the tent.

"Okay people, it's been a tough day and all of us will be grieving. I won't ask any of you to volunteer for tomorrow's escape attempt. You've lost too much already.

"James, I'll go alone with Phillip to free Becky and Marion. You must stay here. As my 2IC I can't put you in harm's way. If anything happens to me, you will take my place."

James protested; his face stricken and his voice emotional. "Please Anna. The cause can't afford to lose you. Not now. Let me go. Please."

"No. It's my responsibility. Understand, James. You would not be my 2IC if you didn't have the ability to lead.

"This will become a war of attrition. We can do no more than wait for the return of God and the Angels of Light from The First World. We wait for as long as it takes. Now go and rest, all of you."

*****

Phillip arrived before Dawn, silently approaching out of the darkness. His stealth was impressive, surprising the guards keeping watch. The first they knew of his proximity was the moment he spoke, "My name is Phillip. Anna is expecting me."

The moment they saw that he dressed as a Shield, one guard lost all reason. "You bastard. A fucking Shield killed my brother, and you dare to come here wearing that fucking uniform. I'll drop you, you bastard. Grab him." Two guards grabbed Phillip and forced him to his knees; the parcel he was carrying fell to the ground.

"You idiots. What are you doing? Anna needs those uniforms." Before Phillip could say another word, a wild kick struck his stomach, driving the air from his lungs and doubling him over in agony.

"I'll kill you, you bastard. This is for my brother," He directed a kick to Phillip's head, but before the kick connected, his fellow guards grabbed their raging companion and pulled him back.

"Let me go. Let me go. He has to pay. Someone has to pay," he cried. The man broke down in desolate tears, tears for the brother he had lost.

Phillip knelt on the grass, heaving air into his lungs, trying desperately to make these guards understand. He could not speak, he could not move, the fire in his belly made speaking impossible.

Through a haze of pain, Phillip heard one of the other guards rip open the parcel he had been carrying.

"What's Anna want with Shield uniforms? Don't make sense." His friend, who was firmly holding the weeping guard, said, "You better take him to Anna. I'll look after Fred."

The guard holding the uniforms and truncheons, dragged Phillip to his feet. He whimpered in pain, swaying drunkenly, and threatening to fall to the ground again. "Oh no you don't. If you won't walk, I'll drag you."

Phillip somehow moved where he was harshly led, almost falling on several occasions. When they finally reached Anna's tent, the guard pushed Phillip inside where he fell at Anna's feet. His uniform was dirty and ripped and covered in spittle. The crowd through which they had walked, had not been kind.

Anna knelt and put Phillip's head in her lap. Tears sprang to her eyes. "Who did this?" she cried bitterly. "Who disregarded my orders?"

The guard looked mystified. "What orders ma'am? We had no orders. This spy turned up and we caught him. He said he wanted to speak with you, and he brought you these uniforms.

"The Shield murdered our people yesterday. What were we supposed to think?"

"I'm sorry, Phillip, I'm so sorry." Anna looked up at the guard. "This is the bravest man I have ever known. He is going to risk his life tonight to try and save two of our people, held captive by the Fae. I can't understand how you didn't know this," she said through her tears. Anna took a deep, shuddering breath. "It's not your fault. Someone has failed to pass on my instructions to the guards. I want to know who it was. Do a bit of digging. We may find a traitor."

The guard left the tent, muttering something about incompetence. Anna sat there weeping softly for many minutes. James walked into the tent and stopped short when he saw Anna weeping at his feet. "What happened?" Who did this?" Anna looked up and all she could manage to say was, "they didn't know." James tried to comfort Anna putting his arm around her shoulders. When she had regained some modicum of control, Anna explained what had happened.

Phillip stirred and looked up at Anna. "I feel like I've been run over by an elephant. Not the welcome I was expecting. Some of your people should fight in the ring.

"All I remember are fists, pain, spit, and someone dragging me here."

Anna looked down at him and smiled a sad smile. He could see that she had been crying. "Hey, I don't look that bad, do I?" It was then he noticed James. "Oh, hi James." Anna and James were relieved to see that Phillip was lucid, despite the bruises and bloody nose.

"Our plans to release Becky and Marion may be compromised," James said. "The guards on duty didn't know you were coming; they didn't receive Anna's instructions."

"We don't know yet whether it was deliberate, or an oversight. But we'll find out," Anna sounded confident.

"Do you think you could sit up if we helped you?" James asked. Phillip flexed his arms and moved his legs.

"No breaks or sprains that I can feel." He tried to sit up unaided and winced. "I think I might have a bruised rib or two." Perhaps it would be better if you helped me up."

Anna and James lifted Phillip into a sitting position and then stood him up so that they could move him to a chair.

"My uniform is ruined. I can't go to work like this." Phillip lamented.

"Until we find out whether we have a traitor in our midst," Anna said, "I don't think you should go to work at all. While we investigate, why don't you clean yourself up as best you can and change into one of the uniforms you brought. James, could you ask someone to bring a bowl of hot water, some soap, and a towel for Phillip. I'm off to speak with Helen. She will know whether we have a traitor in our midst. I shouldn't be too long."

Anna left the tent and walked to the nearby guard post where the rosters were organised and distributed, along with any daily security instructions. The day had dawned an hour before, and the crowd were busy preparing breakfast.

Anna entered the guard post and saw that Helen, the organiser, was already hard at work. "Don't you ever sleep Helen?" Anna teased.

"Good morning, Anna," Helen said cheerily. "You should talk. I'm just following your example."

"You remember yesterday afternoon I gave you instructions for distribution to the duty guards?" Helen nodded and said sure. "The guards on duty overnight didn't receive those instructions."

"What? No, that's impossible. I personally handed those instructions to my 2IC. He wouldn't forget to deliver them."

"Have you seen your 2IC this morning? I'd like to speak with him."

"No, no I haven't. He's probably still having breakfast." Helen led Anna to the large tent where several of the guards slept. All the bunks were empty, blankets folded neatly.

"That's his bunk over there. Funny, I can't see any of his belongings. Wait a moment. I'll try to find out where he is." Helen left the tent. She returned in less than a minute.

"He's gone. Left early this morning. He told the others he had something to do for you."

Helen looked deeply concerned. "He didn't, did he?"

"No Helen he didn't. Your 2IC was a spy for the Fae. We have to assume he's been passing on information. His last act was to sabotage a rescue attempt, meant to happen tonight."

"Oh Anna. I'm so sorry. I should have vetted him more thoroughly. He was so good at his job. It never occurred to me."

"Don't worry about it, Helen," Anna said encouragingly. "I haven't vetted anyone either. How could we do it? The Light Realm doesn't have the bureaucracy and recording systems in place to properly vet anyone. We haven't needed them before. All we can do is trust and be alert." Anna sat on a nearby chair and wearily rested her head on her hands.

"This Dark Fae is changing everything in The Light," she whispered. "We're losing our innocence; I see it in our people, I feel it in the air and in the very fabric of the soil under our feet. I'm tired. I want to go home and pretend that nothing has changed. But running away won't help. The Dark Fae's poison will follow us wherever we go and taint every good thing we love."

More tears formed in Anna's eyes, threatening to fall endlessly in a stream of loss and longing. Anna wiped her eyes in frustration. "Oh Helen, don't mind me. I've just left the company of a brave man beaten up by our guards. I've never seen that before. I'm still in shock, I think."

Helen didn't know how to react, feeling both concern and embarrassment at the same time. So, she did the only thing she could think to do; that felt right. She sat with Anna quietly and held her trembling hands.

A short while later, Anna shook herself out of her malaise and stood. "No time to be maudlin. Thanks Helen, for sitting with me. I feel a bit better now."

"That's what friends are for," Helen said, relieved that Anna had recovered something of her old self.

"See if you can find out what this spy has been up to," Anna suggested as she walked out of the tent. "Your people may know something." Her voice disappeared becoming quieter with distance as Anna returned to her tent.

## The Mortal Realm

Louseefa was overseeing the construction of his new palace. Once finished, Louseefa intended to move permanently out of his old, dark, and dusty quarters and into these grand new lodgings. One step closer to The Light, was his secret desire, but he had justified the change quite effectively, he thought.

What better way for the Dark to take possession of this new Dark Realm, than for the Dark Master to move in.

"How long must I wait for completion of my palace?" Louseefa directed his question to his Architect, one of the few members of this benighted species that had some memory of learning and skills acquired before they died.

"The wait will not be long, my Master. See, the workers swarm the site and have been encouraged to work fast and skilfully." Louseefa did not doubt what that encouragement entailed. He could see several Dark Lords supervising the workers.

Next to the palace was a large, artificial lake filled with fresh, untainted water. This was necessary for The Trial, a formal, almost religious ceremony, where wrongdoers must suffer, without uttering a sound, exquisitely painful oblivion by immersion in water. The stage for such ceremony graced the nearest shore of the lake.

Louseefa had directed that the lake be bordered by plants of every kind, to humidify the air and keep the water clean. Workers did as the Dark Lords required, but they did not understand the need for the unnatural vegetation.

A mighty stone wall was under construction to enclose the palace, lake, and vegetation; with one, grand entrance providing access to both the palace, and the stage, where The Trial took place. The path from the gate to the stage, would become The Way of the Condemned. A fearsome name for a fearsome end.

"How long, Architect? Do I need to ask again?" The architect froze with fear.

"My apologies, Master. Fourteen risings of the sun should see all work completed."

"That is too long. I want the palace finished in four days. Leave completion of the wall until the palace complex is finished. Get more workers if you must. Threaten them with The Trial. I don't care how you do it, but get it done." The Architect knew the unspoken reward for failure. "Now get back to your work." The Architect scurried off.

Later that day, Louseefa called a meeting of the Dark Lords. It was a small meeting, as only five Lords were in the vicinity.

"It has come to my attention, that nothing has come to my attention. Why have I not received regular reports about Light activities across the Realm? Surely there must be something to report."

"That is the strange thing Master," a Dark Lord said. "There is nothing to report. We have found many of the Light portals across the Realm and watch them continuously, yet there have been no incursions. Anywhere. It's as if The Light have given up."

"That is strange, indeed. However, we can't assume that they have given up. They may be planning something, but we can't know what they are planning. We must keep vigilant. Ensure that all my Dark Lords are aware of my wishes." They nodded in assent.

"I have informed the Architect to complete the palace construction work in four days. You will need to drive the workers harder. How you do it is up to you; but do it!"

The Lords filed out of the meeting muttering under their breath. Four days, it can't be done… what will be the punishment for failure? These and other thoughts along the same lines beset the Lords as they returned to the building site.


Louseefa stood alone. He wondered why The Light had not shown any recent interest in the Mortal Realm. It was so unlike them, always meddling and interfering, and now, nothing. It was quite out of character. What could so preoccupy them?

He could solve the mystery by making his own incursion into the Light Realm, to see conditions for himself. He was Light, so why should he not make that journey by Light portal?

Fantasy. That journey could pose too great a risk. If the Dark ever discovered his true nature, Master or not, they would try to kill him, even though he knew they could not. He had already pushed the envelope as far as he dared, with the lake and vegetation in the grounds of his new palace.

But, to look out of his window and see water sparkling in the sunlight, and smell the multi-hued vegetation cleansing the air, were things he had craved for thousands of years. Had not experienced for thousands of years.

Louseefa's arid and hungry soul said that such vibrant beauty was worth the risk.

## Dancing Hearts

Anna walked into her tent. The sun was quite strong outside, so she waited a moment for her eyes to adjust. When she could finally see clearly, standing before her was a changed man. Phillip had done an admirable job of cleaning himself up. Except for a red nose and a vaguely black eye, he looked very much like his old self. And Anna saw his old self through vastly different eyes. She saw a tall, confident, handsome man of about her own age smiling at her. He had changed into his new uniform.

"How do I look?" Phillip did a little twirl to show her his every side.

"Not bad. I guess you'll do." Anna said with an enigmatic smile.

"You guess I'll do?" Phillip questioned melodramatically, returning that enigmatic smile. "I spent hours in front of a mirror trying to make myself presentable, and all you can say is *I'll do*?"

"In front of a mirror, eh? I know that is a bare-faced lie Mr Black Shield. Unless you brought one with you, and that would be a little creepy, there is no mirror in this tent."

"Ah, that is a tiny flaw in my story." Phillip looked comically crestfallen.

"To tell you the truth, I'm as surprised as you are. While you can't see the worst bruises, for obvious reasons, I got off lightly. And no cracked ribs, just very sore. I'll be okay for the rescue tonight."

The rescue! Why had she forgotten about the rescue? This man had driven it out of her head. *Whoa. Slow down and get a grip.*

"The rescue, yes, the rescue…" Phillip looked at Anna surprised by her vague expression.

"Anna, are you okay? The rescue, you know, Becky and Marion, the danger, tonight?"

"Of course, I know about the rescue," she replied more forcefully that she intended. *Oops.*

"I'm sorry Phillip. I was thinking about something else. It was rude. Yes, I think we had better sit down and discuss the rescue." Collecting her jumbled thoughts, Anna began.

"We may have to postpone the rescue or think of another way to free Becky and Marion." Phillip tried to speak, but Anna shushed him. "We have good reason to be cautious. I've discovered that a spy for the Fae has been working in our midst for several weeks. We're trying to find out what information he was able to access and pass on. Discovering what and how will take some time.

"However, there are two things we can be sure of. The Fae knows or is about to learn that there will be a rescue attempt tonight. And he will know that one of his Black Shield officers will lead the attempt. You, in fact."

Phillip sat, thinking intensely. Initially shocked by this news, he soon began to think that the new circumstances offered lateral opportunities. He began to share his thoughts with Anna.

"Do you think it might be useful to have James with us before we start the planning?"

"Right. Yes. Of course, you're right. I'll send for him." Anna left the tent briefly and came bustling back in with an unconvincing smile on her face. "He's on his way."

For some peculiar reason Anna resented James's imminent intrusion. *What's gotten into me?*

A few minutes later, James arrived, and Anna brought him up to speed. Then, Phillip began talking.

"Our original plan was for a group of Black Shield officers to march openly in through the front door of the Government Building, free the women, and get out as quickly as possible. That frontal approach won't work now. We need a new plan.

"Say, we were robbing a bank, and the authorities knew that the crime would happen tonight. How would you approach planning the theft?"

"Very carefully," Anna said with a mischievous grin. *What's with this woman, this morning?*

"Come on Anna, get into the spirit. It's important."

"I know," Anna laughed, "I'm sorry Phillip. I'll behave. Promise."

"Riiiiight," Phillip said sceptically. James was sufficiently observant to notice the change in Anna.

"We're going to plan, dress and act as bank robbers would. We'll need to be furtive, we'll need a diversion, or several, something to keep the Shield occupied. And we're going to need more bank robbers. Is there anyone within your circle who knows how to disable surveillance devices?"

"No one comes to mind, but I can ask around." Anna suggested. "Do you know of anyone James?"

"I think I might. But I can't guarantee he'll agree to help us. If you know what surveillance system operates in the Government Building, he may be able to tell us how to disable it.

"Or I could just take a sledgehammer to the computer systems in the Communications Centre." Phillip offered. Anna and James looked at each other.

"That would work," James said.


"I'm going to draw the layout of the building," Phillip explained. "There's one discreet way to enter. Once we've disabled the communications systems, we'll disperse throughout the building.

"We'll have our own jobs to perform. Several of us will light multiple fires. I will go straight to the prison suite and disable the Shield guards. Once the fire alarm starts blaring, I'll lead the women down the fire stairs and out a side entrance. The chaos caused by the fires and the fire alarms will be the signal for everyone else to get out of the building as well."

"You make it sound straightforward, Phillip," Anna said. "But there is another player in this game, and he knows when and why we are coming."

"Of course, you mean the Fae," Phillip conceded. "Yes, I agree he is an unknown quantity. But I'm going to risk it. I must. I promised Becky and Marion that I would free them sometime tonight. I'll understand if no one else wants to share the risk with me." Phillip stared at Anna and James, determination glowing in his eyes.

"Are you kidding?" James laughed. "After yesterday's bloodbath, volunteers will be itching to take part. Many of us have scores to settle. And destroying the Fae's home will be part of the fun."

"Okay then," Anna concluded, "while Phillip draws his plan of the building, James could you go and round up the most capable volunteers you can find. Tell them that they will need to find black or very dark clothing for tonight's raid.

"Phillip, how many other volunteers do you think we'll need? Anna asked. "There'll be you and me…"

"You're not going," Phillip said firmly. "You and James are too valuable to risk."

Anna looked pleadingly at Phillip. "And you're not? What makes you think that no one here values you? You're brave and honourable, and, dammit, you're valuable… to me." Those last two, little words said it all. Spoken tentatively, barely audibly, those words escaped from Anna's heart before her mind could catch them.

She tried to cover them up, embarrassed that she had so exposed her inner self to the room. To Phillip.

To James. *Oh God, James must have heard. What must he be thinking?*

Anna wanted to sink into the ground. Instead, she became business-like and asked Phillip to continue with his assessment of the escape plan. Phillip looked quizzically at Anna, smiled uncomfortably, and then continued to speak.

"The building has six levels, above the ground floor. I think ten volunteers would give us the flexibility we need and prove a handful for the Shield. Any more might be difficult to manage."

"Right then," said Anna, robustly, "We'll all meet here at 3 o'clock to run through the rescue process, to allocate jobs and familiarise ourselves with the building layout. I'll see about collecting the accessories we'll need, including accelerants for the fires and heavy clubs for banging heads. Anything else you can think of Phillip?"

"Not off hand," Phillip said. "Let's keep it simple."

Simple? Anything but! *I've managed to complicate things in a big way,* Anna thought as James hustled out of the tent – rather more quickly than was necessary.


Anna and Phillip were now alone. She was fiddling with some papers on the table, not with any particular purpose in mind, but to keep her hands busy while she wrestled with her unexpected romantic revelation. A revelation not only to Phillip, but also to herself.

Phillip looked at Anna, the powerful, beautiful, and gifted woman he had only known for a few days. To say she was magnificent, would be an understatement. Anna was all he ever imagined in his fervid erotic and romantic dreams.

He should let this drop for now. His mind demanded he do so. Here and now were neither the place nor the time to pursue a new relationship. But his heart shouted otherwise. His heart would not be denied.

"I, I don't want to muck this up, so I'll ask the question straight out. I need to know whether I'm interpreting you correctly. When you said, 'you're valuable to me', did you mean it as a brother-in-arms, or as something else, a friend, or, or something else…?" Phillip's voice dropped away, uncertain as to what more he could say.

There it was. He'd asked the question. She couldn't run away from giving an honest answer. She looked into the depths of Phillip's eyes, seeing there a longing and an expressive he same way I do. interest surpassing anything she expected. *He feels the same way I do.*

"I think 'something else' just about covers it." Anna whispered.

Phillip offered Anna the most revealing and tender of smiles. "Well, that's good then. I wouldn't want to offend you or be presumptuous. Would holding your hand be too presumptuous?"

Anna pretended to think for a moment. "Mmmm… I think brothers-in-arms shaking hands is acceptable."

Phillip took Anna's hand in his. He lifted it and bestowed a gentle kiss upon it.

"What about kissing?" Phillip asked mischievously.

"On a first date? Mmmm… I don't know about that."

"You consider this war room a fitting place for a first date? Is it a first date? I need to know so I don't do anything too presumptuous." Just as Phillip said the word presumptuous, Anna chimed in with the same word and they both descended into a fit of laughter.

They had cleared the air. They both knew where they stood. During the current madness, they had found something unexpected. Something to hold on to, something to look forward to.

They both realised that progressing the matter in the current circumstances was not a clever idea and they both said as much. The rescue and the ongoing battle with the Fae must be their focus.

There would be a time, in the near or distant future when they could safely explore their feelings, and both were prepared to wait.

## Rescue at a Price

The hours dragged. Midnight had come and gone, and Phillip had not appeared for his shift. Becky and Marion sat nervously, or paced the room wondering what may have gone wrong. Was Phillip's plan discovered? Would the rescue attempt go ahead?

Not knowing was the worst. No word. No hint of any change. "This wait is killing me," Becky declared.

"Shhh!" Marion said. "The guards are speaking outside the door." The women rushed over quickly and pressed their ears to the wood.

The guards were speaking quietly, but not quietly enough. Becky's hearing was acute, particularly since she became Fae, an enhancement that lingered after she resigned.

Becky's face went white, fear replacing the uncertainty she had previously experienced. She heard every word, and the words shocked her.

"My God. They know!" She whispered. "The Fae is expecting the rescue attempt tonight. Marion, this is awful. They know about Phillip. He'll walk into a trap, and we have no way of warning him. What can we do?"

Marion, who had not heard one clear word through the door, save *traitor*, was nonetheless thinking hard.

"We can't warn him, but we can take action ourselves. Shortly, you're going to scream and knock over some furniture, anything to make a noise. When the first guard enters the room and sees you lying on the floor, he'll try to help. Make it clear your distress needs the attention of both guards. Hopefully, the second guard will come in and I'll knock him out with one of the truncheons Phillip brought us. You use the other truncheon on the guard trying to assist you and, by then, I should be able to help you subdue him.

"Then, we can put on our uniforms and walk out of the room. Simple."

Becky's face lit up. The days of inactivity had been killing her. Now this, a chance to do something, make a difference. "We need rope and gags to keep the guards quiet." Becky found what she needed in the room; sashes from the window curtains and material to stuff in their mouths.

Marion looked at the time. "It's 2.30 in the morning. You can take your tumble at 3am. Scream and moan as much as you like. The guards have been on duty for hours, so they'll be tired and bored with waiting — at least, I hope so."

If it were possible, those 30 minutes seemed to drag even more slowly than the previous three hours. But even the most watched of clocks will eventually reach the appointed hour. "Okay Becky, are you ready?" Asked Marion.

"You bet I am, I'll give them a performance they'll never forget. She stood up in her shortie pyjamas and grabbed the lamp at the side of her bed. With a flourish the lamp flew off the bedside table along with a heavy vintage clock. The room went dark. There was an almighty crash as the lamp and clock hit the floor. Becky lay down quickly beside the smashed lamp, hiding the truncheon near her left hand. She screamed and moaned piteously, and one of the guards rushed in to find out what had caused the commotion. He stumbled through the darkness to Becky, who was crying and moaning piteously. "He yelled to his mate, "come and help me, hurry? I can't move her."

The other guard came in more carefully, searching the gloom with suspicious eyes. "Where's…" he didn't get another word out before Marion appeared from the rear side of the door and smashed him on the head with a truncheon. He went down, unconscious before he hit the floor.

The other guard who heard the crack of the truncheon, turned his head toward his mate, and this was the moment for Becky to spring into action. She grabbed the truncheon and started beating the guard mercilessly, though she couldn't reach his head. Marion obliged with another mighty blow that sent the guard reeling to the floor.

"Quickly, help me lean them against the bedposts," Marion ordered. "We'll tie them there. Arms, *and* heads to hold the gags in."

Becky stood and shut the door of the suite. She turned on the ceiling light. They dragged each guard into position and bound their arms tightly to the posts with lengths of curtain sash. Becky stuffed their mouths with wads of material and then tied their heads to the bed posts. More lengths of sash bound their legs tightly together.

Neither had stirred as the women worked. "I hope you haven't killed them, Marion. They're going to have headaches when they wake up. If they wake up."

"Don't worry too much on their account. They're breathing. Okay, into the uniforms." They dressed, and Becky tucked her hair up under the black cap. "Ready?" Marion enquired.

"Not really, but I suppose we have to face it some time." Becky said resignedly.

"We'll take their truncheons with us, Marion advised. "Remember, the Fae knows about the escape attempt tonight. He'll have taken precautions, though why that didn't include moving us and providing extra guards is beyond me. Lucky for us.

"When we step outside into the hallway, act like a real guard. Keep your head down in case of surveillance cameras."

Becky was impressed by how calm and professional Marion was. She knew her stuff, and her demeanour was encouraging. Marion squatted and retrieved the keys from one of the guards. "Nice one, Marion. I wouldn't have thought of that," Becky said with a smile.

They stepped confidently out into the hallway, and Marion locked the door. "We'll sit for a moment and prepare for the next phase," Marion advised. "Shortly, I'm going to take a walk along the hallway, to 'go to the bathroom' and find out where the fire stairs are. Keep your head down. See, on the floor beside your chair, that's one of their tablets. Check it out while I'm away. You never know, we might get lucky."

Marion waited a little longer, then stood and walked down the hall, checking rooms on either side. After 30 metres she saw the bathroom symbols on adjoining doors, and opposite, a set of fire stairs.

She quickly stepped into the male bathroom, took a long drink from the basin tap, and waited in the dark a few minutes for effect; stepped out and continued to saunter along the hallway, checking doors as she went.

About 30 metres from the end, was another set of bathrooms and fire stairs. Marion checked her watch — 3.30 — and opened the door to the fire stairs and took a peek inside. There was a distant noise coming from below. She thought she heard shouting, and a door slam, and quickly shut the door. That didn't sound normal. And then the fire alarm went off.

Marion returned along the hallway at a much quicker pace, shouting as she ran. "Becky, get up, we have to move. There's fire and fighting downstairs and the Fae will be coming for us. I know it.

"We'll get to a lower floor and hide in one of the rooms until we know what's happening."

The two women dashed along the hallway and chose the second set of fire stairs for their escape.

Becky wanted to get as far away from their prison as possible.

They ran down the stairs to the third level and opened the hallway door. Acrid smoke filled the air. They heard shouting and fighting through the dense fog. Marion slammed the door. "Down another floor," she ordered. The same result. "Our rescuers have set the building alight. We're not going to find anyone in this chaos. Further down. See if there's a basement level."

There was. Becky pulled open the door and looked out into the void. Silence and darkness greeted her. "I can't see a thing," Becky said breathlessly. "The place is like a tomb."

"By the sound of your voice, it's a large, open space," Marion said. "I'm going to jam the door open with one of my truncheons, then, we're going to feel our way around the circumference of the basement, to see if we can find a way out. I'll go one way, you go the other, okay? Let's do this quickly."

The women separated and began their search. Five minutes later they met on the other side of the basement. "Everything is locked," Becky lamented. "There's no way out."

"Same for me," Marion confirmed. "Okay, quickly. Back to the fire stairs."

The women rushed back the way they had come and re-entered the stairwell. "Let's try the ground floor."

They raced up two flights of stairs and Marion carefully opened the door just enough for her to peak out, quickly closing it after sighting a Shield officer with his back to the fire door.

"There's a pitched battle out there. Shield Officers and civilians everywhere. The crowd must have invaded the building. And they're ignoring the fire alarm."

Becky looked forlorn. "Marion, what are we going to do? Hide here and wait? Someone may come through that door any moment. And what about the fire?"

Marion made a snap decision. "Back up the stairs to the fifth floor again. Maybe, the air is still clear of smoke."

They were tired and gasping for breath when they stood again on the fifth floor landing. Marion silently pulled open the door and peaked out. No smoke, but voices, several voices. Someone said, "where are they?" A voice replied and Marion knew that voice. She pulled Becky out into the hallway and called loudly to Phillip standing outside their prison door, now open and smashed.

The two parties ran toward each other. Becky could see that one of them was a woman. "Thank God you're okay," Phillip said with relief in his voice. "Nice work with the guards, by the way." Everyone was shouting, trying to be heard above the blaring alarm.

Anna rushed to embrace Becky and Marion. "Thanks, Anna, for helping us," Becky said. It's so good to see you again, although the circumstances could be better."

Marion knew Anna through their regular planning sessions, and she grabbed Anna's hands. "The Fae knows about the escape plan. That's why we had to act. We didn't know what was happening."

"But why are you here, Anna? Becky asked. "It must be bad to drag you away from the crowd."

"Things could be worse, but not much," Anna replied. "The crowd have attacked the building. Bad for them, but good for us, at least for a short while. It will give the Fae something else to think about. He has already been here. You were lucky to get out of the room when you did."

"What?" Marion was shocked. "Has he freed the guards we tied up?" Marion attempted to walk through the smashed door of their prison suite.

Phillip grabbed her arm. "No Marion, please don't go in there. The Fae has torn everything apart, including the guards. Now come, quickly. We must find a way outside."

Becky was distraught. "We left the guards defenceless. My God. How could the Fae do this?"

Phillip looked both women in the eyes and said sternly, "Becky, get a grip. The Fae killed the guards, not you. We need you both to settle down and start thinking. We have to move. Now."

Marion and Phillip led the women down the corridor at a brisk pace.

"Sorry Phillip," Becky said, "just the shock, I guess. Okay, we've checked the floors down to the basement. Smoke everywhere and the basement is locked tight. The Shield are fighting a battle with the crowd on the ground floor. I can't see a way out." Becky's voice held little hope.

"Don't give up yet," Phillip ordered. "We can try getting out the way we got in, through the sub-basement service delivery door. Come on, down the stairs."

"There's a sub-basement?" Marion asked. "The stairs we took didn't go that far."

"On the first floor there's a service lift that goes to the sub-basement, illogical I know as it's the only way to reach it," Phillip announced. "The lift will be difficult to access. There'll be smoke, and the Shield will be guarding it. They know that's how we got in. Let's hope the lift is still working."

As they raced down the stairs Becky said the obvious, "We don't have much choice. The lift or nothing."

Phillip raised his hand urgently causing everyone to stop on the second-floor landing. He placed his fingers to his lips, indicating complete silence. He then pointed over the balustrade. Everyone looked down the stairwell and saw moving shadows on the wall below. Phillip mouthed, "Shield."

"He indicated, by signs, that they should creep down the stairs and then attack the Shield with their truncheons. There was nothing else they could do.

Phillip and Anna in front, Becky, and Marion behind, the group moved silently down the flight of stairs until they could see the feet of the two Shield defenders. Phillip and Anna yelled defiance and rushed down the last few stairs, their truncheons flying.

The Shield were ready for them. *They knew we were coming*! Phillip thought as he aimed a truncheon at the head of the nearest Shield. The man ducked returning the compliment with a deflected blow to Phillip's solar plexus. He winced with the pain but had the height advantage and felled the man with a blow to the head. Anna was fighting the other Shield, managing to grab her truncheon and disarm her. Fear filled her eyes as Anna advanced.

Pounding footsteps from below, announced reinforcements. Anna pushed the Shield woman down the stairs, and she collided with the reinforcements racing upwards. A tangle of arms and legs made the Shield defenders easy prey. Truncheons flew and bones cracked, until a pile of still bodies lay at their feet.

Phillip opened the stairwell door and quickly shut it again. "Dense smoke and some of the offices are ablaze. Take a big breath and turn right in the hallway. The lift is 20 metres further along. Use the wall as a guide. Okay, everyone ready?" Nods all around.

Phillip moved first into the hallway and disappeared. The three women followed touching the wall as they ran. Writhing flames lent an eerie dancing glow to the smoke. It stung the eyes and the heat from the fires was terrible. And still that damnable alarm blared.

Becky and Marion followed Anna until she suddenly stopped. And there was Phillip, standing at the lift doorway. The doors opened, as if by magic, just as the women arrived. Everyone tumbled inside, coughing, and wheezing.

For some peculiar reason, Becky thought of the sign that always graced lift doors, *do not use lifts in case of fire*. She smiled at the crazy thought, despite their desperate situation.

The doors closed and Phillip ordered the lift to descend. Nothing happened. He said *descend* again but the lift stayed where it was. He said *sub-basement* — still nothing. He guessed that once the fire alarm started the lifts stopped as a safety precaution.

Phillip searched for a way out and found it in the lift ceiling. An inspection hatch, large enough for all of them to climb through. Phillip jumped upwards and pushed it with his truncheon. Locked!

"Okay, I'm going to need some help now. Anna, if we three lifted you up, do you think that you could bash your way through?

"I'll give it a go," she answered.

Phillip bent down and placed his arms firmly around Anna's lower thighs and, with a grunt lifted her up. Marion took some of the weight by supporting her feet, while Becky balanced Anna on her precarious perch.

Anna started attacking the locking mechanism with her metal truncheon. Ten, twenty blows and at last the lock gave way and crashed to the lift floor. She lifted the hatch with her truncheon, and it slammed backwards onto the roof of the lift. Grabbing the edge of the hatch, she pulled herself up, until she lay gasping on the lift roof.

"Are you okay Anna?" Phillip asked.

"Just peachy," she gasped. "Weight training would have made that easier."

"When you're ready, I'll lift Marion and Becky. Do you think you can pull them up?"

"I hope so, Phillip. Give me a couple of minutes to recover."

Once she felt strong enough, she advised Phillip to begin. He lifted Marion above his head and Anna grabbed her outstretched arms. With every ounce of strength she had, Anna hauled Marion up so that she could grab the hatch opening. Working together, Marion was soon lying on the roof of the lift.

Becky was the lightest of the four and Anna and Marion soon had her safely on the roof.

Three faces looked down at Phillip, arms outstretched to try and grab Phillip's hand. They couldn't reach it. Anna looked into his eyes and knew that he would not be coming with them. "Phillip, come on. Jump and I'll try and grasp your hand. Please Phillip. You can't leave us here."

"There's no way I can reach that hatch, and I'm too heavy for the three of you to pull me through. I'm sorry Anna. I'll find another way out. Look behind you. There should be a service ladder attached to the wall."

"Yes," Anna said despondently. "I see it." Phillip directed them to climb down until they came to the outer doors of the lift in the sub-basement. "You'll have to prise open the doors. Anna, you know the way from there."

And with that last statement, the three faces disappeared, Anna taking charge and helping the others to reach the ladder. Once they were climbing down, Anna's face reappeared, and tears wet her cheeks. "I don't want to leave you," she said. Phillip looked up with glistening in his eyes and said what he had to say, "But you must, Anna. The others are depending on you." Anna nodded sadly and with a last look of torment, went back to the ladder and started her descent.

Phillip tried to prise open the lift doors with his fingers and they proved most difficult to shift. Once the doors were open sufficient to poke a truncheon through, he used it to help him gradually force the doors back.

Dense smoke billowed into the lift and the fire burned intensely, licking up the wood panelled hallway walls.

He turned left and ran the twenty metres to the fire door. It opened, bumping into one of the bodies lying on the landing behind it.

Phillip would have to risk the battle on the ground floor. There was no other way. The lights were out so he gingerly used the stairway railing to guide him up the two flights to Ground Level.

He opened the door sufficient to peak through. People everywhere. Packed in. He spied several Shield officers, prone on the floor of the lobby. Phillip had to get the crowd out of the building. The fire would burn quickly, taking hold on almost every floor.

Phillip flung the door open and screamed "FIRE ALARM! Can't you hear the alarm?" As loudly as he could. Those nearest him turned in shock. "The building is on fire. Please spread the word. Get out now while you still can."

Phillip pushed past them and made for the main entrance; shouts of fire following in his wake. The crowd surged toward the doors and Phillip barely made it through before the crush at the restricted exit caused chaos.

Those lucky enough to make it through ran off into the darkness; others were trapped and slowly suffocated by the crush of bodies. In desperation, Phillip hammered on the plate glass of the side windows, trying to make the exit wider. His truncheon bounced off the toughened glass. He then stood at the doorway and physically pulled people out of the crush asking others to help if they could. Some did and gradually the numbers and pressure declined, until only the trampled dead remained in the lobby.

So many mangled, mingled bodies, uniformed Shield officers, and men and women from the crowd, lying like discarded bloody mannequins on the floor of the lobby. Smears of blood covered the walls and floors.

Injured and dying sat or lay comatose on the grass outside, sobbing and bleeding, and Phillip felt helpless. He had nothing he could use to tend to their wounds.

In the distance, he saw a face he recognised, the man who had beaten him up just two days ago. Phillip walked over and the man recognised him, looking embarrassed by the chance encounter. He started to apologise, and Phillip shushed him. "No time for that now. Do you know where the hospital tent is?" The man nodded. "Go and tell the medics that they should come urgently, and to bring supplies to treat multiple wounded. That clear?"

"Sure thing. And, and sorry, okay." The man rushed off.

Phillip eyed the scores of wounded and he felt sick to his stomach. To yell *FIRE* in a crowded space — he caused this carnage. *Oh God.*

Phillip looked up at the burning building, flames erupting from almost every window. He looked higher and there atop the building stood the Fae. He was staring into the distance. And then, he looked down, directly at Phillip.

The Fae saw him. The Fae knew him. Phillip shivered and was afraid. He dashed around the side of the building, to the back and came to the door where the women should already be waiting.

No one stood there. The door, however, was open. Running down the access ramp, Phillip yelled into the darkness, *Anna, Becky, Marion*... his voice returned to him as echoes from the silent, confining darkness.

Phillip was distraught. Tears for the dead and wounded... tears for his missing friends... tears for himself, the cause of so much suffering and loss.

The women who trusted in his will and skill to save them, were gone. He had failed. *Anna*... just thinking the name constricted his heart and shame consumed him.

Beaten and alone, Phillip turned and ran quickly back up the ramp and out into the gathering light of a new and terrible dawn. He no longer cared what happened to him. He had failed everyone. He did not deserve to be free and alive, with so many others imprisoned by pain and death.

Phillip began to walk around the building to the front entrance. A voice boomed from above. "Look up, worm! Look what you have done."

*The Fae!* Phillip stopped walking and looked up, as commanded by that terrible voice. The Fae was no longer standing atop the building. He was floating in the air several metres distant from the wall and slowly descending toward Phillip. Two other figures descended with him. *Anna and Becky. Where was Marion?*

As they came closer Phillip could see the fear and confusion in their eyes; they could not move, could not speak. They were completely at the mercy of this merciless monster.

From some hidden depth of will Phillip shouted, "let them go. They cannot hurt you. It's me you want, not them. Please, let them go."

"And why would I do that, worm?" The Fae's voice dripped with loathing and malice. "Why let them go when I can have all three of you, hmmm? *Giggle, giggle.*"

Phillip felt a restriction around his body, pressing harder and harder. He struggled in vain. He could not speak; could barely breathe. His feet left the ground.

Phillip rose, higher and higher, until he could see into the mad eyes of his captor. Those eyes bored into his own, through the flesh and into his tortured brain.

They drew strength from his torment, ecstasy from his defeated body.

Phillip tried to close his eyes. He could not. The Fae wanted him to see. He forced Phillip's eyes to look upon Anna and Becky. "See how they suffer," he hissed. "You must be proud to have caused such misery, promising so much, and achieving so little.

"I saw every move you made; heard every word you said. Nothing about your pathetic rescue attempt was hidden from me. You were all puppets, and I guided you as a puppeteer might, pulling your feeble strings.

"Look upon Anna — oh yes, I see how you feel about her — this traitor who will join you in exile. The tears, the bitter tears of loss; tears not for you. Not for you. She cries for what might have been; if you had been a better man, a better leader and more deserving."

"There will be no Tribunal to judge you all," the Fae screamed. "My judgement is enough. Tomorrow, at dawn, I will take you to the nearest portal and have an end of you.

"The people will witness my judgement meted out upon you. They will see what becomes of those who oppose me. Their defiance and disobedience will wither on a dying vine, else they too feel the flames of the Dark Fae."

These last words boomed from the skies and into the ears of everyone in the city, the entire world, and beyond.

As the Fae flew them away to another place of confinement, he freed the mouths of his captives. Asking more quietly, almost as an afterthought, "where is the woman you call Marion? Surely you know." The smile that accompanied his question was not friendly.

Becky answered, her voice trembling with the strain, "I don't know. She returned to the building to try and help those trapped within. She is more than likely a victim of the fire."

Becky screamed as the Fae pressed harder upon her frail body. "Are you sure? It does not feel right to me. Surely Anna, the smitten warrior, would have gone, not Marion, a mere teacher."

Through gritted teeth Becky said, "believe me or not. I don't care. I'm telling you the truth. Now get on with whatever you intend to do, you evil monster. You're worse than the Dark. You're…" Becky's voice stopped mid-sentence, the Fae freezing her facial muscles into a rictus grin of suffering.

"Oh yes. I am worse than the Dark. People call me the Dark Fae. It has a nice sound to it, don't you think?" The three captives nodded, unable to resist the guiding force of the Fae.

"That's better," he giggled, the giggling disappearing into the sky and beyond the treeline.

The building burned. The walls began to collapse inward onto the smoking pile of debris. A dark figure appeared from the sub-basement doorway, garbed as a Black Shield. Marion looked up and saw that the Fae was truly gone. She had heard every word of the conversation between the Fae and his captives.

Becky had told the truth. Marion *had* returned to the building to try and find Phillip and save others, despite the pleading of her friends. She had used the ladder in the lift shaft to get to several floors, but smoke and flames had defeated her, so she returned to the sub-basement and saw that Becky and Anna had gone. She waited some distance from the doorway, standing silently in the darkness, wondering what to do, fearing what may have become of the women, lost in thought.

Then Phillip arrived suddenly, called out the women's names, but he was too quick. She had no time to reveal her presence. And then — he rose into the air.

She knew the Fae was nearby. Marion dared to peak above, and she saw the drama play out, heard every word. And overcome by her grief, she watched the building burn and fall.

And consumed by the burning and the falling, Marion's grief transformed into determination, and a plan began to form in her mind.

Marion walked into the trees and took the longer, stealthy way back to the Training Centre, out of sight of the surrounding crowd. She stayed dressed as a

Black Shield because the uniform would surely be useful, at dawn tomorrow.

## Exile

The closest portal was located within the government complex. Ironically, the very same portal that Sam and Rose had used so many months ago to infiltrate the horrifying new world of the Dark.

Marion waited in the pre-dawn darkness, hidden by a thick barrier of shrubbery. She dressed as a Black Shield, although she also wore a black cloak.

She had arrived much earlier and had already travelled through the portal several times. Her plan now awaiting fulfilment with the arrival of the Fae and those to be exiled.

The Fae had not bothered to set guards at the portal. The hubris and stupidity of the man was laughable. So confident, so assured of his superiority. He would come to regret his mistakes. Marion would see to it.

Marion was alone. There were no others at the portal. None waiting to see the Fae's judgment executed. No audience to see the Fae's empty victory. He had scared the people off with his bluster and threats. The Fae will be annoyed, Marion thought with a quiet chuckle. Then remembering what had happened the last time the Fae was annoyed with the people. The chuckles stopped.

Shock replaced Marion's renewed foreboding. Strong hands grabbed her from behind and a voice hissed, "what is a Black Shield doing here, lurking in the bushes? Speak, or I'll beat you senseless."

"My name is Marion," she answered firmly. "I was a prisoner of the Fae, but now I am free. I'm here to follow Becky, Anna, and Phillip into the Mortal Realm."

"That's an unlikely story. Turn around and lower your hood. I want to see your face before I smash it to a pulp," the man ordered brusquely.

Marion turned and lowered her hood. "I speak the truth. Hello James, we've met before." James started to speak but Marion interrupted him.

"I was present when the Dark Fae captured my friends. I heard what he said. I saw what he did. I could not let my friends go defenceless into the Mortal Realm. So, I have brought weapons for them." She lifted her cloak aside to show several weapons belted to her waist. "Most are already placed on the other side of this portal. I go where I must."

"Marion, it is you, but how did you get here?"

"It's a long story James." Marion said quietly. "More to the point, what are you doing here?"

"I and a few of my friends have come to try and free Anna and the others. We can't lose Anna. She's our leader."

Marion was alarmed. "Please, please don't do this. The Fae will already be angry that the people have not come to witness his little victory. There's no telling what he will do if you anger him further. Please. Let me do what I must do. If all goes well, our lives will not be in danger when we reach the other side. The portal is not guarded by the Dark. I've already discussed a plan of action with Becky, and we are confident it will work."

"You are willingly going into exile?" James asked in astonishment. "You're wearing one of the uniforms Phillip gave you. Now, I know why. You'll become part of the Shield guard." James thought for a moment and then made his decision. "Okay, I'll do as you ask and try to convince my friends not to do anything stupid. But please convince Anna to return to us as quickly as she can. I fear what may happen if I lose control of the crowd. The Fae will kill us all."

James left Marion to her own thoughts and went to speak with his friends, to convince them not to attempt a futile rescue.


Marion waited until the first rays of the rising sun broke through the trees. It was then that Marion heard the rising beat of many marching feet. The leading line of Shield guards came into view, the captives walking confidently behind them, all accept one. Gerald was among them, walking unsteadily, and clearly not yet recovered from his illness.

The Fae rode behind in a stately black vehicle driven at walking pace by a Shield officer; a fact that amused Marion as drivers were no longer needed in The Light. This struck her as both pretentious and arrogant. *The man can fly, for pity's sake.* A phalanx of guards on either side protected the vehicle.

One of the Fae's guards had dropped behind to adjust his uniform. Marion dared not miss this opportunity. When the man passed her by, she crept up behind and struck him hard with her truncheon. She grabbed him as he fell and pulled him into the shrubbery. Then, she casually joined the guard detail in his stead.

The portal entrance appeared before the group. The Fae ceremoniously stepped from his vehicle. "Where is everyone?" He screamed. "They should be here to witness this punishment. How dare the people snub me."

A Shield guard, who spoke with some authority, suggested that fear had kept them away. "Honourable Fae. The people fear you; they fear your power; they fear what you may do, should they displease you."

This argument appealed to the Fae's fractured ego, and he seemed content with the explanation.

"Take the prisoners forward to the portal entrance," the Fae ordered. A Shield held each prisoner and dragged them without ceremony to the portal.

It was now or never. While everyone focussed on the prisoners and the portal entrance, Marion crept forward and, in this way, stood amongst the frontline of remaining Shield guards. No one noticed her, so entranced were they by the prospect of history in the making. Exile to the Mortal Realm had not occurred since Louseefa's dismissal from The Light.

"For your crimes, I hereby banish you from The Light Realm. Guards, push them through the portal."

The guards did as the Fae commanded. As the last prisoner disappeared, Marion dashed forward wielding her truncheon, and with skill enhanced by desperation, surprised and eluded the guards and disappeared through the portal.

"Who was that?" The Fae asked no one in particular. The guards looked at each other in confusion.

"We do not know Honourable Fae," the Captain of the Guard said, "I will investigate at once."

"No matter. Whoever it was, they are already dead." The Fae pointed a finger, and the portal light went out. The portal collapsed into rubble. There could be no return.

"Well, that's done," the Fae said happily. "Captain of the Guard, you are to inform the technicians that maintain the other portals to disable them and block the entrances with rubble. See that it is done. "You may now escort me back to my new quarters. I feel in need of a cup of tea."

# Part Thirteen - Seeking the Sonciel

Sam was sitting alone under a massive apple tree which grew nearby his modest cottage. He had lost count of the times he had spent under this tree. Time had little relevance here. One day blurred into the next, as rivers merge into the sea, or mist dissipates into the air.

He had come to understand why the arrival of the three travellers had so disturbed the Angels of Light. Acceptance of the visitors' call would require release from thousands of years of intoxicating, undemanding, peaceful existence.

Zadkiel told him that the apple tree was never without fruit, blossom and fruit together, always giving of itself, and always renewing in the sacrifice of giving. Quite poetic, Sam thought, and he could well believe that such wonders exist in a place where time seems irrelevant.

Not all irrelevant, however. He well-remembered one relevance when an apple fell from the tree, but not upon his head, rather into his lap. Would Isaac Newton have explored the mysteries of gravity and motion, had that apocryphal apple fallen into his lap. The interaction of chance and circumstance never failed to surprise him. A falling apple may well have changed history by the path of its falling.

Zadkiel, the appointed spokesperson for the Angels, came and sat with Sam on many occasions. This was no small thing for Zadkiel to do as the boughs of the tree hung barely a whisker above his head. To Sam's eyes it looked comical, though he never dared say so. Rather, he rejoiced in the wonder of conversing with an angel more than twice his own size.

"So, Zadkiel, did you ever have wings, or were angel wings just a creation of mortal folklore?" The Lord looked surprised at the question, asked so baldly.

Had he been haughtier and more conscious of his position, he might have considered the question impertinent. Instead. He responded with deep and resonant laughter. "Oh Sam, you never fail to lift my spirits. I need reminding that you are but a babe in The Light, and the Mortal Realm that was, will still be strong in your memory.

"Let's just say that wings are among the many romantic qualities that various mortal cultures and religions have attributed to heavenly beings. In truth, we have no need of wings." Hearing such things said, reminded Sam of Gerald and his contribution to the pilgrimage.

"A member of our company said very much the same thing and would have enjoyed discussing it with you. The Fae has denied him the opportunity," Sam lamented.

"*God in the Stars*, Gerald Solipsis. Yes, I read the book soon after its publication. Incredibly prescient. I'm not surprised it caused a stir when you were alive. The book certainly caused a stir in the First World."

"It did?" Sam asked in wonder. "You've read it? How? I mean, I'm just surprised that you've kept such a close watching brief on the Mortal Realm, particularly after The Light rejected you so long ago. I just assumed you would lose interest."

"Not at all, Sam. I knew of your journey and of the Testing you and thousands of others endured, from the day you started your pilgrimage.

"But I took especial interest in you and your companions. You are marked for greatness and for a higher purpose that is yet hidden from me.

"Your arrival here has resounded much more loudly than you know. The archives say that you, or someone like you, would come and shake the foundations of the First World. That the time for choice would come. And now, it has.

"The Angels of Light must now make a choice, and we are a little out of practice. I tell you now, my choice is to help you. The others are yet undecided and procrastinate as a result."

"I fear that The Light will not survive undue procrastination," Sam commented. "We've wasted too much time already. The Dark Fae may have already exiled Becky and the others to the Mortal Realm. She was the Fae before the name and position went the way of the Dark. And now, now… she may be dead… at the hands of Louseefa." The sadness in Sam's eyes verged on tears as the realisation hit him.

Sam looked earnestly at Zadkiel. "Is there no way you can speed up the process?"

Zadkiel smiled reassuringly at Sam. "Yes, there is a way. The Angels are meeting later today, and I intend to hasten a decision, one way or the other. Whatever the decision of the meeting, I will help you find the Sonciel."

*****

John and Rose dropped by Sam's dwelling in the afternoon, after a marked and extended absence. "Hey you two. I was starting to wonder where you were. Haven't seen you since breakfast."

"We thought we could use some exercise, so we've been exploring," John answered.

Sam grinned. "Exploring, and exercise? You must be tired from all that exploring," this last word spoken in such a way that John and Rose could be in no doubt as to what sort of exploring Sam meant.

Rose looked daggers at Sam. "Zip it, smart arse. You know exactly what John means." Rose smiled wickedly. "Or will I have to explore your nose with my fist to…"

"Whoa! Truce!" Sam laughed. "Just kidding, my childish sense of humour. So where did you go?"

"We must have walked 20 kilometres, at least," John said. "Beautiful hardly describes the magnificence of this place.

"Completely unspoiled, no one living in the local area. We think the vicinity surrounding the StarLight Portal is for the sole purpose of vetting people like us. A buffer between the Portal and the First World population. So, we've seen a lot of wonderful landscapes, but have no idea how or where the First Worlders live."

Sam nodded his agreement. "That makes sense. It might also explain why few if any First Worlders visit other worlds of Light. We can ask Zadkiel about it soon, I think." Sam explained the contents of his conversation with the Lord of Light earlier.

"But Sam, that's marvellous news," John replied throwing his arms around Rose and whirling her about like a mad thing. "Zadkiel has agreed to help us, whether the others will do so, or not. The Pilgrimage is saved." Rose, dishevelled and nonplussed by John's ecstatic response to the news, gave him a firm slap on the rump. "John, not in front of the children!"

That did it. The laughter floodgates opened, and it was several minutes before decorum reigned once more.

The floodgates closed swiftly with the timely arrival of Zadkiel. He could not enter the human-sized building so the three friends went outside. "You three are in high spirits. I heard your celebration from the other side of the woodland.

"Such wild laughter and celebration are rarely heard in the First World these days. It is refreshing to hear it. This also suggests that Sam has relayed my decision about helping you find the Consciousness. I've just come from a meeting with the other Angels. After long and tedious discussion, which was, frankly, leading nowhere, I told them my decision to help you."

"And what was their response?" Sam asked with some trepidation.

"Surprisingly good," Zadkiel replied with a grin, "clearly relieved that I had taken the initiative. My decision relieves them of the need to decide themselves.

"But then, wonder of many wonders, they quickly made their own decision. If we find the Sonciel, and the Consciousness agrees to come back to The Light, they will join with us then, but only then.

"I cannot blame them for being cautious. They have had endless years of undemanding life and now feel threatened by the invasion of responsibility into their quiet little world. To agree to help us at all is an achievement, I think."

"That does beg the question," Sam mused, "why you have agreed to help us so easily when the others find it so difficult?"

Zadkiel smiled at Sam, appreciating his question. "Very perceptive of you, Sam. Indeed, I did find the decision easier to make. Unlike the others, I have remained intimately involved in the politics and events that make The Light so fascinating.

"I have many eyes throughout the Realm, on every world. They keep me informed of happenings. The other Angels only hear of such things second hand, through me. On occasion I have travelled to other worlds to see things for myself, in disguise, of course."

"I can see how a giant appearing from nowhere might cause comment," Rose chuckled.

Sam was surprised. "Your powers extend to shape shifting? You alone might be a match for the Dark Fae."

"Not so fast, Sam," Zadkiel warned. "My powers may indeed match those of the Fae, but I dare not act alone. It is my duty to seek the support of the Sonciel and the other Angels.

"Only when the Consciousness installs a new God will I happily follow him or her into The Light and Mortal Realms. Until that time, I dare not intervene.

This is more than tradition. This is in our blood, and the ways of the soul must be honoured."

The three friends looked at each other. "So where do we go from here?" John asked the obvious question.

*****

Three hours later, after the sun had set and all had eaten their fill, the friends and Zadkiel sat in the Visitor Vetting Room, which was the same space where Sam, Rose, and John had first met the Angels of Light.

This time, Zadkiel sat with them round a large table, strewn with maps, Archive parchments, and scrolls. He had reduced to human size so that he could speak with them at the same eye level.

Zadkiel spent the first hour of the discussion presenting much of the information that the travellers would need to know before meeting with the Consciousness. He explained that the Sonciel were not persons, organic life forms or anything tangible or physical. "The Consciousness just IS," Zadkiel explained enigmatically. "The energy enabling conscious, ultra-intelligent thought is the totality, the All.

"The name given to the Consciousness is ancient. That name, in the earliest Light Archives, is Sonciel, as you know, both male and female. The Mortal Realm might better understand the name as Gaia, and for our purposes, the similarities overwhelm the differences.

"The earliest Archives speak of an ancient race of beings, the Sonciel, the first intelligence in the universe. Throughout millions of years of exploration and discovery, the entire Universe of Light became known to them. In reality, they became the Universe. Physically, there was nowhere else for them to go, nothing else that they could know. The energy of the stars was subservient to them. They had found no other conscious intelligence in all those years of exploring the Light Universe. That is, until they found The Light.

"The limitations of physical separation, one from another, were an obstacle to complete satisfaction. And so, this mighty race of beings conceived a way to coalesce all their energy and thought into one energy: timeless, ubiquitous; as the source and haven of energetic Spirit in the Universe.

"This coalescence enabled them to merge their life force with both The Light and the Mortal Realm. They are both the source and destination, from which all souls flow and to which the souls of Light return. The souls of Dark do not return, only the pure energy that was part of the whole. In this way, evil cannot corrupt the purity of the source.

"All power lives in the Sonciel as pure energy. Such energy is both given and received in an endless dance of distribution and reaping. The fact that they still participate in this process, indicates that their withdrawal is not complete or irrevocable. They will already know of the tragedies in both the Mortal and Light Realms because of this participation. And that provides us with an opportunity."

"If we find the Sonciel," Zadkiel continued, "if the Sonciel find us, the only way we can speak with them, the coalesced race, is to allow absorption into their energy stream. We will become completely known to them. Nothing will remain hidden.

"The Archives reassure us that absorption is not harmful. Our physical bodies stay unaffected. Only our minds and souls take part."

"Well, that's a relief," Rose said. "I didn't sign up to let the Sonciel eat us." John and Sam chuckled at Rose's discomfort. John gave her a light kiss on the cheek and replied, "don't worry my love, I'll protect you." Rose looked sharply at John but then softened as she saw the love in his eyes.

Zadkiel waited patiently to regain the complete attention of the travellers. "This is not a classroom, and you are not adolescents. It is not wise to speak flippantly of the Sonciel and I'm not sure whether they have a sense of humour." Rose and the others looked chastened.

"I know that I sound like a lecturer, but please understand the seriousness of the information I have given you. The Sonciel will remain hidden from us if we don't seek them with righteous and honest purpose."

Sam spoke up. "Zadkiel, I know I speak for the others when I say that we have travelled too far, risked too much, to fall at the final hurdle. Our flippancy is but one, normal, human reaction to stress or unexpected information. It's a way of dealing with things that might otherwise overwhelm us. We meant no disrespect.

"As you so rightly say, we're babes in the Light and in that sense, we are adolescents. Our mortal thinking is still strong within us, and we have very much to learn."

Zadkiel smiled and reassured Sam that he bore them no ill-will. "You have given me a greater understanding of humanity. Such subtle nuances are easy for the Angels to miss. Thank you for putting me in my place, in the politest of ways.

"Okay, down to business. How do we find the Sonciel? The information that will guide us to an answer is in the documents before us. The ancient scrolls are in the archaic Light language, spoken many thousands of years ago, and you will not understand them. The parchments are more recent documents and those you should be able to read.

"Somewhere, on the First World, is a portal known only by our God, that he used often to visit the Sonciel. Our God is dead, and knowledge of the portal's whereabouts is lost to the living. Our job is to find it, somewhere in these documents. I'll start reading the scrolls while you attack the parchments. Any scrap of information may be vital. Anything that seems peculiar or out of place, note it down in the tablets I have given you. Don't be afraid to ask questions or seek clarifications."

And for the next few hours they read. It was only when the want of sleep consumed their thinking, and frequent yawning became an unwelcome guest at the table, that Zadkiel called a halt.

Leading them outside, he walked them to their dwellings and bid the travellers goodnight. "Sleep well my friends. We have a lot of reading to do tomorrow."

*****

Zadkiel's final sentence, spoken the night before as he bid the travellers goodnight, was not entirely correct. Within the first hour he had found the first clue, in one of the earliest scrolls. It narrowed the search for the portal to one continent. Admittedly, an exceptionally large continent, much larger than North America in the Mortal Realm, a continent named Estrada.

Zadkiel opened the ancient map and pointed out the continent. It was on the other side of the First World, to the east and toward the rising sun. The southernmost parts were within the Tropics, whilst the northern parts reached almost to the North Pole of this world.

"Reaching Estrada will not be a problem," he advised. "But without a more exact location, we might explore for countless thousands of years and not find the portal.

"Keep reading. The answers we seek are somewhere within these documents."

Two hours later, Sam had found something that drew his attention. He worked assiduously to digest, translate, and manipulate the words, and an hour later told the others.

"I've been reading an 800-year-old manuscript, and I've found something that might narrow the search. At first, I was doubtful because the contents were prophesy and story through poetry. I've spent some time trying to make sense of it and, if you'll allow me, I'll read you what I've found."

Sam cleared his throat and read the pertinent words in his tablet:

*"Between the earth and sky there lie*
*three sisters high, one born to fly.*
*Each births a river wild and free*
*that finds its rest in farthest sea.*
*The middle sister tall and fair*
*provides the stairway into air,*
*and those who seek exalted rest*
*must undertake this hardest test.*

*To breach the doorway in the sky,*
*and meet the source of life — or die."*

Profound silence followed Sam's recitation. He looked enquiringly at the others. "It wasn't that bad, was it? I even made it rhyme."

Zadkiel eyes glazed over for a moment, and then, as if waking from a dream, he stood abruptly and shouted, "Sam, you may have found it. Would you allow me to read and compare both the original and your translation? Rose and John might like to have a read as well. We all need to be sure that the information you've found is what we have been looking for."

"Of course, Zadkiel. I was going to suggest you all do that," Sam replied.

Zadkiel studied the parchment and Sam's translation, his face showing no emotion and giving nothing away. He passed the items to John and Rose, who read them carefully.

John displayed little emotion as he finished reading. Rose, however, remained true to form and responded more passionately. "Wow, hidden depths Sam. Hidden depths. Your translation convinces me. But then, what do I know about poetry. John, what do you think?"

"What do I think?" John asked. He reached across Rose and shook Sam's hand. "I agree with Rose. Hidden depths, indeed. You have a gift with words that is rare, and you've captured the heart and intent of the source material. Well done Sam."

The three travellers looked enquiringly at Zadkiel. Sam was on tenterhooks, wishing for Zadkiel's approval. The suspense was killing.

Zadkiel reread the material and read it again and thought carefully for several minutes. Finally, he smiled and gave Sam the approval he looked for. Sam could not understand why he craved their approval, but he was relieved, all the same.

"I see by your expression and obvious relief that our approval is important to you." Zadkiel offered with a smile of gratitude. "All true artists need approval and approbation whether they admit it or not. It is nourishment for the creative soul within. Rose is right, you have a gift Sam."

"Somewhere on this map, are the three sisters mentioned in the parchment. We can safely say that we are looking for three adjacent mountains, each the source of a river that flows to the farthest sea.

"May I suggest that I look for the sisters, while you three follow the major rivers to their source."

"Good idea," Sam said. "And... thanks."

Zadkiel spread the map closer to the travellers so that they could follow the rivers more easily. Silence reigned for a few minutes as each bent to their task.

Sam was following a river upstream that continued to the very centre of the map. He arrived at the source as a finger landed on the map in front of his eyes.

"Here," Zadkiel announced. Sam looked more closely and there indeed were the outlines of three mountains, Sam's river ending in the foothills of the central mountain. There was a faded name scrawled in an archaic language beside the mountains. Zadkiel translated the words for the others. "The words say *The Three Sisters*. We have found the mountains. The next task is to find the portal."

Sam suggested that the source material was clear about the general position of the portal. *"To breach the doorway in the sky...* Those are the literal words in the parchment and the poem. The portal is floating directly above the central mountain. How high above the peak is still a mystery."

Zadkiel reflected on Sam's words and said, "the words may indeed say exactly what they mean. But we would be remiss not to consider other meanings. The writers of these ancient documents delighted in confusing the issue with subtle deceptions and puzzles. The words, *in the sky,* might just mean on top of the high mountain. And the word *breach* suggests that the portal is either closed or hidden in some way and we must find the way to open it."

"There is another complication. Estrada is the home of early humans, an ancient lineage going back to a time when you were living in trees. For millennia we have left them alone, left them free to live as their culture and beliefs dictate.

"They are special, and they value their isolation. Their intelligence is not sophisticated, but they *are* intelligent, in their own way, and they will not take kindly to us invading their domain.

"We must seek permission from the clan leaders in the territories through which we travel. I could fly you to the mountain, but that would be a breach of the first and only treaty ever agreed in The Light. I dare not break what should not be broken."

"But travelling to the mountains from the coast could take weeks," Sam lamented. "I fear that Becky doesn't have that long."

"Ah. There, I believe I can reassure you." Zadkiel answered. "I received a report from my agent on Floriana. His name is James, and you do not know him. But Marion and Becky did. James reports that Marion had organised, secretly, weapons and supplies for the exiled group and stored them in the Mortal Realm on the other side of the portal.

"The Fae had them pushed through the portal some hours ago." Sam gasped and looked stricken. "Wait Sam, there is more, and the words will comfort you, at least for a time.

"Marion risked her own life to break through a line of Black Shield guards and entered the portal after the others.

"Amongst the group were the leader of the God Movement, Anna, a sympathetic Black Shield warrior named Phillip, and Gerald Solipsis.

"James reports that the exiles have supplies to last some days and plan to use the name of Louseefa to gain an audience with the Dark Master. Marion was sure that they would be more valuable alive, as Louseefa's prisoners. Sam, they should be safe for some time."

The travellers were surprised to hear that Anna was with Becky in the Mortal Realm. They said as much, and Zadkiel told them why: Anna's presence in Floriana City as the leader of the opposition to the Fae; a failed rescue attempt; and capture by the Fae.

There were more immediate concerns requiring their attention, however. "Is there no way we can speed up our trip to the mountain?" Sam asked.

"Yes Sam, there is a way. Once I receive permission from the local leader, I can fly you all to the next clan territory. We can leapfrog to the mountain, cutting the journey time by weeks.

Sam was mystified by something Zadkiel had told them. "You say that Estrada is the home of early humans. Surely, that must mean the Sonciel have been part of the human story from the very beginning. Wow, that raises so many questions. It's mind-blowing.

"Were modern Homo Sapiens always intended?" Sam asked. "Did the Sonciel guide our evolution. Was God around from the very beginning. And the Angels?

Are you millions of years old, Zadkiel? I feel faint just thinking about it."

Zadkiel looked impressed and amused by Sam's outburst. "No Sam, I'm not millions of years old. And yes, the Sonciel have always been part of the human story. There are hundreds of questions that you could ask but now is not the time to answer them. Once we breach the doorway and merge with the Sonciel your questions will be answered.

"We'll leave tomorrow. It's a long flight to Estrada so wear something warm."

# Part Fourteen - James Takes the Reins

James had a hard time believing what he had just seen. Marion had fought her way through the Black Shield guards and then entered the portal. Willingly. Recklessness or bravery, he thought the choice moot. He might never know the history now unfolding on the other side of the destroyed portal.

He and his fellow warriors in the God Movement stood together, alone — for the Fae and the Shield guard had departed the scene — alone with their thoughts, as they inspected the pile of debris in front of them. They had heard the Fae's order to disable the remaining portals.

"Some of the technicians that maintain the portals to the Mortal Realm are our supporters," James announced. "I'm sure we can keep some of them functional despite the Fae's reckless order. It shouldn't be difficult to keep the deception from him."

He turned to the other warriors, "Anna's gone and may never return," he said sadly. "As her 2IC, I'll continue her legacy. We may not have the power to defeat the Dark Fae, but we can make his life miserable.

When we return to camp, I want to meet with the Echelon Council of the God Movement.

"We have mischief to plan."

*****

James' first meeting as the new leader was a revelation to many. Once seen as the second in command; second in the requisite skills and contacts thought necessary to effectively lead the Children of The Light; second to Anna in all things; James assumed the burden of leadership with skill and sensitivity. And it soon became obvious that James had contacts of his own.

The Echelon Council bore little resemblance to an army equivalent. These people were not officers, not paid and empowered to give lesser beings orders and to discipline misbehaviour and inferior performance. No, these people were more like scout leaders, empowered to encourage respect for the cause through tireless example. Anna had put together a fine team and James was keen to keep them together.

What better way to gain their support and respect, than to give them some new and encouraging information. "Welcome everyone. I've called this meeting so that I can let you know that nothing will change. Anna is not with us, but her legacy is, and that includes all of us.

"We are all Anna's legacy. And while she's fighting another enemy in another place, we have an enemy here. Our enemy is the Dark Fae. We cannot defeat him by force and overwhelming numbers, but we can frustrate him at every turn and make his existence uncomfortable.

"But, before we discuss how to handle the Fae, I have news for you that will prove enlightening. The mission to the First World has been successful. My contact informs me that Zadkiel, chief amongst the Angels of Light, will help our emissaries find the Universal Consciousness, the Sonciel."

"What about God?" one of the attendees asked. "Won't God return to help us?"

"The soul of the God our distant ancestors knew and revered, has returned to the Sonciel," James replied.

"But that means God is dead. Where does that leave us? The Fae will clobber us!" The attendee was becoming agitated, and his confusion was spreading amongst the other Council members. The volume of distraction threatened to overwhelm James's control.

He hit the table with a metal club. Every head turned at the noise and the chatter stopped abruptly. "Please everyone. Let me finish," James said firmly. "Our emissaries and Zadkiel will persuade the Sonciel to empower a new God to rise, a God who will be sympathetic to the distress of The Light and the loss of the Mortal Realm. We must trust in their skill to convince the Sonciel to return to The Light and give us the God we so desperately need. Anything less, and we fail before our fightback even begins. We owe it to the billions of Light who support us, that we don't lose faith.

"Our emissaries will succeed; I feel it in my soul and Zadkiel is optimistic. At this very moment, our emissaries are preparing to journey to the place where the Sonciel live. Believe in them and God will return."

Convinced by James's speech, heads nodded around the table. The meeting then turned its attention to the matter of thwarting the Fae's activities. The group decided to camouflage resource deliveries through the StarLight network and hide them away for future distribution to the population. The idea was to starve the Fae's supporters into submission.

They would also ask their supporters to return home, many to other worlds of Light, to relieve the pressure on Floriana. The leaders of the resistance agreed these things, especially as the dispersal of the crowd would protect supporters from the Fae's mercurial temper.

They had the signed and sealed support of billions, in many petitions. They had their evidence. The crowd need not stay any longer and burden the local population.

The Council meeting ended on this positive note, and delegates dispersed to fulfil the meeting's decisions.

James quickly proved himself as the leader of the God Movement, and of the massive crowd surrounding the Government buildings. The people were behind him. The Fae had lost all credibility throughout the worlds of Light, and the God Movement had become much more than a fringe revolutionary group. It had become the heart that spoke to the soul of Light. And the world of Floriana had become the focus, where heart and soul merged and spoke an ages old truth.

The people had come in vast numbers. So large was the crowd that the resources of one world could not sustain it. James realised that this situation could not continue, and the Council's campaign began to encourage supporters to return to their homes.

The StarLight portals had become the peoples' portals. The populations on every world, overwhelmed or co-opted the Black Shield, subduing the guards and destroying the Fae's spy network. Resources and supporters flooded the ancient pathways with a new and thrilling hope. And that hope met no resistance. The Fae may be powerful, but he is not God. He cannot be everywhere and know everything at once. James hoped this was the case.

The people had made their point. Many had died as martyrs to their point. Now was the time to disperse.

*****

The Fae thought himself God. A God without worshippers, without worship places. He quickly moved his quarters into another of the Government buildings. But he could not escape the people.

Everywhere the Fae went, as he flew regularly back and forth above the crowd and further afield, he sought a devotion that was not there. So, his flights became a means for intimidation, to remind the people that he wielded the power of life and death and would use it if pushed.

A Dark Fae was predictable. A mad Dark Fae was a nightmare waiting to happen. So, no one dared antagonise the Fae further, having seen already his cruelty and power in action. They ignored him and the doom he dangled above their heads, refusing to look up, to acknowledge his presence. It was a stressful and uneasy truce and the people's refusal to acknowledge his intimidation was itself intimidating. The Fae's insane frustration grew.

The Fae's unpredictability, convinced much of the crowd to disperse, as encouraged by the Council. And it soon became clear to the Fae that the crowd defying his divinity had begun to dwindle. He thought this was because of his intimidation and he giggled in satisfaction, until he learnt the reason the people were leaving.

A week after the Echelon Council meeting, and in the early morning darkness, a hooded figure entered the Government building where the Fae now lived. the meeting with the Fae was pre-arranged, and a locked private door remained unlocked to admit him.

A short lift ride to the top floor, accompanied by two Black Shield officers, ended inside the Fae's sumptuous quarters. The Fae was waiting for him. "Why have you kept me waiting for so long? The Council meeting was days ago. Why is the crowd dispersing and what else do you have to tell me. Speak quickly, lest I torture the information out of you. Giggle, giggle."

"Please, Honourable Fae, I meant no disrespect. I came as soon as I could safely exit the crowd. The guards have been very attentive since your last spy escaped them.

"I have news. The new leader of the Movement, James Boyce, is in direct contact with the First World and has learned that the three rebels you are pursuing have been admitted by the Angels of Light. Further, the chief Angel, Lord Zadkiel, is helping them find the Universal Consciousness."

"But they have not yet found the Consciousness?"

"No, Honourable Fae." Several minutes of silence followed as the Fae's muddled mind tried to make sense of the information. What could he do? How could he stop them from finding the Sonciel? And gradually, amongst giggles and gesticulations, the Fae made a tortured decision. His focus must now be on the First World. He would travel there and cut off the rebellion at its roots. If necessary, he would kill the Angels of Light.

# Part Fifteen - A Different Earth

Becky endured a nightmare. Surely this horrible place could not be anything other. The red gloom, the dry and sapping heat, like death on the skin and in the air she breathed. Nearby, Anna and Phillip lay side-by-side, hands clasped and mouths agape, so desiccating was the heat. Gerald lay a little further away, dead to the world, and oblivious. Becky envied him.

There was another body lying near to Gerald. Who was that, dressed in black as it was? A Black Shield had followed them through the portal. Surely not. No one in their right mind would willingly enter the Mortal Realm. Unless, unless they had a good reason. Becky stood slowly, trying to conserve her energy. This heat, so terrible; so enervating.

She stumbled over to the unexpected arrival. "My God — Marion?" Becky bent down and shook Marion by the shoulder. She stirred and opened her eyes. "Hi Becky, good to see you." Marion smiled weakly and sat up with a groan. Looking around she saw that everyone was here. "This place is even worse than I remember it. And it was only yesterday."

"What? Why are you here? Marion, why did you come through the portal?"

"Because I had to come, Becky. I needed to show you where I've hidden the supplies." Confusion filled Becky's eyes. "I'll explain after we've checked out the others. Come on Becky, let's wake our friends."

The closest was Gerald, but they would let him sleep for now. No need to invite him into the nightmare just yet. Becky and Marion walked over to Anna and Phillip who were stirring uncomfortably. The two women looked down on them, noticing their clasped hands. Becky felt a chill on her soul at the sight, for she could not clasp Sam's hand at this moment. She pushed the thought from her mind. No time to feel maudlin.

Becky bent and shook Phillip awake. His eyes opened and he closed them again. "Go away Becky and let me sleep. It's still dark." Suddenly his eyes flew open, a fleeting moment of terror… "God Becky. Please tell me I'm still asleep and this awful place is just in my head. I feel like I've been hit by a bus." He then realised he was clasping hands with Anna, who was still unconscious. Phillip squeezed her hand gently and whispered, "Anna, wake up." She stirred and grimaced. A soft voice broke the silence, "if this is what it's like to travel by portal, count me out next time."

Becky chuckled. "It gets better the second time around. But we won't be travelling by portal again any time soon. The Fae's destroyed the one we used."

Phillip and Anna sat up and looked in the direction of the portal they had come through. Where there should be an opening, was now rubble.

Then they saw Marion, saying together, "Marion!" Both were surprised and alarmed to see their friend trapped in the Mortal Realm with them.

"Welcome to the new world of the Dark. We can talk later but first we should see to Gerald. Anna and Becky, could you wake him? Phillip, could you come with me, and we'll get some water?"

"Water? Look around, Marion, there is no water." He studied their surroundings and all he saw was dust, rock and dead, burnt tree stumps.

"Marion gave a conspiratorial little smile. "Oh, yes there is. Come with me. She led Phillip to a group of large boulders 20 metres further up the hillside. "I hid the supplies in this deep crevice; didn't want the Dark stumbling across them. There are four backpacks and a carry bag for the weapons."

Phillip was even more confused. "Backpacks, weapons… Marion what's going on? How did they get here…?" Realisation struck. "You planned this. Marion, you did this for us and now you're trapped, just like us."

"Phillip, please, let's get everything down to the group and then I'll explain." Marion had not for one minute thought that helping her friends was a sacrifice. It felt right to do it, so she did it.

They struggled down the hillside with a backpack on each shoulder and together carried the weapons bag. When they arrived, Becky and Anna were comforting Gerald, who was sitting up and staring, aghast at his surroundings. He did not look at all well. He should still be in a hospital bed, Anna thought. The Black Shield had not even given him the dignity of dressing him in suitable clothing. He was sitting there, in the dust in his hospital gown. The cruelty of it left her breathless.

Marion and Phillip approached Becky and Anna and dropped their burdens on the ground. Marion opened a side flap of one of her backpacks and removed a canteen of water. She unscrewed the top and handed it to Gerald who, thankfully, took it from her grip. With hands shaking, he raised the canteen to his lips and took a few sips.

"I'm sorry Gerald. The water will be tepid and not very refreshing but it's the best I can do right now." Gerald smiled weakly and nodded his thanks, too weak to even talk.

By this time, everyone sat on the ground in a circle and studied each other. All eyes eventually fell on Marion, who was uncomfortable under that enquiring gaze. "I guess you all want to know how, and why, I got here.

"I saw the Fae capture the three of you. I heard what he said to you. After he flew off, I went to the Training Centre and stocked up on a few things that I knew would be useful. In the backpacks are food and water, energy drinks, protein bars and toiletries, as much as I could carry."

"There are other things in the carry bag that might also be useful." Marion unzipped the bag and opened it for all to see. Within the bag were several Dark disguises, voice boxes, and, most surprising and useful of all, several shaping swords and wooden clubs.

Anna and Phillip looked at the contents, recognising only the Dark disguises and wooden clubs. Phillip reached into the bag and picked up a sword. "Swords, you brought swords? I've never seen anything like them. So light and strange. They look like water but they feel like steel." Phillip's eyes lit up. "Shaping swords. I've heard of them but never seen one. Amazing."

"The sword you are holding is more than ten thousand years old," Marion said with wonder in her voice. These, along with the StarLight portals are all that is left to us, of the God that once ruled The Light. The swords are deadly to the Dark. I thought they might be useful, considering where we are."

"Useful? My God Marion, this is wonderful. You've given us what we need to survive, at least for a few days; and in doing so, you had to give us yourself as well. You sacrificed yourself for us. I'm… I'm overcome."

Anna got to her feet and sat down beside Marion. She hugged her fiercely, the emotion flowing out of her in waves. "Thank you, Marion, I don't know what else I can say. I'm speechless."

Becky left Gerald's side and walked over to the others, the canteen in her hand. "We need to keep hydrated, particularly in this heat, so take a swig."

Handing the canteen to Phillip, she then kissed Marion on the cheek and reached into the carry bag. "Perhaps you can demonstrate what these strange contraptions do. I'm sure Phillip and Anna would love a demonstration," Becky said with a twinkle in her eyes.

Marion was only too happy to oblige. "I suspect that three of you will have never seen these things, I'll switch one on and show you what it does. She started to sing, and the voice box worked its evil magic. I'm Dreaming of a White Christmas had never sounded so hellish. Phillip, Anna and Gerald were shocked. "This thing is a voice box," Marion announced still speaking with the box switched on. "It makes the speaker sound like the Dark. Becky and I know their language and, disguised, we can pass as Dark warriors." She switched off the box.

"I'll be damned," was all Phillip could say. Anna, sounding relieved, said, "Thanks for switching it off. That sound was ghastly. How can you stand it?"

"It gets easier," Marion explained. "But this is not a plaything. I brought the voice boxes for a reason. Becky, Phillip, and I are going to be Dark warriors. Anna and Gerald, you're going to be our captives and we're taking you to Louseefa.

"We have to reach Louseefa before we run out of water and food. There are only supplies for two days. So, we'll travel in the open and hope we meet some Dark warriors quickly. Everyone clear on the plan?"

Marion handed a voice box to Phillip and Becky. "Phillip, you'll need to dress in a Dark disguise. Becky will show you where the voice box goes. And leave the talking to us.

"I'll scout ahead and attract the attention of any nearby warriors. I don't think Gerald will be able to walk far, even with us helping him. I'll get some food out of the backpacks and some energy drinks. We'll rest for a little while and then we can be off."

*****

Marion and Becky had walked for some time and had not seen any hint of Dark activity. They followed the dry riverbed north for several kilometres. There was desolation and heat shimmer wherever they looked.

Finally, defeated, they turned around and retraced their steps until they saw the slope up which they would need to climb to reach their friends. As they climbed, they saw movement further up the slope; someone, a male voice, cried out midst the unmistakable sounds of fighting. The two women raced up the slope and came upon a group of Dark taunting and threatening their friends.

Marion and Becky looked at each other and then they drew their shaping swords from beneath their cloaks. In silence, they wielded them in a blaze of light and cleaved two Dark warriors in half. They fell instantly as ash to the ground. The other two, taken by surprise, backed away from the lethal swords and cursed the new arrivals, who seemed to them to be traitors.

Cursing and shrieking, they gathered up stones that instantly burst into flame; and hurled their explosive bombs dripping molten rock toward the women. Both bombs missed their target, but only just. Becky was lucky to escape the hit, but still felt the heat and pressure as the bomb grazed passed her sword arm.

In an instant, the women turned defence into attack, rushing and striking the two Dark warriors as they bent to pick up more stones. They, too, fell to the ground as ash.

Four piles of harmless ash, three grateful, unharmed faces, and two relieved Light warriors was all that remained of the brief skirmish.

Becky and Marion scattered the mounds of ash as best they could and joined their friends. "Are you all okay, no burns or injuries?" asked Marion. Phillip stood and embraced Marion. "Thanks to you, we're all unharmed. I struck one of them with a wooden club — it broke off a finger — but the club burst into flames. I threw it amongst the boulders.

"And, would you believe it, the finger regrew before my eyes. Hitting them with anything smaller than Uluru seems to be a waste of time."

"Worth a try," Marion judged. "There is one upside, though. Since the clubs are useless, we may as well discard them; less weight to carry."

The friends spoke quietly for a few minutes, Becky, and Marion reporting that they had found nothing to the north; no movement, no Dark, nothing. "From which direction did these Dark come?" Becky asked. "It couldn't have been north. We would have seen them."

"I do believe it was south, or southish," Gerald offered. They approached us from behind, which would have been south. Yes, definitely south. My eyes are still working, even if the rest of me is not."

"Gerald's right," Anna agreed. "They were making so much noise they had no hope of surprising us. And when they saw us, the shock immobilised them, as if they couldn't believe what they were seeing."

"Just as well you arrived when you did," Phillip added, "neither of us knew their language so I could not speak with them and calm the situation. Dressed in the Dark disguise they thought I was a spy. They'd just begun to threaten us when you appeared. I couldn't reach the swords, so only had the club to use against them.

"But those swords. Wow! Like a hot knife through butter. I've got to have me one of those."

"All in good time McBane," Marion laughed. "We'll have to teach you how to use it before we set you loose on the Dark."

"Fine with me," Phillip said, "when do we start? Er… Who's McBane?"

Marion, feigned indignation. "And you want to be a swordsman. You haven't heard of one of the greatest swordsmen in history? Scottish, 17th century, owned brothels, and gambling dens. Quite a colourful character by all accounts."

"Sounds like it," Phillip chuckled. "So then, when do we start? I can't defend your honour if I don't have a weapon. Although, I must admit, you do quite a decent job of defending it yourself."

Phillip proved to be a quick learner. Marion was impressed by his poise and balance. Only once did his aim let him down when he sliced clean through Marion's left arm. Mortified, Phillip looked for the blood, the terrible injury. There was nothing to see. No blood, no severed arm lying at her feet.

Marion quickly reassured Phillip. "I'm all right. The shaping swords are harmless to us. Pass right through, as if we're not even there."

"God, Marion. You could have told me. I almost had a heart attack." Phillip waited a moment and then burst into laughter. "First round to me, I think, even if I didn't draw first blood."

"Call it a draw and I'll give you a sword. The pupil doesn't master the teacher that easily," Marion said with a grin. "We don't have time to make a real swordsman of you. Just keep it safely in the scabbard and wear it under your cloak. No point advertising our origins too soon."

Becky drew everyone's attention to the fact that time was getting away from them. "We're on a countdown here. We have less that two days to find a group of Dark warriors and convince them we are who we purport to be. No telling how long our water will last in this heat."

Becky gazed out across the once living river valley, the heat shimmer distorting the utter desolation in waves of regret; regret for what had been lost; regret for what might never be restored.

"Becky's right," Anna chimed in, drawing Becky's attention away from her regrets for a past forever lost, and back to the dilemma they now faced. "We need to get moving soon; at least down into the river valley where we'll be more obvious. I'll help Gerald as much as I can, but he's in no condition to travel very far. So, which way do we go?"

"No point going north," Marion concluded. "The only real alternative is south. Travelling west will take us toward the mountains, and I don't know what dangers lie in that direction."

"That makes sense," Phillip added. "Following the dry riverbed south will take us somewhere that Becky already knows, albeit from the air," he said with a smile.

The decision made, everyone prepared themselves for the short march down the slope to the river. This was the same stretch of river that Sam and Rose had crossed a few short months before. At that time, occasional stagnant pools defined the course of the river. Now, even those reminders of another world were completely gone. When the group finally reached the river, they could see that it was dry, dusty in fact, and no more appealing than the desolation that surrounded it.

The gloom was deepening as the sun dropped slowly toward the horizon; now permanently hidden by the turbulent cloud layer. The exiles decided to make camp for the night. Where they had stopped was as good as anywhere else since they didn't need to hide. They wanted to be found.

Anna gave Gerald her cloak to hide his flimsy hospital gown. She thought that such a decent, respectable man must have hated being so under-dressed. His heartfelt gratitude confirmed her thought.

Each of the backpacks stored food and water and everyone ate their fill that night. They saw no point in rationing their food supplies. If they did not find Dark warriors during the next two days, no amount of rationing would help. Rather, it would merely prolong the agony.

Marion was the last of the group to lie down and try to sleep. She spread her cloak on the ground and stretched out on her back, looking up at the clouds, still visible, though the sun had long since set. There was a perpetual ruddy glow in the turbulence, as though flames danced within the clouds. This new world of the Dark was never dark. How ironic, Marion thought as she drifted off into an uneasy sleep.

*****

They knew it was morning because the gloom was not as gloomy. The hidden sun was doing its best to light the world, but the cloud layer was a chaotic adversary, scattering the power of the sun and distorting everything the crippled rays touched.

The exiles had been walking slowly south for several hours, with regular rest stops for water and to allow Gerald and Anna to rest. Marion had made two extended trips ahead to survey the land and thus far had seen no sign of the Dark.

The heat built as the day wore on. Everyone was sweating profusely, and they were quickly depleting their water supply. They could not go much further today. Finding a grouping of charred tree stumps, the exiles took refuge in the centre and spread their cloaks upon the hard ground. They sat and rested their backs on the stumps, sipping water and eating the high energy protein foods that Marion had packed into the bags.

I'm going to make one last sortie south in a few hours when the temperature is slightly cooler," Marion announced. "Becky, could you stay behind with the others, just in case the Dark find you? You know the language and you'll make a very convincing guard."

"No problems with that," Becky replied, glad for the extra rest.

And so, as the gloom started to deepen, Marion left her friends and ventured south once more. She intended to travel as far as her strength would take her, realising that they were running out of time. The hours passed. Still nothing. Damn. No, wait, what's that glow to the west. It looks like a fire, a very big fire. Marion could see that the blaze was reflecting off the low-hanging, cloud layer.

Marion's heart responded, beating rapidly at the heightened expectation. Could it be a Dark camp?

With hope rising, Marion turned toward the glow. She assessed the fire was at least two kilometres distant. Walking quickly and quietly, she reached the base of a slope that shielded her from a view of the fire. There did not appear to be any guard patrols or sentries. Why bother? Marion thought. This was their world now.

She climbed the shallow slope until she reached the top and lay down to assess what lay before her. This was, indeed, a Dark camp. It was enormous. Countless tents disappeared into the gloom in all directions.

At the centre of the camp was the largest campfire Marion had ever seen, and an exceptionally large tent which she assumed served as headquarters for the Dark Lord who commanded so many warriors. Not since her days wedded to the flames had she seen so many of these creatures gathered.

Marion shivered at the thought of it, thankful that the pilgrims had saved her from this nightmare. She could not bear to see any more of it. She slid backwards down the slope and quickly disappeared into the infernal shadows.

They had found their saviours. At least, she hoped they would prove to be saviours. They must convince the Dark Lord to take them to the Master, Louseefa. Anything else did not bear thinking about. Anything else would mean certain death.

Marion vowed to fulfil her unexpressed promise to save the exiles. She would do it. She must do it. The future of The Light may well depend, at least in part, upon her powers of persuasion.

Several hours later, Marion approached the camp of the exiles. She gave a low whistle to announce her arrival and both Phillip and Anna greeted her with a hug. Gerald was asleep, or so it seemed, exhausted by yesterday's trek.

Marion wearily removed her cloak and sat down in the circle with the others. She took a few mouthfuls of water from her canteen, which was almost empty, and announced the success of her journey to the south.

"I stumbled upon a mega Legion of the Dark. Huge! There was a massive fire burning in the centre of the camp. Although I didn't see it, there must be a Dark Lord commanding so many warriors. The headquarters tent was huge. Huge enough for a giant that's for sure.

"Tomorrow is the fateful day my friends. We rise or fall by the tongue, not the sword. If we can't convince the Dark Lord to take us to Louseefa, then tomorrow we die. It's that simple. They will be sure to search us when we arrive at the camp. wearing shaping swords will be an immediate giveaway. We'll have to hide them somewhere we can easily find them again, should we ever return this way."

"What story are we going to give them about our captives?" Becky asked.

"We'll tell them a half truth. I'll say we're emissaries of the Dark Master on a mission to capture infiltrators from The Light. We were watching the portal when Anna and Gerald came through. The Dark Master wants to interrogate them as they will have recent knowledge of intentions and events in The Light.

"I'll ask the Lord nicely to take us to Louseefa or bring the Master to us. Simple."

"And daring as hell," Phillip said. "It's a good story. If I were a Dark Lord, I'd believe it."

Anna took Phillip's arm and said in the nicest possible way, "but you aren't, are you dear. Let's hope the Dark Lord is even more gullible than you," she added with a grin.

Marion chipped in, "whatever happens, we have no choice. No one is coming to save us. We make our own future, win this fight ourselves. So, get into the spirit. Know your part and perform as if your life depended on it.

"Okay, let's settle down and rest. It's a big day tomorrow," she said, lying down on her cloak and closing her eyes. *At least, I hope it turns out to be a big day…*

Over the next few hours, the exiles dozed fitfully. They found it hard to rest comfortably when images of violent death haunted their immediate future. But eventually, everyone drifted off and slept for a time.

*****

It was morning. The gloom had brightened, meaning the sun must have risen above the hidden horizon. Groans broke the silence, as the exiles wakened and moved their weary bodies. "I hope Louseefa has comfortable beds," Phillip complained. "This sleeping on the ground is killing me." Anna, lying beside this man she loved with a passion that surprised her, sat up and kissed him full on the lips. "Stop complaining, you old softy. It could be worse, much worse. Use your imagination and you'll get the picture."

Phillip looked chastened for a moment and then replied, "No thanks. Imagination and reality are blood-brothers in this madhouse. I'll stick with ignorance, much more comforting."

By this time everyone was awake and going about their own business. Marion sat beside Gerald and could see that he was dealing with the hardships a lot better than she thought was possible. "If I'm not mistaken, you're feeling a little stronger this morning, Gerald."

"I do believe you are right. I don't know why, but I feel stronger, lighter somehow. It is as if this adventure is nourishing my body by nourishing my mind. Very strange…"

"You know what I think? I think you're seeing the other half of your thesis played out in front of you. You've seen the reality of The Light, as it has become. Now you're seeing the reality of the Dark as it always was, in all its terrible grandeur. Meeting Louseefa will be the icing on the metaphysical cake."

"Terrible grandeur… I like that," Gerald answered. "Yes, the only thing that will top meeting Louseefa, will be meeting God. And, I suppose, we all hope for that."

The exiles had eaten and drunk their fill, completed their meagre ablutions and had hidden the shaping swords in the obvious place — within the circle of tree stumps. Burying the swords was difficult in the hardened earth, but they managed to dig deep enough to accommodate all the swords, except one. Marion hid that one sword and scabbard in a secret pocket of her cloak.

It was time to leave. Phillip and Becky walked in the rear, ostensibly to guard their captives, Gerald, and Anna. Marion led the exiles from the front and headed south at a slow pace. Although Gerald was feeling a little stronger, he still needed help from Anna.

By the time they reached the place where the glow of the fire was visibly reflecting off the clouds, they had been travelling for many hours and had stopped many times so that Gerald could rest. One more stop, to consume the last of their food and water, and then the exiles were off again, headed west, toward the Dark camp. The next few hours would decide whether they lived or died.

*****

The small group stood atop the rise and looked down upon their fate. As before, the campfire burnt fiercely; the numberless tents filled the plain. So many...

Dark warriors were milling about as far as their eyes could see. Some were training directly below them — target practice, throwing flaming rocks at Light-sized targets. The accuracy displayed over long distances seemed to the group an unfortunate omen of the fate they most feared.

Marion as the chief spokesperson for the exiles saw no point in delaying the inevitable and assumed her character as the Dark warrior in charge. She barked an order that was incomprehensible to Anna, Phillip, and Gerald and Becky quickly translated. Her shouted order attracted the attention of the Dark warriors below. The group slowly negotiated the gentle slope.

Phillip and Becky treated the captives harshly, Becky shrieking Dark insults and threatening the captives. Anna looked terrified, a threatened touch from Phillip was sufficient to send both captives reeling. Gerald barely managed to stay upright and uttered a cry of such despair, that even Marion was convinced by the performance.

Target practice had ceased as the group approached. The Dark warriors started screaming and throwing insults and pushed forward to grab the captives.

Marion screeched an almighty curse. "Keep away you evil bastards. These be not for you. Which o' you lot is in charge?"

An exceptionally large warrior came forward and looked down upon Marion in her disguise. "Who be you, scrawny little worm? Why's you interruptin' me trainin'? And where'd you get that Light scum? I takes them off your 'ands and use 'em for target practice. What you say? Let's 'ave 'em."

"Keep yer 'ands off me captives." Marion stood her ground daring the Dark officer to push passed her. This was the moment. If he touched her, she would burn.

"Me and me mates 'ere be under His protection. The Dark Master, exalted be 'is name, he wants 'em you see.

"Take me to your Dark Lord. He be 'ere, I knows it."

If a faceless thing could look confused and alarmed, this officer would win an Oscar. "Beggin' yer pardon. I's disno' know," the officer said fearfully, moving backwards and almost tripping over his clumsy black feet. "I takes yer to the Lord." The officer spoke huskily to an underling. "Take charge o' the trainin' while I be's away." He turned back to Marion. "Follow me an' keep close. No tellin' what the sluggards 'll do when they sees the Light scum."

Marion felt relief. She'd heard that the Dark warriors were gullible, believing anything if said to them in a commanding voice. But the real test was still to come. Would the Dark Lord be as gullible, more suspicious, more perceptive? No going back now... Marion crossed her fingers under her cloak and the group advanced slowly through the crowd of Dark warriors.

Some brave individuals reached out to grab the prisoners and the Dark officer rebuked them with a shrieked order that Marion could barely translate. It worked, and the crowd moved backwards as one, alarmed by the mention of the Dark Master.

The group arrived unscathed at the headquarters tent, which was, indeed, impressive. The Dark officer requested admittance. The guards disappeared into the tent to alert the Dark Lord of the visitors. The guards soon reemerged and ushered them all inside. Anna and Gerald looked suitably brow-beaten and terrified as they stumbled into the tent. Phillip and Becky stood close behind with arms raised as if ready to strike their captives with fire.

The Dark Lord stood in front of them looking down from a great height. His head nearly brushed the ceiling of the tent, so tall was he. Marion stared up at a face and, pretending subservience, asked for permission to speak.

"How dare you interrupt my discussions. Who are you? Why are there two Light spies with you? Speak."

Marion repeated her story, and the Dark Lord looked more suspicious still. "Why was I not warned of your presence in my lands. I rule here. This is outrageous."

"Beggin' yer pardon me Lord," Marion said obsequiously, "our mission be secret like. We's on a mission to capture these spies and take 'em to the Dark Master, Louseefa, exalted be 'is name."

Marion had taken the gamble she had to take. The Light did not know without question that Louseefa was the Dark Master. But if he was, the use of his name might just convince the Dark Lord of their credentials.

"Louseefa? Not many sluggards know that name. Only the Lords and close advisors of the Master, exalted be his name, know it. Perhaps you are telling the truth. And what are your orders from the Master, little warrior?

"Master Louseefa, exalted be 'is name; he be orderin' us to find the nearest Dark Lord, to take us to 'im. Wants to torture 'em, see, find out what they knows. That's why we's 'ere. *We were right, Louseefa is the Dark Master*, Marion thought with relief.

"You're in luck, little warrior. The Light scum would not be able to enter the Dark Realm. But Louseefa has just taken up residence in his palace a long way to the north."

"I knows this, me Lord, that's whys I asked," Marion replied. Luck indeed…

"We must go outside for this. Otherwise, I'll burn the tent." The Dark Lord ordered his guards to usher the visitors to a clear space outside. "Gather round. We're going for a ride. The fiery tempest will not harm the spies."

Standing close, but not too close, fearing the fiery touch of the Dark Lord, a vortex formed around them, of flames and screaming wind. The vortex lifted off the ground. And then, in an instant, it was gone, its flight too fast for the eye to see.

Marion's gambit had succeeded. They were on their way to meet the Dark Master, Louseefa.

*****

Inside the fiery vortex was almost magical in its strangeness. The exiles rode unharmed on a solid floor of air, the earth far below flashing beneath their feet at incredible speed. They stood facing outwards towards the colourful winds, the Dark Lord in the centre at their backs, although none of them could see him. He was taking great care not to touch his passengers, much to Marion's relief.

Eerie and profound silence belied the violence of the vortex winds. The circular wall of fiery colours danced in rhythmic tides before their eyes and was almost hypnotic in its effect upon the weary passengers.

Marion closed her eyes for fear that she would, indeed, fall under the spell of the vortex. It would not do, to arrive at Louseefa's residence in a catatonic state. She would need to be alert and nimble. A single error of judgement could be fatal.

Marion's story to the Dark Lord indicated that Louseefa would be expecting them. But Louseefa had no idea that they would soon be arriving. This disconnect provided another exquisite test of Marion's skills. *This will be tricky,* she thought, smiling at her understatement.

They had been travelling for several hours when at last the arid ground beneath their feet slowed and came nearer. They were descending rapidly. As Marion looked, she saw a flash of reddish green and something that looked remarkably like a body of water. She blinked, not believing what her eyes had just seen. *I must be going loopy.*

At last, the passengers felt firm ground beneath their feet. The winds slowly faded until the vortex completely disappeared. Becky and Marion were facing directly toward a miraculous landscape bathed in the last rays of sunlight. Before them was a vast garden, trees, shrubs, and grass, surrounding a large body of water on three sides, the whole encompassed by a tall and solid stone wall, still under construction. The clouds above circled an area of clear air, like the eye of a cyclone. The air was cooler, much cooler.

"I be damned," Marion said in wonder, quickly transforming her tone to one of distaste. "What's this doin' 'ere? Ain't natural. We works ourselves 'til we drop, 'til every trace o' green be gone, an' 'ere you brings us to more of it. An' water, *foul be its substance,* what be water for?"

The Dark Lord who had transported them in the vortex, was happy to soothe their shock. By this time, Gerald, Anna, and Phillip had turned around and they stared at the landscape with amazement. "The water is for the Trial," said the Lord. "The green stuff keeps the water pure, or so the Master says. I don't have to like it, same as you, but I accept it as the Master's will.

"Watch your prisoners while I announce your arrival." The Dark Lord entered the nearby entrance way to Louseefa's impressive residence and disappeared.

Several Dark warriors stood on guard some distance away, eyeing the group suspiciously.

Marion spoke softly to the others. "The Dark may see the presence of plants and water here as a foible of the Master, an eccentric test of character, him living so close to a watery death, but we know different. The Light need these things for life. And Louseefa *is* Light.

"Everyone, remember your roles and pray that we're still alive at the end of today." Marion could see the Lord returning. He did not look happy.

"What are you lot playing at? The Master says he's not expecting you. Doesn't know anything about your prisoners. You told me different. I'm of a mind to throttle the lot of you for making me look like a fool. Who are you?"

Marion looked at the Lord, reached under her cloak and revealed the shaping sword, placing it on the ground at the Lord's feet. "We are no threat to the Master. We come seeking audience with him. Forgive us for deceiving you. We thought it was the only way we could speak directly with your Master."

To the Dark Lord's amazement, Marion stripped off her disguise and revealed herself as a child of The Light. Becky and Phillip, momentarily transfixed by Marion's actions, followed suit. Soon, five children of The Light stood before the Dark Lord, looking tired and dishevelled. Gerald still looked weak and unwell.

The Dark warrior guards rushed forward to kill the deceivers. The Lord waved them away.

Becky spoke, without the voice box and in the Dark Lord's language, "thank you, Lord. I was Fae to The Light, now no longer Fae. The new Fae has exiled all of us to the Mortal Realm… to what was once the Mortal Realm. We have information that will be of interest to the Master, *exalted be his name.* Please help us to see him."

The Dark Lord, monstrous as he was, stood immobile, undecided what to do. "You put on quite a performance. You must, indeed be desperate to see the Master. And you could have killed me with that sword, yet you did not. That is either an act of great folly, or of great courage.

"Throw the sword into the water. Only then will I leave you to speak again with the Master." Marion picked up the sword and did as the Dark Lord asked.

The Lord then spoke to the Dark guards. "Watch over these prisoners, but do not harm them. If you disobey this order, you will suffer the Trial." The Lord disappeared again through the entrance way.

Several minutes later, the Dark Lord returned, this time looking much happier. "The Master will see you. He wants to learn how you came to know his name. Your knowledge and story intrigue him. Follow me."

The Lord turned around and walked slowly through the entrance way, ensuring his prisoners were able to keep up; two Dark guards walking behind the prisoners, lest they try to escape. "This Dark Lord is not at all as I expected," Becky whispered to her friends, "he has treated us honourably. Another Lord may not have been so gracious."

"True," Marion answered. "We're extremely fortunate to have met him. It's a miracle we got this far, so let's not fall at the last test. The Master will be intrigued to speak with you Becky as you were once the leader of The Light." Becky acknowledged this assessment with a weary smile.

As the group walked into the heart of the residence, more a palace than a mansion, they marvelled at the architectural features, showing great sensitivity and dexterity with chisel and brush.

Elegant columns lined the hallway, unlike anything they had seen before. Gilded and painted in muted, warm colours, the whole spoke of sophistication. How the Dark artisans achieved this level of precision and skill, without burning everything they touched, was beyond their current understanding.

At the end of the long hallway were a pair of beautifully carved wooden doors which, upon their arrival, opened into a vast space. Directly in front of them, across 50 metres of intricate polished mosaics, was a raised dais with an enormous black marble seat, more likely a throne than a chair. The throne was empty and looked extremely uncomfortable. *Such is the price of power,* Marion thought with a secret smile.

Black crystal chandeliers hung from the vast ceiling that soared impossibly high above the throne room, lighting provided by scarlet candles, too many to count.

Anna was awestruck. "This is extraordinary. I had no idea the Dark could achieve such things."

"Silence!" The Dark Lord hissed in the language of The Light. "You will not speak until the Master commands it. When the Dark Master arrives, you will bow as I do, with eyes lowered. The Master will tell you when you may look upon him. Is that clear. Nod if you understand my meaning." Five heads nodded in unison.

The Dark Lord and his prisoners, together with many Dark warrior guards, waited in silence for the Master to arrive. They stood there in silence for many minutes. The wait seemed interminable as the prisoners grew steadily weaker; Anna and Phillip were having difficulty keeping Gerald upright, his body becoming almost insupportable.

It was at this moment that the Dark Master Louseefa made his grand entrance. *If he thinks we're impressed by his theatrical display...* Phillip thought the performance infantile and unworthy of a Lord of Light, even if he was in disguise. The group bowed, lowered their eyes, and studied the mosaics on the floor.

After some minutes, during which the Master took his uncomfortable place upon the throne, he ordered the guards to leave and lock the door behind them.

"You may look upon me," the Master directed. All eyes rose and beheld the leader of the Dark, resplendent in his Cloak of State and his hideous mask. The Master's speaking voice was sonorous and not at all like that of a Dark Lord. Marion thought he sounded almost pleased to see his visitors.

"The Dark Lord Ephistos has told me your story. I am intrigued. Why would five Children of The Light dare risk the horrors of this realm, just to seek an audience with me, their most hated enemy, sworn by time and by blood? Which of you declares herself to be the former leader of The Light. You may speak."

Becky stepped forward and bowed to the Dark Master. "I am the person, my Lord. My name was Rebecca Pilgrim in the Mortal Realm; before I died and entered The Light. I was chosen the First Among Equals, the Fae, though I did not seek the position. I resigned after your victory over the place we called Earth.

"A new Fae was chosen, a man of political ambition who cared less for the needs of The Light, and more for the power he wields absolutely. We opposed his destructive rule, and he banished us to this place. You are now our only hope."

"How dare you presume to come to me and seek protection," Louseefa said indignantly. "You will not find hope here, not unless you can convince me of your worth."

"My Lord Louseefa," Marion declared, knowing how much she risked by speaking up, "Master of the two realms, may I speak?"

"You have five minutes to convince me to keep you alive. If I remain dissatisfied, you will all burn, or better still, be enthralled to the fire and become Dark. That would be ironic, don't you think?"

Marion cringed at the prospect of fire, or worse, but appeared resolute, determined to convince the Master. This was it, the moment when their quest succeeded or failed.

"We have sought your protection out of self-interest, that is true. But we did so with honest hearts, seeking at first the understanding of your gracious Lord Ephistos. He saw the truth behind our ruse and agreed to bring us to you. When we arrived, our Dark disguises no longer needed, I lay my shaping sword at his feet and begged an audience to plead our case.

"We wish to right a wrong, committed long ago, knowing that you would understand the meaning of the wrong. Together, we hoped to redeem what has been lost, and end the enmity of millennia. To right the wrong."

The prisoners could not see the Master's reaction to these words, hidden as it was by the mask. Marion imagined that her words had shocked Louseefa. Would he take the bait she had dangled before him. Would he refuse to discuss the matter and be rid of them. The seconds ticked away. The silence lengthened. The Master was thinking, deciding their fate.

After many minutes, the Master spoke. "Lord Ephistos, would you leave us. I am in no danger. You have done well today. I will recall you when I have need of you."

*He's taken the bait.* Marion was quietly euphoric.

Ephistos looked surprised by the Master's request, but dared not disobey him. "As you wish my Master." He bowed, eyeing the prisoners quizzically as he turned and left the room.

Once Ephistos had closed the same door by which the prisoners had entered, the Master asked the prisoners to approach him. "We can speak freely. What is this wrong that you wish to right?"

"You know the nature of this wrong, Master Louseefa," Marion said confidently, "God caste you out of The Light many thousands of years ago; you were exiled, as we are now; but forever bonded with us, by blood and by nature, despite the rupture of our realms."

"You have seen through my disguise. Why should I not kill you now and end the danger that you present."

"We are no danger. What would we gain by revealing that you are an Angel of Light? The Dark would kill us. We would have risked everything, to seek your protection — all for nothing? We pose no danger.

"We have a common enemy now, the Dark Fae, who has gone mad, who thinks he is God, who wields his power against his own people. The wrong cannot be righted while he is the Fae.

"We do not blame you for hating us, for doubting our intentions. We saw, by the presence here of the sun, the greenery, and the water, how much you have lost. You need The Light as much as we do.

"Please Master Louseefa, allow us the opportunity to speak with you for we have much to share with each other. Too long have you lived in the Dark. We may be naïve, but we hope that you may one day, re-enter The Light."

Louseefa could not believe what he was hearing. *They would invite me back, unconditionally, little realising that I have my own desire to re-enter The Light; to re-enter not as a mere Lord, but as the Master? These prisoners are indeed naïve.*

Louseefa decided there and then, to play their game for a while, at least. The game would amuse him.

"I suggest we retire to a more comfortable setting and continue our discussion. One of you looks unwell, the man at the back. He needs rest in a comfortable bed. I will ask my physician to treat him, though her experience with Light patients is almost non-existent. Support him while we walk the short distance to my private quarters. He may rest in one of the guest rooms.

"I usually enjoy a cup of tea at this hour. Would you care to join me?

*****

The Master left the throne room by way of a side door and hallway that led directly to his quarters. He clearly did not fear his visitors and walked ahead of them at a leisurely pace. At regular intervals, Dark warriors stood guard, their presence more ceremonial than protective. Thus, they were surprised to see the Master escorting five Children of the Light to his quarters, *without* a security detail.

The guards bowed as the Master passed by, eyeing his 'guests' with obvious distaste. Hoarse whispering filled the hallway once the group had disappeared into the Master's quarters, so surprising and unusual was this event.

A lone whisper may trigger an avalanche. How much more damaging then, an avalanche of whispers.

The Master's private quarters were breathtaking. That was the only way the visitors could describe the artistry in every part and detail. The furnishings were tasteful and comfortable, though not human-sized, carved by skilled artists from native timbers (extinct in the wild for obvious reasons). The soaring ceilings were artfully constructed, rounded ribs of stone meeting at the highest point, where a large, sculpted roundel reproduced the Master's grotesque mask in remarkable detail.

"Would a couple of you follow me to a guest room with your ill friend. I'm afraid the beds are Lord sized and much too high for you to place him on the bed. My

Physician is a Lord of the Dark, so she will clean him up and attend to his needs. Until she arrives, lie him on the provided cushions near the bed. She will arrange for bedding to make his short stay more comfortable. Anna and Phillip carried Gerald the few metres to his room and did as the Master asked.

When they returned to the sumptuous lounging room, the Master picked up a device from its cradle and spoke into it for several minutes. Placing the device back on its stand, the Master responded to the questions he saw in his visitors' eyes.

"The Dark are not interested in technology. This device for example is little better than a taut wire, attached to two tins. But it does the job.

I have arranged the assignment of rooms for each of you. Until I'm satisfied as to your integrity and honesty, guards will see to your needs, particularly exercise, and lock you in your rooms when you have finished your duties. As to your hygiene, there is only one bathroom in the building and that is mine. I will rectify that situation. Once I am satisfied as to your intentions, I will allow you more freedom. Is that clear?"

"Absolutely," Marion answered. "We could not expect otherwise. We're grateful that you've given us the opportunity to speak with you. Prison's a small price to pay when the alternative is death."

The Master chuckled, "well said little warrior. I must warn you, however. If I learn that any of you have revealed my identity in any way, you will all die. Is *that* clear?"

Becky bowed to the Master. "Perfectly. Our survival depends upon your identity remaining secret. We knew this from the moment we entered the old Mortal Realm, your new Realm. Cannot we use our time here as an opportunity to discuss matters of mutual interest?

"There is so much about the Dark that we in The Light don't understand. We're amazed, and humbled, by the craftsmanship displayed here. How is this possible when everything that the Dark touch bursts into flames?'

"In this Realm," the Master explained. "The Dark must physically touch objects to burn. If they prevent the burning, they are then able to create extraordinary things. The reverse operates in the Dark Realm.

"Now before we continue our little talk, would any of you care for a cup of tea?" All the prisoners nodded or *yes pleased*. "For obvious reasons, I'll have to make the tea myself. The main problem is finding suitably sized cups. I collect thimbles so perhaps they might work. I won't be a moment." *Thimbles?* The prisoners were more than bemused.

As Louseefa went to leave the room, there was a loud knock at the door. "Enter!" The Master ordered. The door opened and a Dark Lord stepped over the threshold, carrying a doctor's bag. *Now that's incongruous,* Marion thought.

The doctor waved a couple of warriors inside carrying bedding materials and a makeshift mattress, and the group disappeared into Gerald's room.

Louseefa said softly, "the tea will have to wait until they leave."

The warriors appeared first, bowing low to the Master, and then marching quickly out the door.

The doctor took much longer to appear. When she did, she approached the Master and began speaking in Dark, the Dark Language. After a couple of minutes listening to her assessment, the Master translated for the prisoners who could not speak the language. "As I told you previously, the physician has no experience working with Light patients. Her assessment, based upon observation, is that he is very weak, malnourished, and dehydrated. She recommends food, water, and rest. She did not find any other worrying symptoms such as pain."

Becky bowed respectfully to the Lord physician and, speaking in Dark, thanked her for assessing the patient. "We are grateful to you for helping our friend. It's an honour to meet you."

The doctor seemed taken aback, that a Child of the Light should speak to her so respectfully, and in her own language. Looking uncertainly at the Master, the doctor took her leave, without another word.

"It will do her good to see that not all Light are monsters. The Dark are indoctrinated with lurid stories of Light atrocities from the time they arrive in the Dark

Realm. They hate the Light because of this and have used the Mortal Realm as a plaything to annoy their enemies.

"It has not yet occurred to them, that by taking all human lives in the Mortal Realm, they have cut off the traditional supply of souls to replenish their numbers. They are the last generation. Unless… there is another source of course, but let's not speak about that shall we? Now, to the tea." The Master disappeared into an adjoining room through a hidden doorway that materialised before him.

Marion spoke what the others were thinking. "So far, so good. We've achieved what we intended. And imprisonment can't be a bad thing, given where we are." The small group of willing prisoners moved over to the large window and looked out upon the strangest view they had yet seen in this ruined Realm. The extensive green growth and the large body of water seemed out of place, surreal and disturbing, and Becky wondered how the Master had managed to get the Dark to accept this unnatural intrusion into their world.

"I can understand why the water would be needed for the Trial," she said, "but the plants — that must be hard for the Dark to understand."

"Did you notice, when Louseefa spoke about the Dark," Anna asked, "he spoke in the third person, *they*, and *them*? He leads them, but he doesn't consider himself one of them.

"Louseefa misses The Light. He surrounds himself with food and water, things that the Dark don't need, because *he* needs them to nourish his body and his soul. After thousands of years pretending to be something he's not, he still craves the life of the Light."

Phillip eagerly supported Anna's statement. "I'm amazed that Louseefa has kept his sanity for so long. A weaker personality would have succumbed long ago."

"That's a matter we'll have to agree on," Becky assessed. "He seems perfectly sane, but is he, really? We must watch him closely. He craves The Light, that's obvious. He could return through a portal at any time. For what purpose? We need to find out.

"Louseefa hides his bitterness well, but his grievances run deep. Sharing tea with us doesn't mean we're friends. He'll be watching us while we're watching him."

Marion was relieved that the others felt as she did. "My friends, all that is true. Let's enjoy tea with Louseefa but remember where we are. Louseefa orchestrated The Fall despite knowing the Dark would lose a ready source of souls to renew their numbers. What are his intentions? To feed the Children of Light to the Dark? To do that he will need to conquer The Light and the Sonciel. Or is he sincere in desiring to return to his own people, without recrimination or agenda?

"Be wary, everyone. Sweet words in the mouth of an enemy may hide bitter intentions." Marion could see

Louseefa returning. She whispered, "take care and be careful what you say."

Louseefa set a large tray on a high table. "I see you're admiring the view. The water and the greenery remind me of The Light. And that greenery will ensure you don't go hungry. There is a thriving vegetable garden, fruit and nut trees, and berry vines, all within a separate walled garden. You'll get to know it well as you will tend the garden every day, under guard, of course.

"The best seating I can offer you are those large cushions in the corner. Grab a few of them and bring them here. We can chat comfortably while we drink our tea. It's an herbal blend of my own devising. No milk I'm afraid, but we do have sugar and lemon."

Phillip and Anna went and grabbed several super-sized cushions, and the prisoners sat, looking up at Louseefa. He poured himself a cup of tea and handed the heavy tray to Phillip who set it down on the floor amongst the cushions. "Please serve yourselves. Will you excuse me a moment?" Louseefa's face transformed before their eyes, replaced by a very large human face, the most exquisite human face they had ever seen, luminous translucency notwithstanding.

The indrawn breaths were audible. Louseefa *was* an Angelic Lord of Light. He had the face of an angel and Marion blurted out, "You're beautiful." She covered her mouth, shocked by her outburst, but quite overcome by the face before her. "I'm sorry my Lord. I don't know wha…"

"Hush Marion. This is the same face that God exiled to the Mortal Realm. Nothing else about me is as it was before that time. Do not see goodness where there is none. The years of exile have changed me, and you would do well to remember that — all of you." Louseefa spoke these words sternly, but not aggressively. Marion thought she heard regret in Louseefa's voice. *Or had she imagined it?*

"Let us reach an understanding, here and now. You are prisoners here, but you are also my guests. I hope that we may be able to share many moments of convivial conversation, a pleasure of The Light I have missed and long to experience again. By day you can work in the garden and ensure our food sources are bountiful. I hope at least one of you is a keen gardener. As there are no insects, you will need to pollinate the flowers by hand, a tedious task, you'll agree, but a vital one.

"I enjoyed gardening when I was alive," Becky offered. "I had a knack for it. I don't know about the others, but I would welcome the work very much." Heads nodded around the circle of *guests*. They had no choice at all save one, grow and gather food, or die of starvation. No choice at all, really.

"Thanks for the tea," Phillip said, "very refreshing. I don't know where you obtained the leaves in this desolation we once called Earth, but sharing your supply with us is most generous."

"Generosity does not feature in my estimation. Everything I do is for a purpose. You will understand more a little later when I show you several secret storage rooms. The Dark know nothing of these rooms, and I'd like to keep it that way. Understood?" Heads nodded vigorously.

"Speaking of rooms, at this very moment, your accommodations are being prepared in another wing of the residence. Craftsmen are providing you with human-sized furnishings and clean bedding. Each of you will have a private bathroom, though the Dark do not understand the need. I will ensure that you are made as comfortable as possible in captivity.

"In return I ask for your cooperation and company. I trust that is not too much to ask?"

"My Lord, Louseefa, what you offer us is more than we could ever have expected or hoped for. You have given us sanctuary. In return for this undeserved sanctuary, we will give you what you look for, and more. We will give you loyalty. I will give you loyalty. We are of the same blood, though separated by eons, and blood always knows its own.

"We are exiles, same as you, sentenced to death by a Fae who could not tolerate competition or opposition."

"I would know more of this." Louseefa said. "How is it that the Leader of The Light could do such a terrible thing. God did it once before, but he no longer rules The Light. And now you tell me that the Fae has done it again."

"The Fae is not sound of mind." Becky said bitterly. "The power he holds has driven him mad, and he lashes out against his own people."

"You were Fae. You ruled The Light as we conquered the Mortal Realm. Why did you not use your power against *us*?"

Tears sprang to Becky's eyes as she recalled her humiliation. "The Advisory Council of bureaucrats and politicians would not allow me to aid the defence of the Realm. We lost and I resigned. Simple as that.

"The Constitution of The Light, written after your exile and the rejection of God, gives the Fae power but limits its use, at the discretion of the Advisory Council, the remnants of the diminished Angelic Council, of which you were once a member."

"You had power, but you did not use it." Louseefa said in wonder. "I did not know that integrity and humility still existed in The Light. You were, indeed, a remarkable Fae, and you have paid a terrible price for that integrity."

"Now, on a more mundane matter, can any of you cook?" Louseefa asked. Becky, Marion, and Phillip indicated as much. Louseefa looked delighted. "Marvellous. The Dark have no need for cooking since they don't eat. You may imagine how frustrating that has been over the past several thousand years. Creating one's own meals from nothing becomes repetitive and tedious and takes on an institutional blandness. I long for the taste of freshly harvested and cooked food.

"I think our partnership here can be of mutual benefit, don't you agree?"

"Oh yes," Marion gushed. "It would be an honour to cook for you." The others looked at Marion uneasily, not recognising the voice of the sensible and careful woman they knew. *What's gotten into her? It's as if she's under a spell or something.* Becky knew that Louseefa had *something* to do with it. What else could have caused Marion's uncharacteristic behaviour?

Becky stared at the others, pleading with them to be careful. Her eyes conveyed the urgent message. They stared back, Phillip nodding imperceptibly.

"It's almost dark now," Louseefa said, "so too late for you to explore the food garden and those secret rooms I mentioned earlier. There will be time enough tomorrow. Have you finished your tea?" Everyone saying that they had, Marion looking up at Louseefa with an adoring smile.

"Place your thimble cups on the tray." With a flick of a finger the tray lifted from the floor and followed Louseefa out of the room.

Becky whispered to Marion, "what's gotten into you? You're not yourself Marion. We can't trust him, at least, not yet."

Marion looked at Becky, wide-eyed — and then winked. "How do you like my little performance? I'm not laying it on too thick, am I?"

"*Yeees*! Gees Marion, I thought he'd put a spell on you. Ease up a bit. You scared us half to death."

Marion looked around the group. "Sorry guys. I'll tone it down. But, wow, he is beautiful, right?"

Anna smirked and looked at Phillip. "Don't worry dear, you're beautiful as well, and your beauty runs deeper. And you cook as well." Phillip took Anna's hand and kissed it lightly.

At that moment, Louseefa returned to the room and lowered several plates of food to the floor, in front of each prisoner. Then, as if by magic several crystal wine glasses appeared, followed by bottles of aged French wines and juices.

"Please help yourself to the refreshments. After you've finished, I'll call some Dark warrior guards to escort you to your cells. The alterations to your rooms are not yet completed. I have arranged for hot and cold running water in your bathrooms and this is delaying the work. Plumbing is not something the Dark are familiar with."

"Thank you, my Lord, that is most thoughtful," Marion replied, in a more characteristic voice.

Everyone ate and drank in silence, until hunger and thirst were satisfied. Louseefa gathered up the empty plates and the bottles and they followed him dutifully into another room. Tinkling glass and the sound of running water indicated that something was happening, then silence. Louseefa reappeared, waved his hand casually and the doorway disappeared.

"It's been interesting talking with you all," Louseefa said with a captivating smile. "I'll call the guards now if I may and let you have some time to yourselves. Tomorrow is going to be busy for you. There is much you need to learn. But I hope we will have time to continue our discussions. By the way, two of the rooms have connecting doors. Phillip and Anna may use those rooms when they are ready. Excuse me for a moment." Louseefa's eyes took on a faraway look and his head transformed into the mask, seamlessly affixed to his body.

Louseefa left the prisoners alone for a moment. Anna was looking a little dazed. "How did he know about us, Phillip? I've tried hard to keep it to myself. So have you. Somehow, he saw it. I don't like this at all."

Marion grasped Anna's hands, "Anna, he had only to see the glint in your eyes, the way you look at Phillip and your body language. It wasn't so hard. Please don't fret about it. We're all subject to the same scrutiny and we'll all have to be on our guard. He'll try to make us open up more than we should, and to say things better left unsaid. You know what I'm talking about…"

At that moment, Louseefa re-entered the room, leading a number of Dark guards. "The guards here will accompany you to your cells and will lock you in. If you need anything, ask your guard. If you don't speak Dark, the guard will seek an interpreter.

"I'll say goodnight." Speaking Dark abruptly, Louseefa ordered the guards to remove the prisoners.

Louseefa stood alone in the grand lounging room, standing near the large observation window. He had snuffed the lighting. A shaft of pale moonlight washed his body of colour and nuance, leaving Louseefa exposed and diminished. Something momentous had happened today. His feelings were conflicted and his attention piqued, and he didn't know why.

For the first time in thousands of years, Louseefa's sense of purpose was challenged. He felt less in control of events. Were these visitors from The Light a blessing or a curse?

Finding out, would decide whether his desire to conquer The Light was achievable, or just a foolish dream.

# Part Sixteen - Race to the Three Sisters

Zadkiel met with the pilgrims the next morning. Sam looked bleary-eyed and Zadkiel guessed that he had had difficulty sleeping. Sam could not be completely assured of Becky's survival in the Dark Mortal Realm. He knew that chance and luck would play a role, and the uncertainty ate at him and would do so until they were reunited.

"Good morning, everyone," Zadkiel said cheerily. "A wonderful morning for a flight. I see you've taken my advice and dressed warmly. You'll need it. We'll be flying high, and the flight will take approximately three days.

"Before we leave, I must tell you something I learnt last night. The Dark Fae, as you call him, has taken the StarLight portal to Piaf. My informant believes he is on his way here to stop you reaching the Sonciel."

This news alarmed the travellers. "Then we must leave now," Sam cried, troubled by the threat.

"We will," Zadkiel said, "I've met with the other Angelic Lords and Ladies of Light and warned them of the Fae's intentions. Should the Fae reach the First

World, and there seems no doubt of it, he will have difficulty breaking through the barrier that first barred your entry.

"If he manages to do this, he will then have four Angelic Light to deal with. Their combined power outmatches anything the Fae can throw at them, at least, that is what I hope. Whatever the case, the Fae does not know where we've gone and extracting the information from an Angel will be nigh impossible. They will flee from him, if necessary, and that will create further delay. So, time is not as limited as you think. All the Archives have been well hidden, and he cannot seek for clues without finding that source material. We'll get to the Three Sisters before the Fae."

Zadkiel's confidence strengthened Sam's resolve. He would find the Sonciel; he would go to the Mortal Realm and rescue Becky. Anything else was unthinkable.

All was now ready for them to leave, save for one detail. Zadkiel explained this detail by demonstration; shape shifting into an enormous seabird with taloned feet, a bird capable of carrying ten passengers and their backpacks. Hearing the bird speak in Zadkiel's voice was disconcerting to say the least.

"Forgive the mishmash of species, but I will need taloned feet to enable a take-off from solid ground, once I'm in the air I'll transform them into webbed feet for travel over water.

"I'm going to fly high, so high that oxygen will be in short supply. That will not hurt me, but, without protection of some kind, you would all die. So, while I fly, I will surround you with a hermetically sealed and pressurised bubble, as if you were travelling in a high-altitude aircraft. The air should last you several hours and when your oxygen needs renewing, I will descend, lower the barrier, and give you a little relief from the cold. My abilities only go so far, and I can only warm you a little. We will repeat the process as many times as is necessary.

"Are you clear on what is about to happen? Three heads nodded vigorously, Sam marvelling at the beauty of the bird Zadkiel had become, despite the disconcerting claws. Huge — as large as a humpback whale — with enormous wings, it seemed to him that birds were playing a big part in the lives of the pilgrims since they died during Armageddon, and before (in John's case). He missed Guardian, a beautiful hawk that accompanied his first pilgrimage; in reality, a shape shifted Becky sent to protect him. They merged in his heart and soul and would ever be thus, as free spirit, as life itself.

"I'll rest on the ground," Zadkiel advised, "but you will still need a ladder to ascend to my back.

"Sam, you can find one in the barn at the back of your cottage." Sam dashed off and soon returned with a sturdy ladder that would easily do the job. "It's so light," Sam marvelled. "Alright guys let's climb."

The three travellers climbed the ladder wearing their backpacks and with thick blankets slung over their shoulders. Even with the great bird lying on the ground, the climb was arduous, at least three metres, perhaps more. The extra weight they each carried didn't help, and the three passengers arrived at the top breathing hard. They sat down between the wings and found that Zadkiel had provided an outgrowth on his back which they could securely grasp during times of turbulence. There was also a sturdy support for attaching the ladder. *Zadkiel thinks of everything*, Sam thought.

"Are we ready?" Zadkiel shouted. "Yes," the three friends said in unison.

"Okay, hold on tight, until we reach cruising altitude." Zadkiel stood up and began to run; run faster than a mortal bird had ever run. He would need to, to create the lift his wings needed. One massive flap of those wings and Zadkiel took off. His passengers held on as the bird quickly ascended and the air grew colder as the slipstream buffeted them. Then, in an instant, the biting wind ceased. Zadkiel had created the hermetic bubble which would allow the passengers to breathe.

The passengers felt a warmth growing beneath them, the higher they rose, but the air was still frigid and becoming colder the higher they rose. It was not easy holding on tightly and at the same time covering themselves with blankets, but they managed it. Once Zadkiel's flight levelled out, they let go of their handholds and adjusted the blankets.

The passengers settled down for a long flight and Sam, weary from his lack of sleep, soon dozed off.

Their journey to the Three Sisters had begun.

## Serpent's Breath

The Fae was alone. Everyone had deserted him. The Black Shield had all but disbanded, so many having defected to the God Movement or been killed by the mobs taking control of the StarLight portal network. His Advisory Council was nowhere to be found, many having fled through the portals to hide on other worlds of Light. He did not need them, any of them.

What he had to do, he would do alone. But what could he do to assert his dominance over The Light? His madness and paranoia provided the answer. He would put the fear of God — of him — into every soul on every inhabited world. His thoughts became more muddled, his visions increasingly outlandish and preposterous. He settled upon a chimera creature from his childhood, from memories born of ancient myths and tales in popular culture.

The Dark Fae would become a dragon, no, a serpent. The Realm of Light would learn to fear the Dark Serpent. Oh yes, they would bow to him, and if not, they would burn. He would transform where the gathered peoples of The Light on Floriana could see him; see him and fear him.

Without another thought, the Fae obliterated the main window in his quarters and jumped out, descending to the ground with a declaration of awesome sound that reached all ears in the city. Heads turned and thousands of eyes and ears heard the Dark Fae's declaration of war — against his own people.

"Behold, Children of The Light. You will not love me, but by God, you will fear me. Every world of Light will feel the burning breath of the Dark Serpent." The occasional giggle did nothing to enhance the drama of the moment.

Instantly, the Fae began to transform into something larger, something more terrible than any child's nightmare could ever conjure. The head and body of a legged serpent, wings of a giant bat, scaled, armoured, and spiked from head to lashing tail, all in deepest, Darkest black, save for its eyes, which were the chilling red of blood. The nature of this fantastic beast said much about the disordered Fae's flight from reason and reality.

As large as a blue whale, the Dark Serpent lifted into the sky, its mighty wings obliterating the sun as the creature flew overhead.

Swooping low over the crowd of God Movement supporters, the serpent gave the appalled onlookers a touch of its power. With an ear-splitting roar the scalding breath of the beast left a trail of death and destruction in its wake. The breath of the beast was not fire but heat, terrible heat, that burnt or melted everything it touched. Tents burned and people crumbled instantly into ash.

James was one of the appalled onlookers. The path of the beast had narrowly missed his tent. "It's the mad Fae. Dear God, he's going to burn us all," a panicked man screamed as he rushed by. People were running aimlessly in all directions, desperate to escape the breath of the serpent.

James stood, transfixed, helplessly watching the destruction of all his hopes for The Light. How had it come to this? The Fae was worse than the Dark, much worse. He was here.

Over the next hour, James received reports of the serpent's destructive path across the city and wider afield. And then came the appalling news. The Fae had attacked the StarLight Centre and flown through the largest portal to Piaf. James knew what this meant. The Fae was heading to the First World to stop the pilgrims reaching the Consciousness, the Sonciel.

What he did next, served as a rock thrown into the centre of a pool. Spreading waves of change and chance were set in motion; no telling what the outcome might be. Would those waves slowly subside; or would they become tsunamis of division and loss that swept The Light away?

The warning must be given. James called his partner and 2IC, and, together, they found a quiet place in the Headquarters tent where James told Charles of his misgivings. "I must warn the Angels of Light, dear heart. They need to know that the Fae is coming. Watch outside for me and ensure that no one comes near while I speak with Zadkiel."

James removed a heavy metal case from a locked trunk and opened it. Inside was something that looked remarkably like an old-fashioned two-way radio. But this was no ordinary communicator. Supplied by the Lords, the device worked in the same way that portals worked. God power enabled speech between different worlds and even different universes if necessary. The sophistication was way beyond James's technical ability, and the ability of anyone else in The Light.

James activated the communicator and sent the warning signal to Zadkiel, who answered promptly. James told him of the Fae's dangerous and bizarre behaviour, his shape shifting into a massive flying serpent, and that he was coming to the First World.

"You are sure that he is coming?" Zadkiel asked.

"As sure as I can be, without following the serpent's tail," James replied. "He's taken the StarLight portal to Piaf, where, no doubt, he will rampage a little to show the people who's boss. But even if he did this on every world of Light it would not unduly delay him. He is coming."

Zadkiel thought for a moment. "This is evil news, but not beyond our expectations. I and the pilgrims will leave early tomorrow as planned. I'll make sure the Fae cannot follow us.

"Have faith James. We will bring God back to The Light. Have you informed the other contacts that the Fae may attack their worlds? They need to take precautions."

"I'll do that now my Lord. I thought it prudent to contact you first."

"Thank you, James. And we know each other well enough to dispense with formality. No more my Lord. My friends call me Zadkiel."

"Thank you my..., Zadkiel. I'll make those calls now. Have a safe and successful trip." The call ended and James quickly informed the other worlds of the Fae's passage. Whilst speaking with the contact on Piaf, James heard screaming and confusion in the background and knew that the news was coming too late to save those who were dying as he listened.

James recalled Charles to his side, stood, and embraced him tightly, sighing out his grief. "What a bloody mess," James lamented. "I warned Piaf too late. People were dying as I gave the news. It was horrible. At least the other worlds have a chance to take precautions but how do we protect ourselves from something so monstrous?"

"At present we can't. But some time in the future we may have champions worthy of the fight." Charles gave James a kiss on the forehead. "Have faith James. God and the Angels of Light will return and rid us of the Fae and the Dark."

"You're the second person today to tell me to have faith. Zadkiel said the same thing. Perhaps, I'm no longer fit to do this job."

"That's not true," Charles said with vigour. "You can't carry everyone's grief and suffering on your shoulders. We all have to share the burden, and we will.

"Forget about fighting. Fighting can't help us now. Standing together and helping each other can. You should focus on leading the Movement by encouraging and supporting people, not training them for a war we can't win. Leading the recovery is a big enough job for anyone.

"Why not tell the crowd to disperse, go home, and wait for news from the First World." Charles had said all he could say. It was up to James now.

James sat silently for a long time, stroking his part-ner's hand unconsciously, and staring into his startling blue eyes. Then he sighed, and this time his sigh spoke of acceptance and understanding. "You're right of course. If my thinking had been clearer, I would have seen the truth of it long ago and much more persua-sively asked people to return home."

James stood and embraced the man he loved, for a second time. "Thank you, Charlie. Okay, enough talk. Let's start helping the people outside."

James locked the communicator in its trunk, and taking Charles's hand walked out of the tent.

*****

The Fae felt elated. Such power, such wild abandonment. Each building destroyed, each soul obliterated, was as food for his megalomania and madness. The Dark Serpent flew towards the StarLight Centre and surveyed the destruction below. The burning buildings and piles of ash in the streets spoke tellingly of the Fae's terrible power.

A packed crowd of terrified Light surrounded the Centre, all jostling and fighting together to pass through the portals and escape. For most, there would be no escape.

Without warning the serpent swooped upon the crowd, bestowing death with the touch of its breath. Obstacles crumbled before it, people burnt to ash. The serpent spared no one, women, children, or men. Only those on the periphery, 200 at best, lay wounded, writhing on the ground, moaning with pain from limbs either horribly disfigured or burnt to stumps.

And as it flew into the entrance hall of the StarLight Centre, its massive wings scythed through walls and shops on either side. The serpent shrank, though still massive, and approached the largest portal, leaving large piles of ash in its wake. Shrinking again, the Serpent flew through the portal and emerged in the unsuspecting world of Piaf.

The Dark Serpent expanded, and the murderous process was repeated, repeated on every world of Light. Before leaving each world, the serpent announced in the Fae's booming voice, "I am the Dark Fae, the Dark Serpent. I am your God and your future. Bend to my will or die."

On his path to the First World, the Dark Serpent murdered tens of thousands and laid waste to entire cities and towns. This was no longer a Heavenly realm. Not Nirvana, not any kind of resting place for love and peace. The Dark Fae had recreated a new Hell to match the Hell of the Dark Realm.

Only the hope that God would return, kept people sane. For those who lost hope, the promise of Heaven was lost, along with their sanity.

After many hours of senseless destruction and death, the Fae finally passed through the portal to the First World. The Dark Serpent was, for a time, no more, and a smaller, less frightening being, stood in utter darkness. The Dark Fae raised his hand, and it glowed brightly, sufficient to light the space. What is this? A prison? The Fae screamed, "you cannot hold me. Open these walls and let me out. I command it!"

Nothing happened. "Angels of Light, where are you?" The Fae said in a sing-song voice, accompanied by giggles. He screamed, "if you won't obey me, I will destroy the wall and the First World along with it."

Still nothing happened. The Fae tried everything he could think of to shatter his prison. Absolute vacuum and maximum pressure would not work because the portal was still open. He tried terrible heat, enough to melt rock, and nothing happened. After several failed attempts he finally found the answer. He tried low-frequency, mega vibration and explosive force together directed at the wall, and it shattered.

The Fae saw in front of him another wall and tried the same approach to break through. It did not work. The wall stood strong and unscathed. Somehow this wall defeated everything the Fae threw at it.

He explored above the balustrade onto the observation deck, shrunk to the size of a bee. He searched every connecting corridor and room for a way out. Nothing, no obvious doors, no seams, no fractures or weaknesses. This place was hewn from solid rock.

The Fae's exasperation built. His muddled thinking was overwhelmed by the strength of his confinement. He sat with his back against the wall, looking like a labourer taking his rest. Tears fuelled by frustration and rage coursed down his cheeks. The open portal lay before him. No! I can't go back. I won't go back defeated. There has to be a way.

Hours passed and the Fae drifted off to sleep. He sat there asleep in the darkness, oblivious to his confinement. And with the passage of several hours, his tortured mind rested and recovered a semblance of rationality.

He awoke in darkness and remembered his confinement, but this frustrated him no longer. For during his sleep, the Fae had dreamt an amazing thing. Where overwhelming power, size, and force had failed, a more subtle approach might work.

Standing, the Fae collected himself for a moment, visualised what he needed to do, and slowly disappeared, evaporated completely.

But he had not disappeared. To an observer it would seem that the Fae had evaporated; but the Fae was still present. He was present as a blizzard of elementary sub-atomic particles, without charge or mass, or any other feature that could interact with the atoms that formed the wall. The Fae had become the improbable, something unknown to mortal science that once was.

Each particle was rational and attentive to his will. At fantastic speed, the particles moved through the wall, no need to dodge atoms on the way. Yet it took some hours to reach the other side.

The particles emerged outside the wall in vibrant sunlight. Each particle could see and assess its surroundings. Staying in his nebulous state, the Fae floated over the surrounding landscape finding a few empty cottages and a large stone-built complex more distant.

The Fae assumed that this building, given its size, formed the living quarters of the Angels. His particles passed through the walls and scattered throughout every room searching for the Lords or an indication of where they had gone.

He found nothing but spartan furnishings, simple comforts, and silence. The traitors and the Angels had gone. How could they live in such squalor? The Fae would not lower himself to the level of servants. When this was all over, he would build the grandest of palaces, as befitting his divinity, even if he had to exhaust The Light to do it.

At the centre of the stone complex the Fae found an immense room, the walls lined with shelves, and rows of huge tables and chairs which he guessed were designed for research. It looked a lot like a medieval scriptorium designed for giant monks. He imagined those aging monks painstakingly creating their illuminated manuscripts.

He had found the famous Archives. Except, there were no Archives. The shelves were bare. The Lords have hidden them from me. Why do that, unless there was something in the Archives that might aid his search for the traitors.

The Fae's frustration was beginning to build again. I must have missed something. Nothing disappears without a trace.

In desperation, he scattered himself throughout the region, looking for a clue, for anything that he had missed. The Fae had created a hive mind, his consciousness choreographing the search, collecting, and storing any snippet of information, any sight or sound that might point the way to the answers he sought. Each particle incorporated the memory of clothing touching the particle, so that upon reuniting, the Fae would reappear fully dressed. He learnt this little trick the hard way, having appeared naked on the outside of the wall after his first deconstruction attempt.

After lengthy investigation, the sun was declining toward the horizon. In an hour it would be dark. The Fae's consciousness recalled his questing particles, and the Fae reappeared in the communal space of the Angels' spartan edifice. The Fae then increased to match the size of an Angel, primarily to make his overnight stay more comfortable.

He had gathered himself to this space for a reason. Sifting in his mind the meagre pile of clues, he found only two that were worthy of investigation. The first was in this room, a globe showing the continents, seas, rivers, and mountain ranges of the First World.

The traitors had left this place because they knew where to go. But they would need a guide and transportation. One Angel, at least, must be travelling with them.

The Fae studied the globe. The complexity was spectacular. The surface was not flat, but rather three-dimensional. Exquisite details in colourful 3D provided so much more information than a two-dimensional map would do. The Fae realised that once he determined where the traitors were heading, he could use the globe to show him how to get there.

There was a mark on the globe in the centre of one of the continents, with a name written beside it; but the Fae could not read the script. He searched the globe for other marks, not associated with rivers or mountains and found none. Even the Fae's less than rational mind, could deduce that the mark represented his location. The continent was large, the largest on the globe, and far from any other continent. Wherever the traitors were travelling, it would take days to get there, even flying.

The second clue was more enigmatic — two giant footprints, a right and left foot — in a place where they should not be. Only two prints. It was as if an Angel, yes, it must be an Angel, had alighted there, took flight again, or simply disappeared.

The Fae giggled. He was enjoying himself, solving little mysteries and familiarising himself with the place where the Angels of Light had lived for thousands of years. But no more. They were surplus to requirements;

no longer needed; relics of a dead past. And enemies of The Light. They were helping the traitors from Floriana and that made them traitors as well. And for their disobedience, they would die.

*****

The Fae had slept soundly, the sleep of one who felt neither guilt, nor shame, nor anxiety. The sleep of the just and the good.

In his disordered mind, the Fae *was* the only good, the only champion of truth and justice — *His* truth and *His* justice — all else was sacrilege. Today he would learn the false truth of his enemies. He needed to know the whereabouts of the false God.

After a large breakfast, courtesy of the Angels' cold room and pantry, the Fae prepared himself to explore the mystery of the footprints.

He decided to walk for a change. The weather justified a walk as it was a beautiful day, not a cloud in the sky. A majestic heavenly vault in sapphire blue, shielding the Heaven beneath. The juxtaposition was amusing, the Fae giggling at the prospect of making this a living hell for the Angels. He just needed to find them.

It was not a long walk, but he would have to cross the river and head for a line of hills he could see in the distance on his left. He entered a forest of tremendous trees. They were gargantuan, like oversized ancient oaks, and they formed an unbroken canopy either side of the river. He had seen no animal or bird life as he walked. The silence was unnerving, as if the forest had taken a breath and held it. The Fae assumed any creatures who came near him could smell the Dark Serpent upon him. *No wonder they fear me.* He giggled.

The river blocked his path. It was broad and running swiftly, but the Fae continued walking, his flying ability just keeping his feet above the water. *A neat trick,* he thought with amusement.

It was now a straight walk to the line of hills where he would find the footprints. The particles that found them were leading him unerringly toward his target. And much sooner than he expected, the Fae was there.

The footprints were beneath a deep overhang of rock, jutting out of the side of one of the hills and concealed by a thick copse of trees. He would never have found them, but for the billions of inquisitive Fae particles sent out to saturate the region.

The Fae bent down and inspected the footprints noting that they were side by side, left and right, facing the wall at the rear of the overhang. The feet were clearly unshod, noting the impressions of each toe. He tentatively touched one of the prints, fearing to damage it but he soon realised that the prints were solid indentations. Just like dinosaur footprints, he remembered seeing when he was a mortal child.

*Very odd.* The footprints were there for a particular purpose. To open a door, perhaps? To activate some other process? The Fae removed his footwear and, ensuring his foot size matched that of the prints, carefully stepped into the indentations. He felt a tingling sensation. Nothing happened. He waited several minutes. Still nothing.

The Fae sat down and pondered the matter. The prints were the lock. The size of the foot was not the correct key, neither he assumed was the weight. What else could the footprints read from the sole of the foot that would disengage the lock. The answer was obvious, even to the Fae's incoherent mind. What he lacked in methodical reasoning, he made up for with cunning. The devious mechanism was in the genes. The lock recognised the entity standing in the lock by its genetic signature and provided access for the genetic makeup of the Angels. And only the Angels.

If he was correct, then the lock would never recognise him, no matter how long he stood in the footprints. *Damnation!* The Fae was becoming frustrated again.

Then he stopped, stood absolutely still, and, with a cunning smile realised that the answer to his dilemma had been within him all along. The Fae sat and put on his footwear. Then, visualising what he most wanted at that moment, slowly dematerialised, and disappeared.

The Fae particles explored every cubic centimetre of the hill and burrowed into the ground beneath. For the first few minutes they found nothing. And then when he was starting to think that the search would, indeed, find nothing, a single particle stumbled into a void and found something.

All the Fae's particles rushed to the space, though the Fae remained insubstantial. His conscious mind could see and hear, and he studied the large room that the particle had found. Both vestibule and living area, the space was sparingly furnished, though a grand marble statue graced the centre of the room.

Beautifully carved, the ancient statue depicted a mighty being, presumably *the* God that exiled Louseefa, wielding a mighty sword, about to behead a *writhing serpent*. The image was much too prescient for comfort and the invisible Fae turned away in disgust. Nothing else in the room attracted the Fae's attention so he directed his particulate body to enter one of the connecting rooms, the one he chose situated on the opposite wall, beyond the foul statue.

He had found the hidden Archive. The huge space was a replica of the room he had found in the Angels' living quarters. But this time the shelves were laden with scrolls and ancient manuscripts. As before, the space housed oversized research tables, the lighting provided by a glowing ceiling. There was no one here. The tables near him were empty.

Then the Fae saw several scrolls resting haphazardly on a table at the rear of the room. He floated closer. Why were the scrolls lying here on the table, and not returned to the shelves? Why was one scroll partially unrolled, as if something, or someone, had disturbed the researcher? And where was the researcher now?

The Fae's conscious particles searched the room and found no sign. There were no doors in the walls, so where did the researcher go? The particles searched through the walls and finally found what the Fae was looking for, a small space, like a priest's hole, with an exit tunnel ascending toward the surface. The Fae floated into the tunnel and followed it upwards only to find the way blocked by a wall of solid rock. Walls could not delay him. He poured through the fabric of the wall like a wraith and reached the surface, where he saw a giant figure racing away through the trees. *Got you*!

As if from nowhere, the Dark Serpent popped into existence, felling trees, and scorching hill and earth as it grew to massive size. The serpent rose high into the air and saw its enemy running through the trees. The Angel would know something big was coming. The sound of crashing trees would tell him as much.

"You cannot escape me Angel of Light," the Fae's voice boomed across the treetops. "Surrender, or everything you know and love will burn."

The figure kept running. *Why doesn't he shape shift and fight me*? The thought that the Angel might be scared of him, energised the Fae, setting his brain atingle. The serpent rose and sped ahead of the Angel and breathed upon the trees, blocking his escape with fire.

There could be no escape. The Angel stopped running and turned away from the scorching flames. He hung his head in defeat and despair. The serpent shrank and lowered to the ground, breaking trees on the way as it shifted from serpent to Fae. He stood behind the Angel in the serpent-made clearing.

"Turn around and let me see your miserable face," the Fae commanded. "Or are you not man enough to face me?"

The Lord turned and stared directly into the Fae's eyes. The Fae blinked. "A woman? A Lady of Light. How quaint. And which one are you?"

Defiantly, she declared, "I am the Lady Seraphine. How dare you trespass upon our world of consolation."

The Fae exploded. "*Your* world? *Your* world? No!" The Fae screamed. "Not your world, not any longer. You have already defiled your consolation, your isolation, by letting the traitors in. And now you look to supplant me by helping them.

"This will not happen. Where are the traitors?"

"I have no idea where any visitors are," which was the truth. Are they not in their cottages? I know nothing as I do not meet with the other Angels, my brothers and sisters. I prefer my own company." This was not the truth, and the Fae sensed the deception.

"Do angels make a habit of lying? I must say, I'm shocked.

"Now, enough banter. Where are the traitors, where are they heading? If you don't tell me what I need to know, I will forcibly extract the information from you. And you wouldn't like it; not the way I will do it. *Giggle, giggle.*"

The Lady, though seemingly beaten, stood defiant and remained silent. "All right, witch, you give me no choice." The Fae seemed to evaporate like steam from a kettle as his conscious, subatomic particles flooded the air and violated the Angelic body. The particles now interacted with the very fabric of Seraphine's internal world.

She went rigid, not knowing what was happening. Too late she tried to resist. The pain was exquisite as the particles explored every atom of her body, inflaming pain receptors and violating her very soul. Still, she stayed silent.

The particles entered her brain and sought out neurones as they flashed and fired, and slowly, the Fae saw what he yearned to see — memories of a meeting between the Angels and the traitors, division between the Lords and Ladies, a scrap of paper, a poem so meaningful to her, so dangerous.

This memory perplexed the Fae. Why should a poem be so significant? What does she fear? The Fae particles quested deeper and learnt nothing more. They searched the fabric of her robe and found, hidden in a secret pocket, the incriminating scrap of paper.

At once, Seraphine knew that her resistance had been in vain. She cried a desolate cry of anguish. Overcome by her failure and suffering, Seraphine collapsed to the ground and fainted.

The Fae reincorporated, searched Seraphine's robe, and found the artfully hidden pocket. He extracted the paper and unfolded it. Scrawled on the page, with crossings out and additions, was a poem, written in Sam's hand, though the Fae did not recognise the handwriting. "*The Three Sisters*? What's so significant about three sisters?"

The Fae quickly read the poem, then reread it, trying to interpret the meaning. And then, he knew. "*Three sisters high, the doorway in the sky, meet the source of life... this poem describes the way to the Consciousness. Stairway... The three sisters are mountains. Mountains appear on maps, or a globe of the world. The globe*!

He looked at the unconscious Lady lying at his feet. *I wonder why she didn't fight back. It's almost as if she sacrificed herself, as if she knew that she could not win.* The Fae giggled, uncertain what to do with her. He could not leave her free. No telling what mischief she might get up to. He decided to take her with him, back to the Angels' residence and bind her. He would be long gone before she freed herself from her bonds.

The Fae and Seraphine's body lifted into the air and returned at speed to the residence. He deposited her in the communal living space, creating psychic bonds that would eventually free her, long after he had left to find the Three Sisters.

Then the Fae rushed to the globe that had so fascinated him earlier. He might spend hours locating the Three Sisters in the traditional way, so extraordinarily complex and detailed was it. But the Fae was not limited by tradition. He had billions of eyes to do the searching for him.

Fading once again into particles, the Fae enveloped the globe, simultaneously identifying every feature upon its surface. In one millisecond, he had found the mountains that led to the doorway in the sky.

The Fae had found identifying features on the land-mass that the Angels called Estrada, a continent on the other side of the world. The traitors would need several days to reach that continent; longer still to find and climb the correct mountain.

He need not hurry. Tonight, he would eat and rest comfortably. Tomorrow, he would enter the race to the Three Sisters — and the traitors would not know that he was coming after them, until it was too late.

## Seraphine's Pebble

Seraphine awoke from her long, disturbed sleep. Every part of her ravaged body screamed with pain and violation. How long have I slept? Where am I… what happened? For some time, she lay there, disoriented and disturbed by the visions that plagued her reawakening. Pain, fire, it was all so confusing.

And then she remembered. The flying serpent, the terrible heat, the Fae's power and his disappearance into nothingness, the entering and her violation, the poem, The Three Sisters…

Seraphine screamed in mental agony. The Fae knew, the serpent knew and was now flying to Estrada to stop Zadkiel and the pilgrims. "I have to stop him. We have to stop him," she screamed aloud. Seraphine cried bitter tears at the frustration of it all.

Seraphine's scream of anguish had been heard. A Lady and two Lords of Light rushed into Seraphine's room and attempted to calm her agitation. "The Fae knows. He will kill Zadkiel and the others. Please! We can't let this happen." The other Lords looked at each other, confused by Seraphine's outburst.

Shining, golden haired Aurora, along with Haniel and Anael, soothed Seraphine's heated outcries, gently willing her to slow her breathing and galloping heart.

Over several minutes, Seraphine's agitation subsided — and then she burst into tears again. "I failed. The Fae is more powerful than we believed. One Lord of Light, alone, cannot defeat him. And now, he is flying to Estrada to kill Zadkiel. He and the pilgrims do not know that the Dark Serpent is coming for them…"

Seraphine's voice trailed off as the appalling truth of her words threatened to send her over the brink again.

Aurora spoke up. "Seraphine, please tell us everything that has happened, everything that you can remember." Seraphine dampened her tears and told what she could recall.

She told them of being disturbed in the secret Archive; of escaping through the tunnel; the flying serpent blocking her escape with fire; the overwhelming power that she could not resist; the Fae's dissolution and her agonising violation.

The others were shocked. "How could he violate you? How dare he do this to a Lady of Light," Haniel cried.

"The Fae dissipated like steam, and then I felt him inside me, every part of me. I dared not use power to fight back. It would have been futile. So, I let him believe that I was no danger to him. His disappearance trick is something new. None of us have ever attempted anything remotely like it. He found the poem. He is on his way to The Three Sisters."

"Then we can do nothing," Anael said. "We can't defeat what we can't see."

"No!" Seraphine cried. "We can't abandon Zadkiel and the others. We must learn the Fae's new trick. Five Lords and Ladies of Light, together, can defeat the Fae. We must learn this knew power of dis-corporation and fly to Estrada as swiftly as we are able."

Aurora, Haniel and Anael looked at each other, indecision and doubt written in their eyes. Finally, Aurora could stand the silence no longer. "Seraphine is right. Zadkiel is the best of us. We cannot abandon him and hand The Light Realm to the Fae. We've wavered for too long. We either seize this opportunity or fade into oblivion. A simple choice.

"I'm going with Seraphine," said Aurora decisively. Haniel was the next to relent, leaving only Anael to squirm with indecision.

"How do we know if we can perform this new trick?" He asked. "I don't think I can do it."

Seeing that the others were accepting her call for action, Seraphine re-entered the debate. "When the Fae disappears, he must still have some substance. How else could he pass through solid rock, enter my body and reemerge as the tangible Fae? What if, the Fae doesn't disappear into nothingness. What if he transforms into the tiniest of particles, far smaller than an atom? The Fae's mind must still control his particles because he can dissolve and reconstitute at will.

"The fact that we have never thought to do this before, should not prevent us from trying."

*****

Several hours later, after Seraphine had rested and nourished her body and mind, she, Aurora and the

Lords gathered together in the Common Room and calmed themselves, attentive to the task they were attempting.

"Think of nothing but your body," Seraphine whispered. "Visualise it dissipating into billions of tiny particles, control them with your mind."

The first attempts were erratic and not at all convincing. Aurora and Haniel learnt quickly, Anael was having trouble. "Anael, you are failing because you believe you can't do it," Seraphine admonished. "But you can do it, you can. Just believe."

Slowly, as the Angels grew more familiar with the process of control and the feelings involved — including the embarrassment of reconstituting naked, an omission which they quickly rectified — they felt confident to take their new skills further. They learnt to pass through furniture by partially dissolving at the touch of something solid.

The real test would be solid rock. They first tried passing through the dividing walls of the dwelling, with immediate success. But these walls were not more than a handbreadth thick and posed no obstacle at all.

An hour later, the four Angels of Light stood in the Visitor Vetting Room. Seraphine looked at the broken wall that had sealed off the Portal Room. "See how the Fae used force to break this wall," Seraphine explained. "But the wall in front of you is undamaged. He could not break it. This wall is many metres thick, solid rock. So how did the Fae get out of this room?"

"He passed through the wall," the other three said together, delighted with the revelation.

"And if he can do it, so can we," Seraphine said triumphantly. "Remember, it may take many hours to pass through, so keep calm and you will eventually emerge outside."

The four Lords of Light stood silently together, then slowly faded and disappeared from view.


Several hours later, Seraphine and Aurora were the first to appear in the sunlight. They were the most driven. The next to appear was Haniel, an hour after the others. The three waited for Anael to appear. Another hour passed and there was no sign of him. Seraphine said as she slowly faded, "I'm going back for him. This may take a while."

Seraphine re-entered the wall and spread her particles wide to ensure she did not miss Anael as they passed each other.

Two hours into her rescue mission she detected his soulful signature. Her conscious particles rushed towards it. There he was, a swarm of his particles converged in a small space. Seraphine's consciousness reached out and touched the mind of Anael. "What has happened?" she asked. Seraphine's voice in his mind startled Anael. When he spoke, he sounded flustered and tired. "I've been dodging bits of the wall for hours, and now several of my particles are trapped in that large ball of energy. What am I doing wrong."

If Seraphine had a mouth at that moment she would have smiled. "Anael, you don't have to dodge the constituents of the wall. Think of yourself as insubstantial and pass right through them. Try it to free your trapped particles. It will work." He stopped all movement and willed his particles to escape their prison by floating through the streams of energy. It was as if his particles were hidden from the wall and not present at all.

"It worked," Anael's voice sounded relieved. "Thank you, Seraphine, for coming. I might never have escaped, but for you."

"Okay, let's keep the conversation for later. We've got a date with the other side of the wall. As fast and as straight as we can."

For those waiting outside the wall, their wait lasted another 90 minutes. Inside the wall and at the speeds the particles were moving, time was relative and seemed to pass more slowly. But, at last, all four Lords and Ladies of Light stood on the other side of the wall, Anael looking sheepish as he explained his elementary error.

Enthused by the success of their newfound skill, the Angels returned to the residential Common Room.

Aurora was especially animated. "Yesterday I was asleep and didn't even know it. Today I feel more alive and involved than I have in thousands of years.

"I don't know what you threw into the water, Seraphine, but it certainly stirred things up. I no longer feel threatened. We have a purpose now. When do we leave for Estrada?"

"As soon as we can," Seraphine answered. "Before we go, there is one other thing I would ask of you. We must merge our bodies and minds, and thus our powers, into one body, one mind, and we should do it now. Fighting the Fae with the combined power of five Angels of Light, will be much more effective than acting separately. Will you do it, and whose body will act as the vessel?"

Aurora unsurprisingly was the first to answer the questions. "I will do it. We must. And who better to carry us than Seraphine, who woke us up. What say you, Haniel, Anael?"

The two Lords of Light waited a moment, not wishing to commit themselves until they were certain. Finally, they looked approvingly at each other as Haniel said, "Aye, we will do it. Seraphine will be our vessel."

"I must travel swiftly," Seraphine said, "faster than any bird has ever travelled and higher too, non-stop, all the way to Estrada. We must catch the Fae before he has a chance to attack the pilgrims. Prepare yourselves, we will merge within the hour.

The Lords separated and each went to their room. Seraphine stopped momentarily by an anonymous stretch of wall and waved her right hand. The stones parted to reveal a space, and lying within, a sword,

God's sword — the Celestial Sword. A weapon befitting supreme majesty. Beautifully crafted, bejewelled and shining with some hidden power. No one had dared touch that sword since God had left them. Seraphine was sure that the time was now right to wield it again. With this sword Zadkiel will defeat the Fae, she thought as she fastened the scabbard to her girdle. And then he would present the sword to the new God of Light, anointed by the Sonciel.

All was now ready. "Merge with me sister and brothers," Seraphine commanded. "Link your minds with mine. We have a long flight, and I will need to draw upon your strength to speed us to our goal." Not having done this before, they nervously awaited their turn to dissipate and merge. Each disappeared and gently entered into Seraphine, seeking the mind that would nourish their unity. Anael was the last to enter.

The totality they felt with the merging was breathtaking; all thoughts expressed through Seraphine, similarly, the other senses, sight, hearing, touch; everything absorbed and expressed as one being. The effect was exhilarating.

Seraphine walked outside. She conveyed a thought to her interior passengers. "Prepare yourselves. I am now going to transform into a swift bird of prey, large enough to carry your weight with ease, but small enough to cut through the upper atmosphere at speed. We do not need the pressure of atmosphere to fly."

And so, Seraphine transformed into a majestic bird with impressive, streamlined body and wings. The bird was large, perhaps the same mass as an Angel of Light, but science could not explain how this bird could fly, so high and so far.

Seraphine ensured to hold the Celestial Sword to herself, thereby acknowledging to the other Lords that she carried it. None demurred or questioned her decision to bring the sword. They all knew the immensity of the forces in play.

Seraphine lifted off. Her quadrupled flying power enabled her swift ascent into the thermosphere and disappearance from sight, so impossibly high did she fly. Following the faint echoes of the Fae's disturbing passage through the skies of the First World, Seraphine flew unerringly towards Estrada, towards a destiny that none of them could yet discern.

# Part Seventeen - The Agony of Ignorance

James was exhausted. The Fae, the Dark Serpent, had gone, disappeared through the portal to the First World. The Light welcomed this reprieve, but for those who knew the Fae's intentions, the doubts and fears they felt were just as destructive as the Serpent's rampage.

Every inhabited world of Light had felt the destroying breath of that foul serpent. Casualties and damage were immense. The cost in lives and livelihoods was incalculable, so great was the task of recovery. James felt that should the Fae return, they would know that the pilgrimage to the Sonciel had failed. The Light would never recover. He rested his weary head on the desk in his new office, within one of the otherwise deserted administrative buildings, and tried to sleep.

An hour later, Charles walked into the office without knocking and saw his partner sitting at his desk, apparently asleep. He tiptoed in and closed the door quietly. He sat down in front of the desk and waited, grieving for James and the terrible burden he carried. Charles had been labouring just as hard and he too was weary, but the buck stopped with James. Demands, decisions ad infinitum, the burdens of leadership never let up, and that came with a terrible cost.

After perhaps half an hour waiting in silence, Charles saw James stir, sit up and stretch, and look blearily around the office. He saw Charles sitting quietly opposite him, concern etched across his face. "Hi Charlie. I didn't hear you come in. Sorry, I shouldn't sleep in the middle of the day. Too much to…"

"Of course there's too much to do," Charles interrupted, "There will be too much to do for years, for who knows how long." He grabbed James's hand fiercely. "You've been rushing from crisis to crisis without a rest, travelling incessantly. You're so absorbed by the minutiae that you've lost sight of the bigger picture."

James was shocked by his partner's vehemence. "I… No, this is my responsibility. I've…" his voice trailed off.

"It's the responsibility of all surviving Children of The Light. We agreed this shortly after the serpent created such destruction. How can you have forgotten? You are not yourself.

"We have to believe that the pilgrimage will succeed. Until God returns The Light needs effective administration. We need a government whether the Fae comes back or not.

"Call a meeting of the Echelon Council and appoint Managers for all the critical areas of renewal and repair on every world of Light. We need to get people back to meaningful employment, get the children and older students back to school. Train doctors. Open hospitals, grow and distribute food. The list is long. You need skilled administrators to handle the logistics and keep oversight of first responders.

"All these things need dedicated teams on every world of Light. You may be in charge, but you can't do it all. Give others some responsibility." Charles stopped, feeling breathless after his impassioned speech.

"Hey, where did that come from?" James asked. "I'm just a little tired, nothing more. It's been hectic for both of us, but it will get better."

Charles had not finished. "No, it won't James. You're not God so stop trying to act like it." James attempted to protest.

"I'm afraid for you, alright," Charles admitted. "I can see what this is doing to you. I can't lose you, but I will if you keep this up. It's only been a few days and look at you. Exhausted, unable to think and see clearly. Unable to share responsibility. Unable to hear what others around you are saying.

"I can't stay and watch you killing yourself." Tears flooded his eyes and streamed down his cheeks.

James stumbled to his feet, his weariness expressed in every tremor and sway. "You would leave me?

Now? I need you, Charlie. Your support keeps me going."

"And that's why I can't stay," Charles wept bitterly. "I can't remain complicit in a crime you're committing upon yourself." He turned away and walked out of James's office.

It was brutal. It was shocking and he cursed himself for doing it. But he could see no other way to shake James from his suicidal path.

James fell heavily back onto his chair. Shock was too small a word to describe the horror and emptiness he felt. He was too tired to cry; too tired to think. He lay his head on his arms and trembled with the confused emotion of it all. As time passed, James's body stopped its trembling, his breathing slowed, exhaustion carried him away and he slept, for the first time in days.

*****

He awoke in complete darkness, realising he had fallen asleep in his office. *What time is it?* "Lights on," he said aloud. Nothing happened. *That's weird. The power was fine* — James checked the time — *12 hours ago*. He had slept for 12 hours. He checked his tablet communicator and saw it was almost dead. The power had been out for many hours, and it was 3.00 in the morning.

James stood up and held onto his desk to steady his balance. He needed a torch. There *was* a torch, somewhere. *Where was it? Think!* He fumbled about in the desk's drawers, hoping to feel the small device in the darkness. *Nothing!* There was one drawer left. He squatted and opened the drawer, checking every part. The drawer was almost empty. He reached further into the drawer and finally felt the familiar metal cylinder, right at the back in the very last corner he checked.

James sighed with relief. He drew it out and stood with a groan. Pressed the power switch. A strong beam of light illuminated a small painting on the far wall. Dropping the beam toward the floor, James followed the beam out of his office and walked the short distance to his quarters.

There was nothing he could do until morning. He went to his bedroom and silently opened the door, turning off the torch. He did not want to waken Charlie. Undressing as quietly as he could, James slipped beneath the sheets.

Absolute silence. No sound of breathing. James tentatively reached out to assure himself that Charlie was there.

He was alone in the bed. No Charlie. James sat up and called out his name. No answer.

*Where was he? He would have said...* and then a realisation that floored him. Confused memories of a heated argument the day before, and then, then Charlie walked out. He was gone. His anchor was gone.

James was having trouble organising his thoughts. Everything was a muddle. What was the argument about? He had been so tired. He remembered the vehemence in Charlie's voice, but the words, only occasional snippets, disjointed and maddeningly significant. What had he said?

James spent the hours until daybreak, lying awake, trying to organise his memories of yesterday's argument into something vaguely coherent. At the same time, he was grieving his partner's absence.

Finally, James understood why Charlie had left. He thought about the days since the serpent's rampage, how he had tried to single-handedly heal the worlds, reacting to events, meeting needs here and there and doing some good for those who crossed his path. Billions of others were left unaided.

Charles was right. He saw it now. He'd been running about like a headless chicken; unaware it was already dead. This was no way to rebuild a civilisation. It was unlike him not to delegate and make decisions by consensus. *It must have been the shock,* he thought, trying to find an explanation for his behaviour.

He determined to call a meeting of the Council as early as it could be arranged. Meanwhile, he would search for Charlie and beg him to come back.

First things first, he needed to get to the power station and find out what had happened. James got out of bed in a more positive frame of mind, had a cold shower to clear his head and dressed, wearing the cloak that denoted his rank. The long sleep had cleared his head and given him a sense of renewed purpose. He set out to find anyone who might be able to tell him what was going on.

There were no autocabs on the streets and he could not book a cab because his tablet had finally died. Perhaps the cabs too had died like his tablet. It was a long walk, and he did not reach the power station until mid-morning. It was becoming clear to James, that Floriana and the services that made it tick, were falling apart.

James looked at the impressive structure before him. The fusion power plant that provided all the power for the city and its surroundings was actually beautiful; Glass and rose gold metal, shining in the morning sunlight and shielding the power source within.

James had seen no one on the streets during his long walk, and that did not change when he entered the building. The place was silent, empty. He thought his best chance of finding help would be at the heart of the building, the Operations Centre that controlled the production and delivery of power.

James followed the signs, passing no one on the way. *Not good,* he thought, *how could I have been so blind to what was happening?* At last, he arrived at the impressive Operations Centre entry door. It was locked. He needed a genetic disc to open it. Taking out his disc he tapped it to the reader and, much to his surprise, the doors slid aside. His surprise was not because his disc *could* give him access, but rather, that it *did*. Where had the power for the reader come from?

He walked into the Centre. All the equipment seemed to be active. *They must have an internal, dedicated power system,* James realised, answering *the mystery of the door.* He looked around but could not see anyone. He began a search. It was not until he reached the centre of the large space that he heard voices.

"The reactor is creating power." A woman's voice. "The problem is on the external distribution side. The technicians needed to fix any issues haven't reported for work since the Fae's rampage." Another voice, speaking more softly, commented, but James couldn't make out the words. He hurried toward the voices and just before he arrived recognised one of the voices. He rushed around a wall of whirs and flashing lights and fell into Charlie's arms.

Momentarily startled, the two speakers soon realised who had arrived. "Charlie, I'm sorry for upsetting you. I was wrong." James looked into his lover's eyes, tears threatening to spill down his cheeks, "Please come back."

Charles returned the hug. "I never really left. How could I. You are my life. But I had to try and make you see reason. You must admit the ploy worked." He laughed out loud, so happy was he to see James much recovered.

James pushed him away and looked at Charlie's beaming face. "It was a ploy? You never had any intention of leaving me?" Silence reigned for an uncomfortable 30 seconds and then James laughed out his sheer relief. "It seems *tough love* can work. You *bastard*." James embraced Charlie fiercely. "Don't do it again," he whispered.

A loud clearing of her throat reminded them that someone else was present. They both turned to the woman dressed in the power centre uniform.

"James, this is Jan Grant, the manager of operations. Jan, this is…"

"I know who he is," she said with a welcoming smile. "Good to see you, Leader. Quite the one for dramatic entrances aren't you."

James looked sheepish. "Yes, sorry about that. I should have called out to let you know I was coming. I heard what you said about distribution issues. Is that a problem for the integrity of the reactor?"

"Not as yet. We have sufficient free space in storage to last for several more days," she said. "The problems are with the distribution network. The Fae damaged or destroyed a lot of infrastructure. The last working distribution station gave up the ghost last night.

"I can't contact any of the technicians."

"There must be a way to hook into the citywide public address system. Is there any kind of transmitter here that we could use?"

Jan slapped her forehead. "Of course. Why didn't I think of that? I should have. It's unforgivable."

"Don't punish yourself about it. Lots of us haven't been operating as we should. The shock of the Fae is to blame." James looked meaningfully at Charles.

"The public address system has a hardened and dedicated power supply, meant for just this eventuality. It should be working for the most part. But how do we hook the transmitter here into the system?"

Jan blushed. "Already done. For public safety reasons, you know."

"Okay then," James announced. Give me a moment to collect my thoughts. I'm going to address the people. Jan, could you go and turn on the transmitter and tell anyone who is listening that I will be speaking shortly. Ask them to ensure that their friends and family are able to hear my speech."

"Will do." Jan rushed off.

"Charlie, I want you at my side, just in case I forget to say something relevant."

"I'll always be at your side, you know that." He squeezed James's hand. "Why don't we give it fifteen minutes so that people have time to gather and listen?"

"As always, sage advice. Thank you." James returned the squeeze.

Fifteen minutes later James and Charles were seated with Jan in the Communications Space. There was no obvious microphone. "We can speak freely, Jan said, "I've turned the transmitter off until you are ready to speak."

James nervously held his page of speaking points. He had no time to write a proper speech. This may well be the most important moment of his life.

James nodded to Jan, and she turned on the transmitter. James began to speak.

"Dear friends, I am speaking from the Operations Centre within the Floriana Fusion Station. With me are the Manager of Operations, Jan Grant and my 2IC and partner, Christopher Boyce. This is James Reid speaking.

"This speech is long overdue and for that I am truly sorry. The shock of the Fae has left us all devastated, including myself.

"But I have woken up. Someone has reminded me why we are here, now, midst the destruction of all we hold dear. We have been gifted, by God, or by chance, to join together and heal the wounds we see all around us.

"The task seems insurmountable, endless, impossible. But The Light is where everything can be possible. We can't do this as souls acting alone. With the combined purpose of billions, we can make a real difference. The Fae has gone. In all likelihood, he will not come back. Whether he does, or not, we owe it to ourselves to make our own destiny and solve our own problems.

"How do we do this? Firstly, we need effective government and administration to triage priorities and organise responses. With that in mind I ask that all members of the Echelon Council meet in the Administrative Building, two days hence, at 10 o'clock in the morning. Once the power is back on, we can communicate more easily, so ensure that those who may not hear about this meeting get the news.

"Secondly, I plead with all those who are able, please return to your jobs. If you need help to make that happen, advise your local Councillor. We need farmers to return to the land to provide food. We need teachers to reopen the schools so that our children can continue their educations. We need doctors and medical teams to staff the hospitals, many of which are partially or completely closed. We need technicians and service providers to help repair our physical infrastructure and provide all of the services that our people expect. We urgently need electrical technicians to repair the electricity grid. We need manufacturers to start manufacturing again and small businesses to reopen.'

"If you have skills in administration, or you think you might like to contribute and learn new skills, advise your local Councillor. The Administrative Building is currently empty. I am the only occupant. I want the place buzzing with activity, with people dedicated to the health and welfare of all. Together, we can rebuild our world, and all the worlds of Light.

"So, my third request, is that we have faith in the essential goodness and decency of our people. Commit ourselves anew to the task of healing the wounds that divide us, to make The Light inviting again. I'll be working with you to make this a reality, and my office staff will always be available. On that note, if anyone thinks they may possess skills that can help me run a very busy office, and who think they might be able to work with a novice like me, get in touch. We can build something new, something good, together."

"Friends, one last thing. We have lived through days of great trial. Many of you have suffered and lost so much during this time. It may seem impossible to think of the world returning to any kind of normality, let alone that you might play a part in making it happen.

"My invitation is for you to take that leap of faith and help us heal and renew our world. In so doing, you may just find the healing that you and your family need as well.

"God bless you all. Believe. God *will* return."

James nodded to Jan, and she turned off the transmitter. He looked at Charles who was seated beside him. "How'd I do? Not too much was it?" Charles looked back in wonder. "You said it all. You *were* listening yesterday, or at least your heart was. No way was it too much. It was, it was wonderful, James." He threw his arms around his partner and embraced him with a fierceness that he had never felt before. Jan nodded her agreement with Charles's assessment and smiled with relief that rebuilding could now begin.

If they had been observing the city from above, they would have seen crowds of people emerge from their homes and stand together in the streets to listen to James's speech. Many people embraced while they hung on every word. The speech was what they needed to hear, they longed to hear.

When the public address system fell silent, an eerie hush fell over the city, as if time had paused. Then, a spontaneous cry of extraordinary intensity and passion broke the silence. Such passion had not been heard in The Light since the days of God. A billion souls began to chant *God will return,* over and over the chant repeated. It reached the extremities of the city and beyond, as more and more people heard the chant and joined in.

The chant penetrated every part of the city. It was even heard in the Operations Centre.

Over the next few hours, a great crowd converged on the Fusion Power Station and continued the chant. James emerged from the building and stood at the top of the entrance stairway in the bright morning sunshine; Charlie on one side, and Jan on the other. The three of them clasped hands and raised them over their heads to salute the multitude, ecstatic at the sight.

And so began the Great Renewal of the worlds of Light.

# Part Eighteen - The Shores of Estrada

Zadkiel alighted on a tropical beach at the southwestern edge of Estrada. The pilgrims looked at their surroundings in wonder. A placid azure and turquoise sea to their right and verdant tropical vegetation to their left, a vision straight out of a tourist brochure.

"Wow!" Rose cried in admiration, overcome by the untouched beauty around her. "This is amazing, the kind of place I've dreamed of for a holiday. Zadkiel, you've brought us to Paradise."

"Well, to be pedantic, I could say we were already living in Paradise," Zadkiel suggested, "but I know what you mean. This continent has never seen a chainsaw, never seen a developer, never seen tourists."

"One tiny side benefit of Armageddon, if I can call it that," Rose said with a chuckle. "I doubt many greedy, billionaire developers made it into The Light. What's that Bible story about camels and the eye of a needle?"

"Rose, you are young in the Light," John admonished gently. "It's never wise to treat a tragedy such as Armageddon so shallowly. Every failure to enter The Light, may be a tragedy for others, a partner or a family. We can never know the true circumstances of every individual who makes it into the media, notorious or otherwise." Rose lowered her eyes and kept quiet after that friendly rebuke.

Zadkiel entered the conversation. "Well said John. We'll rest here for a while, but the journey isn't over. We need to fly east along the coast until we reach the mouth of the river that we'll follow north to the Three Sisters.

"I'll drop the bubble and allow you to breathe the air. But please stay where you are. We're trespassing and the last thing we need is to draw attention to ourselves."

The air was much warmer, wafting as the gentlest of breezes, carrying the exotic scents of sea and land — the salty tang of the sea, mixed with an abundance of floral fragrances from the forest. The pilgrims stood up and stretched as the last leg of their flight had taken many hours. Sam winced as he tried to ease a cramp. "I never did like flying much. Aaaah, that's better."

The pilgrims ate and drank a little from their supplies and then lay back to rest in the warming sunlight. Sam looked up at a flawless blue sky, breathing the cleanest, most invigorating air he had ever breathed. Rose was right. It would be sacrilege to destroy such beauty and grandeur.

"Do many people live in this part of Estrada, Zadkiel?" He asked.

"No, most peoples prefer the woodland and savannah country much further to the north," Zadkiel replied. "It is closest to the climate and landscapes that their ancestors knew when they were mortal. We know very little about Estrada. The locals do eat meat however, so there must be some native wildlife for them to hunt."

Rose was about to make a quip about cannibals, but on this occasion, chose discretion over a cheap laugh. John and Sam looked at Rose, as if expecting her to say something. "What?" She said, irritation in her voice. "Gees, you get a reputation for making wisecracks…" John and Sam laughed uproariously, and Rose joined them a little later.

"Sorry, dear Rose, but you can't blame us," John chuckled.

"I'm having some difficulty understanding what the mirth is all about," Zadkiel said. "Humans are a strange and enigmatic species but endearing in their own way."

"Tasty as well," Rose quipped, setting John and Sam off again.

"Aah," Zadkiel remarked, getting the link with his mention of meat. "I think I understand the joke now. Alright, settle down pilgrims. We've got a three-hour flight ahead of us, so hold on tight."

Zadkiel, in his guise as the massive seabird, waddled into the sea and started running, augmented by the power of his wings, his great webbed feet churning the water at impossible speed.

Gaining the lift he needed to take off, the bird soared into the air, skimming a rocky headland that jutted far out into the water.

For most of their trip, the ocean had been placid, because as John observed and Zadkiel confirmed, the First World did not have a large moon as Earth did, there were no tides. Though a combination of temperature variations in the water, seismic activity, the world's rotation (28 Earth hours), and atmospheric conditions at sea, created enough disturbance to make life interesting for the few mariners on the First World. Only once were the travellers delayed, by a powerful, but swift moving storm that whipped up some impressive waves.

The flight along the coast was impossibly, and impressively scenic, as Zadkiel flew only 500 metres above the water. The lush tropical rainforest met endless sandy beaches, lapped by limpid waters, the colour changing from azure, to turquoise, to green, to deep blue. It was all quite magical, and the travellers hardly said a word during the flight.

At last, a wide and deep estuary appeared, signalling the end of their short flight along the coast. Zadkiel circled overhead until he found a suitable place to land, a sheltered cove that enabled Zadkiel to gently meet the water and glide to shore. He waddled up onto the sandy beach. "We'll stay here for a few hours. Please climb down to the sand when you are able and take your backpacks with you. I'll then transform into my usual form. We need to discuss what we might expect on our way upriver.

Sam and John untied the ladder and Zadkiel lowered to the ground so that his passengers could safely descend. One by one the travellers climbed down to the sand. The last to feel the assurance of ground was Rose, who knelt down and pretended to kiss the sand. "Oh, thank you, thank you. It's so good to be back on the ground. No offence Zadkiel, but flying is for the birds."

"None taken," Zadkiel said as he transformed into an Angel of Light. "I'm not all that keen on flying either but needs must." He gave Rose a conspiratorial smile.

The travellers settled themselves and ate from their supplies, the meal augmented by a bottle of white wine, fruit juice and drinking glasses, that Zadkiel presented with a flourish. "Neat trick Zadkiel," Rose said, suitably impressed. "I could have made a fortune back on Earth if I had that ability."

"No Rose," John replied with a smirk, "if you had that ability on Earth, you would have been locked up by the CIA or some such organisation and experimented on like a lab rat." Rose couldn't argue with the logic.

As they ate and drank, Zadkiel started the conversation with two warnings. "The peoples of this continent are primarily warlike. We may see conflict on the way. If negotiation proves impossible or dangerous we will withdraw and travel on. We can't afford delay because we don't know whether we are being pursued.

"With that in mind, I'm shortly going to transform into a bird of prey and travel far to the east and south to see whether the Fae is pursuing us. If he is, we must dispense with diplomacy and fly to the Three Sisters as quickly as possible. Be ready to leave immediately upon my return."

"You really think the Fae could break through your defensive wall and overpower the other Angels of Light?" Sam sounded more concerned than sceptical.

"Yes Sam, I do. This Fae is powerful and ruthless. His madness makes him unpredictable. No one can prepare for that kind of unpredictability. He may be able to do things that a more rational mind would never contemplate.

"The last thing I will say is that the further we travel north, the cooler the climate will become. By the time we reach the Three Sisters it will be cold. There may be snow. Your thermal cloaks and boots will be critical for your survival.

"I'm leaving now and will be away for three or four hours, no more." As Zadkiel said this, he transformed into a bird the size of an eagle and took off, doing a circuit of their surroundings to ensure there was no lurking danger near the pilgrims.

Satisfied, Zadkiel rose high into the cloudless sky and disappeared at impossible speed to the east. The pilgrims settled down to wait. The sunlight was strong and soporific and soon they sought somewhere nearby to rest in the shade. They slept.

They were startled awake by screams and confusion as hands roughly grabbed them and dragged them to their feet. Sam woke up to see a nightmare staring at him, yelling words he did not understand. John and Rose were similarly restrained by strong and un-friendly hands. Surrounding the captives Sam saw a band of about 20 warriors, all daubed head-to-toe with strange and fearsome emblems. They carried lethal clubs, and stone knives that looked extremely sharp.

Sam realised who these warriors were. The warriors were wearing war paint. This was a raiding party intent upon… what? Killing their enemies? Taking prison-ers? If so, for what purpose?

Rose was thinking the same things. She was terribly afraid that her unspoken joke about *cannibals*, was coming back to bite her.

The three prisoners stood at the centre of a garish mob, naked but for feathers and paint. A larger warrior walked up to them and stared each in the eyes, screaming in a strange guttural language with whistles and hoots thrown in.

The words may have been unknown, but their intent left none of the captives in any doubt. They *were* captives. Resistance would see them dead. John, Rose and Sam offered no resistance and stood quietly while the storm broke around them.

Sam looked to the skies hoping for Zadkiel's return. He was their only hope. But there was no sign of him. The warriors pushed and buffeted the pilgrims into the dense, tropical undergrowth that adjoined the sand, and the group disappeared from sight.

True to his word, Zadkiel returned within four hours and landed with a flourish.

"As I feared, the Fae is coming," he cried. No one answered. Zadkiel looked around and realised he was alone. The pilgrims were gone. Zadkiel changed into his usual form and searched the place where he had left them. The backpacks were there, untouched, as if forgotten. *No.* The pilgrims would not leave without their backpacks, not if they left willingly. He searched further afield and at the back of the secluded beach, where sand met the trees, he found the evidence he feared. The sand disturbed by many feet, a fallen feather, a photograph dropped upon the sand. Zadkiel picked it up. A smiling couple looked out of the photograph. *Sam and Becky,* a little younger, before they entered The Light.

Sam would never leave this behind, unless the photograph was a message. The pilgrims had been forcibly taken. They were being held captive, somewhere in that vast forest.

*What have I done?* Zadkiel bemoaned this ill-fortune. He should have searched more thoroughly, before he left the pilgrims unprotected on the beach. He had been careless.

The raiding party, or whoever these enemies were, must have hidden from him, for fear of the menacing bird circling in the sky.

This was disaster. A flying, malevolent serpent was mere hours away and he had lost the pilgrims under his protection. He had to find them quickly, release them safely and then race for the Three Sisters. Disaster indeed!

A gigantic eagle-like bird of prey materialised on the sand. Zadkiel seemingly absorbed the backpacks and ladder and with a massive flapping of wings lifted high into the air and began his urgent search.

Instead of flying directly to the mountains far to the north, Zadkiel flew in circles above the rainforest, searching for signs of the fleeing humans. He had to find them quickly. Failure may lead to the complete destruction of The Light.

With increasing urgency, Zadkiel used his keen eyesight to search every patch of forest, every animal trail, every flash of light, every movement, anything that might reveal the recent passage of his quarry.

At last, after a frantic hour of searching, Zadkiel found the sign he was looking for. Imprints of many human sized footprints fleeing northwards, further into the forest.

Zadkiel realised that the sight of a gigantic bird would cause the humans to hide from him again. So, he attempted something he had not tried before. He willed himself to disappear from view. The giant body faded to nothing, and the air returned to stillness and silence. *Why hadn't I done this on the flight along the coast. They must have seen me. Botheration*!

Hidden eyes now followed the humans, without alerting the warriors to danger from the skies. Elevated as he was, Zadkiel could see where the party was heading. He spied several ribbons of smoke wafting lazily into the sky, rising from a large clearing in the rainforest. As they drew closer, Zadkiel spied at least thirty primitive dwellings constructed from forest vegetation, thatched roofs held aloft by wooden poles, with scant walls providing little privacy or protection from the weather.

A larger, impressive Meeting House graced the centre of the village, the tribe milling about, awaiting the return of their warriors. As the party came into view, the tribe, as one, greeted them with a thrilling shout of delight that filled the air with their tonal joy.

The warriors holding the captives walked toward the Meeting House and threw their prisoners to the ground. An impressive figure appeared from out of the building's shadows, a leader of some description, with multi-hued skin-paint outlining swirling tattoos that seemed to dance as the body moved. The chief's head-dress was startling and much grander than any previously seen.

He looked down at the three Light humans prostrate on the hard dirt of the camp. He spoke in the same strange language that the warriors spoke. Equally un-intelligible. He was commanding or demanding something, the captives deduced that much. But they did not understand. They could not answer.

The chief was becoming irate at the insolence of these defenceless captives. He shouted louder and with greater threat, hauling Rose bodily into the air and squeezing her neck with his hands. Rose struggled but could do nothing.

It was at that moment, Zadkiel reappeared above the village and made an almighty cry of victory, as if to say, *I've found you, I've come for you. There's no es-cape.* The villagers scattered with cries of alarm, but the chief and the warriors held their ground, defiant be-fore the massive bird above their heads. Zadkiel willed the chief to lower Rose, and he was unable to resist.

The warriors threw knives and war clubs at the bird, and all were swept away by a storm of wings. The mighty bird lowered, and as it did, it transformed into an Angel of Light.

The chief and warriors fell to their knees and placed their foreheads on the ground. Sam realised immediately that they were worshipping Zadkiel.

The three pilgrims stood, Rose looking distressed by the red welts on her neck that would likely become spectacular bruising. They walked to Zadkiel's side. "Impeccable timing," John said with a grin. Rose rubbed her throat and answered hoarsely, "not that impeccable. A couple of minutes sooner would have been nice. But thanks Zadkiel. You saved my life."

The Angel approached the Chief and warriors, speaking in that same strange, guttural language. The supplicants rose to their feet and stared at the shining translucent figure before them. Zadkiel spoke at length, the chief occasionally answering in a much more friendly voice. If a guttural, primitive language could communicate awe, the chief's voice was communicating it.

At a sign from the chief, the remaining villagers left their huts and approached the Angel. They fell to their knees and began chanting a hypnotic repeated scale of musical notes. The pilgrims realised that these people knew of the Lords and Ladies of Light. They worshipped them! Had probably worshipped them for thousands of years.

After further discussion, Zadkiel held out his massive hand and the chief placed his own much smaller hand upon it. A pact of some description had been sealed. The chief ordered his people to move back, away from the Lord, and the pilgrims did likewise. They knew what was about to happen.

Zadkiel transformed into the mighty bird of prey and the ladder appeared as if from nowhere waiting for the pilgrims to ascend.

Without delay the pilgrims obliged, finding at the top of the ladder their backpacks arranged neatly on Zadkiel's back. They knew the drill. They retrieved the ladder and held on tight as Zadkiel lifted high into the sky at an oblique angle to aim the downdraft from his wings away from the fragile village structures and into the surrounding forest.

They were on their way again. The bubble reformed as they lifted high into the sky, so high in fact, that the curvature of the horizon could be clearly seem.

Zadkiel's voice, made unintelligible by the rarified air, caressed the pilgrim's minds directly, calming them and comforting them.

Then Zadkiel spoke to Sam alone. "If you check your backpack, you'll find something inside that you had lost, deliberately, I suspect."

Sam lifted the flap of his pack and found the precious photograph atop his other belongings. "Zadkiel, I knew you'd find it." Sam cried with his mind. "I hated to leave it behind, but I thought it was the only way to communicate our abduction."

Zadkiel answered, "the nature of your loss, that you would leave something so special behind, confirmed my belief and spurred the urgency of my search." Zadkiel's voice sounded impressed. "Quick thinking Sam."

Then Zadkiel spoke to all the pilgrims together. He told them the gist of his conversation with the village chief, explaining the urgency of their quest and warning them of the danger approaching from the south.

"I told them to douse their fires and hide in the forest until the serpent had flown overhead. The Fae is no more than four hours behind us, and I am mightily relieved that I managed to find you as quickly as I did."

"So, you saw the Fae," Rose said. "A huge serpent with wings! That's novel. I guess it takes a snake to think of a snake…" the joke fell flat as everyone contemplated the evil news.

Forming the words in his mind, and trying to relieve the tension, Sam commented, "the tribe worshipped you, Zadkiel. God and the Angels must have made quite an impression all those thousands of years ago."

"*That* we did," replied Zadkiel. "I should know as I was part of the delegation to Estrada, when we agreed and signed the Treaty. These people have long cultural memories.

Rose re-entered the conversation, feeling somewhat peculiar. Communicating without spoken words was a strangely intimate experience. "I for one am delighted to wave those savages goodbye. They might have killed us all had you not arrived when you did."

An extended silence reigned in their heads. "Zadkiel, are you there?" John asked.

"Yes, my friends, I am here. I was just trying to find the words to tell you something that you might find distasteful. "Rose, there was no might about it. They would have killed you. In their eyes you were fair game."

Rose voice sounded weakly on the ether, expressing all the fears that she had felt. "Fair game? As in food? They were going to eat us? Bloody hell."

Zadkiel laughed in their heads. "Yes, Rose they *were* going to eat you. What did you think the campfires were for? I eased their disappointment by promising to bring them back plenty of meat, after we slay the serpent."

"Well, that's alright then." Rose sounded indignant. "We can't have the cannibals going hungry." John, Sam, and Zadkiel laughed uproariously, both aloud, and in their heads.

"Oh, dear Rose," Zadkiel said, clearly trying to regain control, "you are a delight. Thank you for bringing so much laughter with you. You lighten my heart."

Conversation at an end, Zadkiel put his mind to the flight, accelerating hypersonically, threatening to break free of the planet's gravity well, so fast was he flying. Inside their protective bubble the pilgrims rested comfortably, unaffected by the massive physical forces around them. No overwhelming pressure battered their bodies, defying the laws of physics as they understood them.

The three passengers watched the continent far below, fascinated by the tiny ribbon of river winding its wiggly way into the north, at last disappearing into the hazy light beyond the horizon. They were headed to the Three Sisters and a future lay before them. A destiny none of them could fathom, could understand or know, until its time had passed.

A Light storm *was* coming and Sam willed desperately that they were the riders in the vanguard of that righteous storm. He dared not think otherwise because Becky was waiting.

**The End**

# Addendum - Time Strands

Time, it seems, is relative. In the Mortal Realm, time moves according to rules theorised over many centuries and more recently by Albert Einstein in his Theory of Relativity. Time speeds up, time slows down depending upon certain theoretical conditions being met. In the years since Einstein formulated his theory, physicists and Quantum Mechanics have further complicated the picture.

But what happens in another universe/dimension? Does time move in exactly the same way as it does in our universe? Does it even exist? Do the same theoretical expectations apply? The answer to all these questions is the same. We just don't know. We can theorise and deduce, but, at present, we cannot know.

Common sense might suggest that there is no reason to think that time is the same across multiple universes. However, constructing a universe-hopping work of fiction where time moves differently in each, throws up all sorts of challenges. How could a writer manage the flow of events and maintain dramatic structure?

Well, as you will have realised, this writer could not. So, I made the decision to see time as the same in all three realms — Mortal, Dark, and Light.

The only variables at play are the date and time of arrival at one's destination; the former based upon the time taken to complete one orbit of the planet's sun, and the latter based upon the rotation of the planet.

Climatic conditions upon arrival are based upon the axial tilt of the planet, if any, and the position of the planet in its orbit. On Earth the axial tilt is 23.439281 degrees off the vertical (averaged over a 40,000-year cycle) — hence Earth's seasons.

Once we accept that time is constant across all three universes, the business of writing becomes much easier. So, the writer can hop from realm to realm and interweave various story lines, thus creating tension within that common timeline.

We have left Book Two with everything to be resolved. Three of our pilgrims, Becky, Marion and Gerald are in the Mortal Realm, held captive by Louseefa, a Lord of Light masquerading as the Dark Master. When last we saw them, they were taking afternoon tea with Louseefa, having convinced a Dark Lord to fly them to Louseefa's new palace.

A universe away, on the First World of Light, the other three pilgrims, Sam, John, and Rose are in a desperate race to the Three Sisters with Zadkiel, an Angel of Light. They are being pursued by the Fae, in the guise of a gigantic flying serpent. The Fae is in turn being pursued by the four remaining Angels of Light.

The pilgrims have just been saved from a gruesome end by Zadkiel, and are now flying high above Estrada, bound for the Three Sisters.

Elsewhere in The Light, the citizens of Floriana and every inhabited world of Light have united to begin re-building their shattered lives. Will James be successful in shaping an effective government? What will happen to the political class that failed The Light so badly? Will the Fae return to Floriana and other worlds of Light to inflict further misery upon the people?

These questions, and many others you may think to ask, will be answered in the next instalment, *Book Three — The Light Rising*.

Thank you for reading Pilgrims of the Fall — The First World. The first instalment of the trilogy — Lost Paradise, is also available as an e-book for Kindle and in print, on Amazon, and is also available on Book-topia.

You can order print editions (plus postage within Australia), through the author.

Email: christopherlevy4@me.com
Follow me on Facebook or send me an email.

# Acknowledgements

I would like to express my deepest gratitude to the following individuals, whose support and encouragement have been instrumental in the creation of this book.

To my family, for their unwavering belief in me and for providing the love and motivation that sustained me throughout this journey. Your support has been invaluable. I especially wish to acknowledge my partner Ian, who has patiently put up with the disruptions that writing a book can cause.

To my friends, who offered their insights, constructive criticism, and endless encouragement. Your perspectives have enriched the narrative and sharpened its focus. My friend, John, in particular, has followed the journey of Sam and Rose from the very beginning, from the time when they were just characters in a poem.

To my mentor and designer, Jan-Andrew Henderson a heartfelt thank you. Your expertise and dedication have greatly enhanced the quality of this work and without your guidance and input, Pilgrims of the Fall would never have been published.

To my beta readers, who took the time to read the early drafts and provide honest feedback. Your input has been crucial in shaping the story and refining its elements.

Finally, to all the readers who have embarked on this journey with the pilgrims. Your enthusiasm and passion for the story fuel my inspiration and drive.

Thank you all for being a part of this incredible adventure.

# About The Author

Christopher is 75 years of age and has been writing, off and on, for 50 years. Only recently has he rediscovered the urge to write after putting down his pen in the 1980s and, only intermittently, taking it up again to compose a few lines here and there. This late flowering of his craft and the desire to share his creations with others, was serendipitous in that he rediscovered his earliest works, forgotten in a drawer, and began to read.

Much of this earliest work was in verse form. Thus, it came as no surprise to him that his first novel found its roots in a long, allegorical poem.

"To have discovered this facility for creative fiction, so late in life, is the most frustrating experience of a life replete with frustrations and might have beens," Christopher says.

It is natural for human beings to grieve the loss of things left undone. So, he has thrown himself into the task of creating a body of work and making it available to others before his inevitable passage into Light or Dark.

So many ideas, so many stories, so many genres, so little time.

Christopher is an avid swimmer and reader, adores baroque music and singing in choirs, and lives with his partner in a retirement community in Brisbane, Australia.